Prai

"A haunting story _____ ing the past, and acce _____ with readers long after they've read _____ see what Roads has planned for us next!"

—*Harlequin Junkie*

"Roads does an excellent job ratcheting up the psychological suspense as she brings together two damaged individuals."

—*RT Book Reviews*

"Dark, sexy, emotional, edge-of-your-seat, romantic suspense with a touch of paranormal thrown in...I was enthralled from the start!"

—*Guilty Pleasures Book Review*

"Hoooo boy! I'm not sure how Ms. Roads does it, but I'm still amazed by her capacity to write the most heartfelt, innocent, and beautiful love stories woven into the darkest, most twisted plot lines."

—*Edgy Reviews*

"*Saving Mercy* is another example of why Abbie Roads's books will always fascinate me!"

—*The Book Disciple*

"*Saving Mercy* left me with the worst book-hangover I've had in a long time. I tried to start another book the next morning, but it just wasn't an Abbie Roads book."

—*My Trending Stories*

Also by Abbie Roads

FATAL DREAMS
Race the Darkness
Hunt the Dawn

FATAL TRUTH
Saving Mercy

NEVER LET ME FALL

ABBIE ROADS

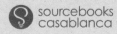
sourcebooks
casablanca

Published by Sourcebooks Casablanca, an imprint of Sourcebooks, Inc.
P.O. Box 4410, Naperville, Illinois 60567-4410
(630) 961-3900
Fax: (630) 961-2168
sourcebooks.com

Printed and bound in Canada.
MBP 10 9 8 7 6 5 4 3 2 1

Be a ray of sunshine in someone's cloudy sky.

Chapter 1

THERE WERE ONLY TWO OPTIONS OPEN TO HELENA Grayse—survive or die. Never had that been clearer than on this night. Her final night in the Fairson Reformatory for Women.

The lights were off, the shadows deep, and the minutes until morning passed slower than the previous ten years. Her heart throbbed, locking her in hypervigilance. She lay on her bunk, her gaze darting erratically around the darkened women's dorm while she strained to hear even the slightest of sounds.

The Eight Sisters Posse had despised her the moment she'd crossed the prison's threshold, placing her firmly at the bottom of the food chain. At the time, she hadn't understood their insta-hate, but over the years, they'd taught her all about it.

She was better than they were. Not really, but that's what *they* thought because she wasn't a junkie, had an education, and—the thing they hated most, the thing they wouldn't forgive—she acted innocent. She hadn't bothered to tell them she really was innocent of murdering her boyfriend, Rory Ellis. They wouldn't have believed her anyway. No one believed a felon.

Dorm B contained bunk beds to conserve space. Five rows of five beds, double stacked. Fifty inmates. Prison overcrowding at its finest. Her bunk sat dead center in the room. Four of the Sisters slept in here. Better odds than eight on one, but still daunting.

Carrie Lane slept in the bunk behind her, head-to-head with Helena. One freedom they possessed—which way to lie in their beds. "Lena?" Carrie whispered so quietly, it was barely a breath of sound.

She hated being called Lena, but that was her prison name. Chosen for her. And like everything else in here, she'd had to live with it. She'd never particularly liked Grandma's nickname for her—Helen—but now she'd sell what was left of her sanity to be called that again. That was the power of nostalgia.

"You know they're coming for you tonight." Carrie's words contained no real emotion. No concern. Just a passing along of information. "I hope you have a plan."

If she had a plan, she wasn't going to share it with anyone. Trust didn't exist in here.

Cuts, scrapes, bruises, and broken bones happened when the Sisters were being nice. Tonight—the eve of her release—nice wasn't part of their plan. This was their last chance to kill her. They'd almost succeeded countless times before, but by some double miracle, she'd survived a gang shanking, asphyxiation, and things she didn't want to think about.

Across the dorm to her left, someone sighed. At the same time on her right, there was a faint rustle of blankets. Was that sigh more than a sigh? Was it a signal? She sounded paranoid even to herself, but paranoia had kept her alive. Barely.

She turned her head and looked toward the rustling blanket sound, but saw no one. Only two more rows of women sleeping quietly. That was a danger sign all its own. Things were noisier during the night. It had taken her years to get used to the noise of sleeping with forty-nine other women.

Breathing. Coughing. Sex. Sniffling. Snoring. Farts.

But tonight, there was just that one sigh. A signal from the Sisters.

Her body vibrated from a terrible combination of fear and impatience. Why didn't they just hurry up and make their move? End the awful anticipation that had its jaws clamped around her.

Two bunks behind her and one to the left, Bertie started snoring. The older woman was silent as the night if she lay on her side, but turned into a lumber mill every time she lay on her back. Whoever bunked underneath Bertie inherited the job of kicking the bottom of Bertie's bed until the older woman rolled over. Or else no one in the dorm would get any sleep.

Bertie kept the racket up, the noise grating and annoying and ominous. Paranoia told Helena that Bertie's snoring was part of the Sister's plan. Disguise the sound of their movements—their attack—with Bertie's chain-saw snores.

From the corner of her eye, Helena spotted the first Sister. She crawled in the left aisle, her movements slow, silent, steady. A second Sister crept on all fours up the right aisle. It was too risky to stand because of the cameras. If the corrections officers paid the tiniest bit of attention, they'd be able to see the movement. But the COs weren't paid enough to be *that* observant.

Helena would just bet the remaining two Sisters were coming from behind her. They always attacked in numbers.

Less than five seconds stood between her and death.

"They're coming," Carrie breathed. Her warning surprised Helena, but there was no time to dwell on it.

Her mind kicked into hyperdrive, sorting through options. Forward was blocked. Behind her was blocked. The guard station would be no help—they'd just tell her to go back to bed. Or if they did help her, they'd expect *payment*. Would blowing one of them be worth saving her life? Could she let her body be used for their pleasure in order to survive the night? Not if she couldn't live with herself afterward. And she couldn't. She'd rather die fighting. Or running. Running seemed like the better option. She'd fight when cornered like she always did, but right now, she'd run.

In one fluid movement, she rolled to the left off the bunk and onto the floor between the Sisters coming from the front and the back. She recognized both of them and sent a silent thank-you skyward that they were both big girls.

"You dead," one of them hissed.

Helena dived perpendicular underneath the bunk across the aisle from hers. The bed sat so low to the ground, she banged her shoulders, the sound echoing like a gong through the dorm. *Shit*. If the guards came in and she was out of bed... Extra time on her sentence when she was so close to freedom she could brush it with her fingertips... That just might break her in a way nothing else in here had been able to.

Helena's head and shoulders exploded out the other side of the bunk into the aisle. A hand snagged her foot, halting her momentum.

Adrenaline roared through her body. She kicked her

free leg like a Rockette, connecting with something solid. An *oomph* of pain sounded at the exact moment her foot was released.

She shot out into the next aisle and continued forward, going underneath the last row of bunks pushed against the wall. Only an inch or two of space separated her and the bottom of the beds. In her hiding place, the darkness was deeper, the feeling of claustrophobia nearly overwhelming. It smelled of dust and the warm, musky stench of body soil from the hundreds of women who'd used the beds above her.

Score one for always being cold. She'd gone to bed wearing her dark-blue sweatshirt and pants. The dark colors blended into the shadows. The two Sisters she'd seen had both worn their white T-shirts—they practically glowed in the dark.

She slid along the cold floor, using her hands and feet to propel her. Her hip bones scraped against the concrete, the material of her sweats not nearly thick enough to prevent the bruises she could feel forming. Her breath rasped in and out of her lungs, loud as an overweight ogre with asthma. She needed to quiet herself. There wasn't one woman in this whole dorm who wouldn't give her away if a Sister asked her directly. Her best bet was to keep silent and keep out of sight.

Hide-and-seek as an adult didn't carry the same appeal as it did when she was seven.

The guard station behind a wall of glass was in the front of the room. She slid that way.

Surely the Sisters wouldn't murder her in front of the corrections officers. And surely the COs would intervene if they actually saw her being attacked—especially if it happened right in front of one of the cameras. They wouldn't want the investigation or the paperwork a dead inmate would cost them.

She stopped at the end of the row, looked all around, saw no one in the aisle, then moved out into the open and back over underneath the bunks she'd initially used to escape. The Sisters would expect her to cower against the wall. But she intended to move back to her row. They wouldn't expect that. Hell, maybe she should move back to her bed. They really wouldn't predict her being there.

"What the—" A woman's startled voice cut off with a thump and slap.

Helena twisted just enough to look behind her and to the left. A Sister landed on her hands and knees three bunks back. They couldn't fit under, so they were going over.

Great.

Helena stared at the guard station and willed CO Holbrook to look up at the monitors and see the Sisters crawling in and out of the aisles. But nope. He was tapping away on his cell phone. Probably playing a damn crush-the-candy game while she was in here fighting for the right to keep sucking air.

Helena peeked out into the aisle to her right. Empty.

Quick as she could, she slid out into the aisle and under the middle row of bunks. Her row. She held her breath to listen and craned her neck to see if anyone was coming from any direction. Maybe all the Sisters were in the far aisle checking for her. No way was she that lucky.

"Goddamn it! I'm trying to sleep," an inmate shouted. A Sister moved off a bunk into the aisle, squatting on her haunches, her back to Helena. The woman gestured with her hands, pointing to the row just on the other side of where Helena hid. They must've realized she wasn't hiding over there against the wall and were all coming back.

Helena made her move. Quiet in a way she never knew she could be, she slid out from under the bunk, across the aisle, and underneath the set of bunks she'd just left. Thank God the Sister didn't have eyes in the back of her ass.

This back-and-forth, back-and-forth felt like a tennis match. Could she do this all night without them finding her? The odds were not in her favor.

The Sister crawled over Helena's empty bunk into the aisle beyond.

Another Sister landed in the aisle, hands-and-kneeing it until she moved up and over Helena's empty bunk and went into the aisle beyond. "What the fuck?" Carrie yelled the words at a volume sure to draw the CO's attention. "That was my hair you just ripped out."

At the guard station, CO Holbrook stood and looked out the glass into the darkened dorm.

Yes!

"Get off me!" Helena yelled the words at nearly the same volume as Carrie. Her voice snapped and broke. Her throat scratched from disuse, and best of all, no one would suspect her of yelling. It had been nine years since she'd last uttered a word out loud. Not since her first grade three concussion from the Sisters. After that, keeping her voice to herself had seemed the only way to keep ahold of her soul.

Holbrook's face transformed from an expression of merely listening to full-on rage-monkey because he was going to have to do his job. He turned away from the window and headed for the door leading into the women's dorm.

Oh shit. If Holbrook caught her out of bed... Helena sprint-crawled underneath the bunks until she was across the aisle from her bed. She dived the remaining feet, jumped into her bed, and ripped the covers up over her body.

A Sister materialized on the right.

Instinct and self-preservation raised Helena's hands just in time to protect her face. The shank sliced open Helena's palm, just before she caught the Sister's wrist, preventing the weapon from gouging out her eye. With both hands, she fought the superior strength and weight of the Sister pushing the blade down.

A light blazed on, and Helena saw her blood dripping down her hand, meandering to her wrist, then winding a path toward her elbow.

The Sister's pressure on the weapon shifted, and for a moment, Helena thought she might survive.

Could she be winning? Could she outmatch the Sister's weight with sheer tenacity and a will to live?

Pain exploded in her gut. Breath woofed out of her. Her body went on lockdown from the gut punch. No oxygen came in. None went out. Her grasp on the Sister's shank hand slipped, and she caught the blade just a few inches from entering her eyeball.

Psychedelic spots formed in her vision. Her arms shook. She couldn't hold off the inevitable for much longer.

Shouting all around them. Male shouting. Shouts from the inmates.

The blade was so close, Helena could see brown smears covering the sharpened edge. Dried blood? Her blood? From the last time they'd tried to kill her?

The Sister's body shifted, tilted, her full weight bearing down on Helena. She couldn't help it—a scream filled with anger at the unfairness of life erupted just before the blade pierced her.

Thomas Brown drove toward a pain and purgatory he couldn't deny. The only light in existence came from his truck's high beams guiding him up the low hills, down the shallow valleys, and around the crazy twists and turns. The night and road conspired to soothe the smoldering anxiety that had taken him over ever since he'd gotten called out on this case.

For one indulgent moment, he fantasized he was alone on the planet. No people. No pain. No death. A smile stretched the scar on his cheek uncomfortably—a bitch slap back to reality if he'd ever felt one.

The dancing gray lights of patrol cars suddenly came into view at the bottom of the next valley.

A scene he was familiar with, except tonight for some reason, those gray lights were a glaring reminder of what he *couldn't* see. Color. His memory told him those flashers weren't plain. They were red and blue. At least they had been before his stepfather kicked him in the face at just five years old.

Brain injury, optic nerve damage—the diagnoses didn't matter—the result remained the same. Total and complete absence of color. He missed the everyday colors the most. The chestnut warmth of a dog's fur, the ruby red of a ripe apple, the calming azure of a cloudless sky. He imagined all these, but tried not to. The act of remembering put a lump in his throat that made him yearn for a beauty he'd never have.

A life without color was a life without passion. And lack of color wasn't even the worst of it.

Thomas pulled up and parked behind a long line of patrol cars. Every car in the county had to be out here. Murder was big news. He flicked off the headlights and killed the engine while he took in the scene.

Past the cars, a group of officers huddled off to the side. A mottled shadow of sorts settled around them. Parts of it were dark, parts of it were light, and parts of it were as wispy as tendrils of fog. Even though he hated seeing the shadow, it carried a frightening beauty.

The first time Thomas had seen the shadow was when he'd awakened from his stepfather's kick to the face. Lacking an adult vocabulary, he'd called it a shadow monster. Over the decades, Thomas had come to call it by its real name. The shadow of death.

The officers congregated in a large group, sipping from steaming mugs, chatting, and laughing as if they were tailgating for their favorite team instead of at a crime scene. Murder was a sobering event. *There but for the grace of God* and all that rang truer in the presence of a body whose life had been taken. But not here, not tonight. He shouldn't be surprised. This was exactly the kind of department Thomas's stepfather ran.

Normally, Thomas didn't get called out on cases this close to home, but Sheriff Robert Malone had called the Ohio Bureau of Criminal Investigation and specifically requested Thomas. *Fucking interagency cooperation.*

There was something more than a little suspicious that Mom's memorial service was tomorrow. Especially since Malone knew the only way to get Thomas to interact with him was on the job. Was the guy going to try to talk him into some public show of family solidarity for the service? *Screw that*. When it came to Malone, the only emotions Thomas could find were shame and hatred.

He should leave. Drive off before anyone noticed him. But there was the greater good to consider. Solving a murder might prevent another murder. Then there was his more selfish motive—every case he helped to solve, every perpetrator held accountable, eased a tiny bit of the anger and hurt that Malone would never be brought to justice for what he'd done.

Thomas sucked in a slow, resigned breath, got out of the truck, and walked past the first of the parked patrol cars. A snowflake caught in his eyelashes, melted to a droplet, and fell onto his cheek like a frosty tear.

Across the expanse of squad cars and flashing lights, he spotted Malone in the crowd and wished he hadn't. His shadow loomed large and dark and roiling like the blackest of smoke—a warning to stay away.

Thomas's heart jogged around his chest, his lungs felt like they were in the middle of bench-pressing four hundred pounds, and his body superheated from bad expectations. Muscle memory. After all these years, Thomas still reacted to Malone with the terror of a frightened child.

His footsteps faltered. He froze, buried under an avalanche of bad memories.

Get over it. Grow up. He should be used to the fear of having to be near Malone by now. He wasn't. Just seeing the man made him *feel* like a helpless child. Yeah, he had four inches and forty pounds of muscle on the guy, but that cowering child inside him could not be reasoned with.

"Thomas?" A gnarled, old man's voice spoke from beside him. "Are you all right?"

Thomas recognized the voice—Pastor Audie, who the kids had called Pastor Oldie when Thomas was a child. The man wasn't just old; he was ancient. And a dead ringer for Gandalf the Grey.

Thomas turned his attention to Audie. The old man's thick, gray beard reached halfway down his chest, and his long, gray hair was cut the same length. Thomas half expected him to be wearing a wizard's hat and carrying a staff. Instead, Audie wore a long, baggy coat that looked way too big for his slight frame. A thick, knitted cap with a jaunty yarn ball covered his head, and a bulky scarf wrapped his throat.

The thing Thomas liked most about Audie was the light, ethereal shadow that flitted and swirled around him like dancing butterflies. It was the kind of shadow that Thomas could watch all day for its beauty.

Audie's face was a weathered map of life, but carried a calming acceptance. He reached out with a thickly mittened hand to touch Thomas's arm and looked him directly in the eye instead of at the scar covering half his face.

The old injury covered his cheek, ran up his temple, and spanned a portion of his forehead. Despite age fading the brightness, most people still stared. Thomas didn't mind. He wore the scar proudly. It was a blazing condemnation of Malone and his actions. Didn't matter that no one else saw it that way. Malone knew. That was enough for now.

"Are you all right?" Audie repeated the question.

Thomas's gaze wandered to Malone and the darkly dangerous shadow of death writhing around him. *Was he all right?* "No," he answered truthfully. Audie was one of those people you couldn't lie to. Who would have the audacity to lie to an elderly pastor, Gandalf look-alike or not?

The old man squeezed Thomas's arm gently, bringing his attention back to him. "I know this is hard for you." An understanding that shouldn't exist lived in his eyes.

For a flash of a second, Thomas thought Audie meant it was hard for him to be near Malone. But no one knew his painful secret. As a child, fear of Malone had super-glued Thomas's mouth shut. What Audie really meant was that it was hard being out here working a murder scene when tomorrow they were burying his mother. Audie didn't know that Thomas's mother hadn't given two shits about him. If she had, she wouldn't have let Malone beat him.

Thomas didn't know how to reply to Audie's heart-felt words, so he opted for a subject change. "What are you doing out here?" It wasn't exactly the middle of the night, but it was cold and snowy and no place for a man who had to be pushing ninety.

"I ask to be called every time there's an unexpected death in the county…to offer comfort and guidance to those in need." The pastor's voice contained a latent sadness.

Thomas couldn't help it; he looked at the party-like

scene playing out in front of him. No one needed comfort here, except for himself, and just by his presence and concern, Audie had done the job.

"I don't drive at night anymore." The old man's teeth began chattering on the last word. "I caught a ride with one of the deputies."

Thomas reached into his coat pocket and took out his keys. He hit the remote start on his truck and unlocked the doors. "How about you wait in my truck while I work, then I'll drive you home?"

A smile fired on Audie's face, shaving decades off his appearance. "I'd very much like that."

"I'll be back in a few minutes," Thomas called over his shoulder, threading his way between the parked patrol cars. From this distance, he could see the body lying on display in the middle of the road. Something about that felt wrong. It was hard to put his finger on what. Maybe it was how everyone seemed to ignore it, and no one seemed to care that a life had been stolen.

Malone walked up to the body, gazed at the ground for less than two seconds, then headed back to a pack of officers.

"Looks like a full moon tonight." Malone's voice came out deadpan and flat. The officers didn't laugh. Nope. They guffawed. The sound of their merriment was wrong—so fucking wrong—when a human being lay dead on the pavement.

Thomas glanced skyward at the thick padding of clouds blowing bits of snow over them. Malone had said, *Looks like a full moon tonight*. Full moon? The thing wasn't even visible. The joke wasn't funny. The words didn't make any sense.

Yeah. Cops were masters at dark humor, but this went beyond that. Where was their indignation that a life had been taken? But he shouldn't expect anything less. These were Malone's good ole boys.

Malone and the officers were in a huddle, not paying attention. *Good.* If Thomas was lucky, he might be able to get in and get out before anyone noticed him. If he was unlucky, which seemed to be his norm, Malone would notice him and try another male-bonding exercise on him. Wasn't that a crack to the nuts? The guy who'd caused all Thomas's problems now wanted them to be best buds. If it was his way of seeking forgiveness for what he'd done… Fat fucking chance.

A portable light was aimed down at the dead guy. All around him, a nebulous and faint shadow of death hovered. Thomas was going to commune with the fading residue. Though that wasn't the *official* explanation of his ability. His superintendent simply thought he was able to make accurate extrapolations from minimal evidence. Wasn't like Thomas could explain communing with the shadow of death. That'd only earn him an all-expenses paid vacay to a locked-down psychiatric facility.

As he neared the body, the musky scent of unwashed flesh, pot smoke, and those death scents—urine and feces—hit him like an invisible wall. The dead guy wore a dark sweatshirt with jeans, both covered in splotches of something. Dirt? Without color, it was hard to tell. He lay on his side in a slightly stretched-out version of the fetal position.

Thomas walked around the body, careful to stay away from the fading fragments of the shadow of death.

The dead guy's complexion was grimy and smudged

as if he were a few weeks over due for a shower. His jaw hung open just enough to make out blotchy, rotten teeth. Bushy, greasy, light-colored hair topped the guy's head. He either had a wicked cowlick or was suffering from a chronic case of bedhead. His pants had slid down, revealing the white globes of his ass.

So that was the reason for Malone's full-moon comment.

Every one of those cops who laughed was a degenerate. A low-life scum sucker who deserved to have his testicles popped like a pimple.

Thomas crouched next to the body, entering the shadow of death. An odd heat settled over him. A sensation that mimicked the feeling of sunshine, or maybe that was the fires of hell reaching across space and time to warm him on this frigid night. He couldn't know for sure.

It was against procedure and protocol, but he grabbed the waist of the guy's jeans and hiked them up over his ass—the only bit of dignity he could offer.

He'd also just contaminated a crime scene. But Malone shouldn't have called him in if they hadn't already bagged and tagged and logged everything into evidence. Thomas's analysis called for a hands-on evaluation. By the time he got done, the integrity of the scene would be fucked to hell from his sweat and touch DNA.

It was time to work.

Thomas went down on his knees near the guy's face. His heart revved, on the verge of overheating. He inhaled slowly to calm himself, but nothing other than leaving the shadow of death would help. Bad shadows always made him feel bad, the same way that good shadows like Audie's eased him.

His hand trembled as he placed his palm alongside the guy's temple. Ring finger and pinkie on the guy's forehead, thumb and first finger on his cheek, middle finger hovering over the guy's closed eye.

Heat burned into Thomas's fingers, then his hand, and up his arm, expanding into an inferno. Sweat oozed from his pores, a bead of it slipping down the channel of his spine. He braced himself. Clenched his teeth so he wouldn't cry out. Then pressed his middle finger to the man's eyelid.

An inferno of agony shot from the guy's eye up through Thomas's body and into his own eye framed by the scar. A grunt of animalistic pain ripped out of him. Misery bounced off the walls of his skull. A kaleidoscope of color exploded in his vision. Why was it that only during these pain-filled moments did he finally see color? The unanswerable question drove him mad.

And then the shadow of death shared the man's life with Thomas.

It was like watching a time-lapse video, except deeper and more real. Images, thoughts, and feelings flowing through him as if all this man's experiences from birth to death were now Thomas's.

Thomas could feel the carefree joy of a child on Christmas morning. The innocent arguments with an older brother. Learning to ride a bike, falling off, skinned and bloody knees, but getting back on. Learning to drive. The pain of a first heartbreak. College. A good job as an accountant. Then the tearing, burning, searing agony of a car accident that should've killed, yet left him alive with a destroyed body. A body that couldn't function without pills. And when there were no more pills, he'd turned to heroin to survive. A decade of being enslaved to the high. The terrible things he did to get his H. Lying. Stealing. Selling himself.

One last score, and he would be done. His mother and brother would be so happy, and this time, he wouldn't let them down, and he wouldn't let himself down. But first, a goodbye to his greatest friend and worst enemy.

A man in a car, face hidden in shadows, but holding out a baggie full of his favorite flavor as an offering. Sex for H was no big thing, especially when his medicine made him feel no pain. He climbed in the vehicle, dosed up as the man drove them out into the country. Didn't care about anything. Nothing. Enjoyed the high as long as it would last, and it never lasted long.

Needle after needle, high after high. Until they all blended together into a floating euphoria. And when he was too weak to dose himself, the man did it for him until...

Nothing. Blackness.

Thomas ripped his hand off the guy's face.

The pressure in his own eye eased, but this time, something was different. He still felt connected to the shadow. *No. No. No. Impossible. No way.* He never had this reaction after taking his hand off the body.

He lurched to the side to escape the remnants of the shadow and the fires of hell raging inside him.

Suddenly, he felt the frigid ground on his palms and through the knees of his jeans. The coldness was such a relief that if a body hadn't been lying there, he would've stretched out right there in the middle of the road and luxuriated in the soothing coolness.

The heat burning inside him faded.

"Tommy." Malone's voice came from behind him.

Thomas's heart seized, then started shivering. His innards shook, and he gulped air. Adrenaline laced with the urge to fight or flee galloped through him. But he could do neither. He wasn't strong enough yet. What the hell was wrong with him?

And he fucking hated being called Tommy.

"Tommy, are you all right?"

Audie had asked the same thing, but with Audie, the question had come from genuine concern and caring. From Malone, it meant Thomas needed to get his shit together and not give the man an opening.

"Tommy…" And there was the stepfatherly concern in his tone.

Thomas sat back on his knees but didn't look at Malone.

Get up. Get out of here. A heaviness in his limbs prevented him from moving.

Time to divert Malone's attention. The last thing he needed was for the guy to touch him or try to help him. There was something especially awful about Malone's shadow of death. It penetrated somehow, kinda like this dead guy's had done.

Thomas gestured with his free hand toward the dead guy. "Heroin." When Malone didn't say anything, Thomas finally looked up at him. The shadow of death around the man undulated and pulsed like a living thing. Thomas tried to ignore it, but his mind transported him back to all those times when he'd been a child and Malone had loomed over him, about to hurt him.

His heart moved from shivering to vibrating. He

fought back the irrational fear that kept trying to take him down.

Malone's eyes never deviated from Thomas. They roamed over him, taking in his face, lingering on the scar, then going to his hair. "I figured as much."

Huh? So much time had passed with Malone staring at him that Thomas couldn't even remember what the original question had been. He pointed at the corpse to force Malone's attention there, but the guy's focus remained fastened on Thomas.

Thomas started to stand. His legs jangled, but he got upright. Probably couldn't take a step without falling on his face, but at least now he could meet Malone as an equal. Actually, more than an equal, since he was so much taller. His heart calmed as he looked down his nose at the smaller man.

He was going to tell Malone the basics, then get the fuck out of here. The guy could read the rest in his report. And then there were the things he wouldn't include in the report. Things like how sad it was that drugs had stolen another life. This guy had a mother and brother who loved him. Who would've done anything to help him get clean. This guy had potential. He might've gone on to do great things. To contribute to the world in a positive way.

But Thomas didn't tell Malone any of that. "This guy's name is Jeremy Tucker." Thomas sketched in the most pertinent information about Jeremy being an addict seeking one last high and the man who kept to the shadows and forced Jeremy into an overdose. "This was murder."

"Murder?" Unfiltered shock sounded in Malone's

voice. He finally looked away from Thomas to the body, scanning the dead guy as if he should be able to see evidence to corroborate Thomas's words. There was none.

"Yeah. Mmmuurrrrddddeeerrrr. Why the hell else would you call me out here?" Thomas didn't rein in the attitude. "You'll find enough heroin in this guy to kill five other people." It was a little weird that Thomas could know such things without the benefit of a tox screen. But that was why he was considered a special consultant. "The guy who bought his sexual services was careful to keep his identity in the shadows. Which makes me think murder was his intention all along."

Malone's gaze swept Jeremy Tucker top to bottom, looking for evidence. "How could you know any of this just from looking at the body?" His words weren't the challenge they should be but were curious more than anything.

"Trade secret." This wasn't the first time Thomas had been asked how he knew things, and it wouldn't be the last. "If I told you, I'd have to kill you." His tone conveyed a little too much glee to be a joke.

Thomas dropped his volume so only the two of them would be able to hear. His lips and mouth ripped back over his teeth in a snarl of pure disgust. "Quit with the devoted stepfather routine. Don't think that just because Mom's memorial service is tomorrow, we're going to pretend to be a happy family. We're not. We never will be. I fucking hate you." He sounded childish and didn't care.

Malone's expression crumpled as if Thomas's words had wounded him.

Something about that, about the man's absolute inability to recognize the harm he'd inflicted, was a match to the powder keg of rage Thomas carried inside. He drew his fist back, prepared to rain down a lifetime full of pain. Give the man a beatdown that would probably land him in the hospital and Thomas in jail. It would be worth it. Oh, so worth it.

A movement from the corner of his eye caught Thomas's attention. Audie slowly made his way between the cruisers. Even at this distance, Thomas could make out the look of concern on the old man's face. Thomas half expected him to yell out some profound words and bang his staff on the ground. If only he lived in a fantasy world instead of reality.

Thomas's rage died. Whatever he wanted to do to Malone, he couldn't do it with Audie watching.

He turned away from Malone but spoke over his shoulder. "Say a prayer of thanks to God and Gandalf… Audie just saved your life."

Chapter 2

THE SKY ABOVE HELENA WAS A MILKY-BLUE MASS, SO expansive, so infinite, that she felt small and exposed underneath its dome. After a decade in prison, it was disconcerting not to have walls around her and a ceiling above her.

This was freedom. A thing most people took for granted. As pathetic as it sounded, she was going to have to adjust to it.

She walked through the cemetery looking for the grave, eyes skimming name after name until she found the one she was looking for.

RORY RAY ELLIS
BELOVED SON
JANUARY 28, 1990–AUGUST 27, 2008

The granite stone was small and simple. Not the giant monument she'd expected Mrs. Ellis to erect over her son's burial place. Red and white plastic poinsettias ringed the grave, and on top of the stone was a Reese's Peanut Butter Cup—Rory's favorite. Mrs. Ellis must've visited the grave recently. Funny how she and Mrs. Ellis both had the same idea. Rory also loved the iced sugar cookies from Franklin's Bakery. Helena reached into her coat pocket, withdrew the bakery bag, and slid the iced cookie out onto the gravestone next to the Reese's Cup.

Franklin's Bakery was where they'd gone on their first date. They'd sat at one of the little café tables chatting and eating those cookies until they were both high on sugar and each other.

She'd loved Rory the way any naive girl could love a boy. Their relationship had been a sweet exploration for both of them. It hadn't been complicated or difficult. It had been nice and easy and, for her, different. He had been her first in so many ways. Her first boyfriend. Her first lover. Her first heartbreak.

"Oh, Rory." She whispered the words, not quite ready to let the world have the full volume of her voice. "Everything was so normal one moment, then the next, you were dead, and everyone blamed me." The situation had been horrible all around, but one thing had made it even worse for her—knowing that someone had killed Rory and gotten away with it. She wanted to promise him that she'd find his real killer. But she didn't make promises she couldn't keep.

No tears came for Rory. Just as she'd had none for her grandparents when she'd visited their graves, minutes ago. The only thing she felt was regret that so many people's lives had been shattered. Rory's. His mother's. Her grandparents'.

She tore her gaze away from the gravestone and the pain it represented.

A man stood no more than fifty feet from her. Tall and… Strong came to mind. It was more than the width of his shoulders; it was something about the set of them, as if he carried a heavy burden. His hair was so dark, it rivaled the majesty of the night sky. But it was his eyes that enthralled her.

From that distance, she couldn't see their color, but she could see kindness in them. Maybe it was the way they tilted down at the outer edges to lend a strange understanding to his expression. But then his lips moved, sliding upward, into a look of undiluted male satisfaction.

Her heart warmed under his appraisal, and the weirdest sensation came over her. It took a moment for her mind to match a word to the feeling—pleasure. She basked in the glory of his attention. Everything inside her wanted to go to him. Meet him. Talk to him. But the thought of speaking, of sharing that piece of herself that she'd kept hidden away for so many years... The mere thought terrified her. Her voice had been the only part of the past ten years that she'd retained control over.

All the warmth she got from being the center of his focus turned to ice. She wasn't fit for public consumption. Fairson had fractured her as neatly as a broken bone. Now she needed time to heal. Oh, and that wasn't even taking into consideration her status as a felon. As much as she wished it wasn't true, people would judge her for the rest of her life on that murder conviction.

She couldn't bear to look at him any longer, couldn't bear to see him looking at her. Without any hesitation, she turned and walked away. Her legs felt gangly and awkward, as if they didn't want to obey her bidding, but she forced her feet to keep moving.

Don't look back. Don't look at him. Don't you dare.

She clenched her fists so tight, they shook. A deep, throbbing ache formed in her palm where the Sister's blade had sliced her. Exactly what she needed. She thrust her fingers wide open, stretching the injury, allowing the burning pain to vanquish all thoughts of the man.

One step and then another, she walked through the wrought-iron cemetery gates and headed out of town toward her next destination. The cold didn't bother her. She'd planned to be outside all day and had made sure to purchase thick, warm clothing.

She followed the strip of road as it wound its way through the naked woods and low hills. Salt crunched beneath her insulated boots, the sound rhythmic and soothing. Occasionally a car passed, but for the most part, she was alone. Alone was nice. Alone meant she was safe. Safe from the Sisters for the first time in ten years.

Some women spent years planning for their wedding. She'd spent the past decade planning for this day. The day she walked out of Fairson.

She used to fantasize about Grandma making all her favorite foods. The joy of sleeping in her own bed. But Grandma and Grandpa had died in a car accident on their way to visit her three years ago. And then she'd had to sell the house...

It'd taken a while, but she'd formulated a new idea. Visit the graves of everyone she'd lost, visit the Bear, then find a place to stay. She'd give herself one night— maybe two—to say a final goodbye to the life she used to lead and then move on. Move away from this place that represented so much pain.

The Bear was up next on her list.

It surprised her that she'd developed such a strong yearning for the totem while in prison. The old carving hadn't figured into her pre-prison life all that much. But for some reason, she longed to see it again. Wasn't like she had anything better to do.

She reached a shallow valley between two hills and

was able to look up to the top of the next hill and see the Bear alongside the road. Excitement coursed through her. She picked up the pace as she started up the hill.

A woodpecker drilled against a tree alongside the road. A squirrel darted in the underbrush. Birds sang to one another across the woods on either side of the road. These were familiar sounds. Sounds from her childhood. The sounds of innocence. She would never get her innocence back, but at least she had her freedom. She opened her arms wide and tilted her face to the sky.

Suddenly, her guts tingled and twitched like a nest of spider babies had hatched in her intestines. She recognized the sensation—knew it all too well. Someone was watching her. She whipped around, eyes scanning the road behind her. No one was there. No vehicle. She was alone. But that creepy, crawly feeling wouldn't go away. And this was why she hadn't gone to meet that guy in the cemetery. She was a paranoid mess. Her body might not be in Fairson, but Fairson was in her mind.

Stop it. You're out here. They're in there. You're safe now. She chanted the words to herself and locked her gaze on the Bear.

When she was a child, the old carving had seemed gargantuan. As an adult, she'd expected to be underwhelmed by its size, but the opposite was true. It was larger than her memory.

The Bear was positioned so it faced her as she walked up to it. He stood on hind legs, mouth open, lips ripped back over its teeth in a snarl of pure menace as if on the verge of a violent attack. Only she didn't find the Bear's appearance scary. She found it protective, almost like the threat was aimed at everyone else. Not her.

She walked directly up to the totem and discovered she only came up to its lower chest.

It was childish and a bit crazy, but she threw herself against the carving, hugging the beast as if he were a long-lost friend. The wood was cold and rough against her face, but comforting at the same time. She closed her eyes and held on tight, pretending the Bear enfolded her in his embrace, keeping her safe and warm against his large body. She imagined she could smell the natural musk of a living being and the warmth and vitality of a heart beating underneath her cheek. Almost without realizing she was doing it, she pictured the man in the cemetery holding her this way.

Her mind drifted back to childhood, to a time before pain and hurt dominated her world, a time when she'd visited this place with Grandpa and he'd told her the story of how the Bear came to be.

A young medicine woman used to live in the region. She had the ability to soothe the spirit with a touch and heal the body with her herbs. Her tribe prospered greatly from her abilities, but there were others who believed no woman should carry such power. They sought to harm her. But the medicine woman was always surrounded by the strongest of warriors—all seeking her favor and her bed. All except for one. Her bravest warrior asked nothing of her, but silently devoted himself to her.

The medicine woman fell in love with him and his simple loyalty. Theirs was a love for the ages. The kind that soothed and frightened, for its power was strong. She soon became with child.

On the day of her daughter's birth, the village was attacked. Her brave warrior saved her but lost his life trying to prevent their babe from being stolen. Devastated at the loss of her warrior and child, the medicine woman found solace in only one thought. Her brave warrior's spirit lived inside their daughter. She resolved to find her babe.

But no matter how far and wide her remaining warriors searched, they could not find her tiny daughter. Deep inside, she knew her babe still lived, but for how long? Every sunrise, she conjured a spell of protection for her child. A spell enchanted by her own blood and fueled by the tears of a grieving woman and mother.

Days passed into months, and months passed into years until her daughter would have been a woman's age. And still the medicine woman cast her spell every sunrise. A mother's love never dies.

Then one day, a man entered the village, carrying a woman in ill health. The man's body bore the mark of a corrupt spirit, and the people were frightened of him, demanding his life for befouling their sacred space. However, the medicine woman was not afraid of the man. She feared nothing except the death of her daughter.

"I am Bear. And this is Fearless." The man spoke directly to the medicine woman. "She is afflicted and needs medicine." Bear settled Fearless at the medicine woman's feet and offered to sacrifice himself for Fearless's healing. But when the medicine woman gazed upon the woman, she saw not a woman, but the babe she had birthed all those years before. Her child had been returned to her as a woman.

Through the medicine woman's blood and tears and magic, she had conjured a man who saved her daughter

from those who'd enslaved her. Bear sought to protect
Fearless above all things.

He offered again to sacrifice his own life so that
Fearless—her daughter—could be healed. But now only
Bear himself had the power to heal his woman. And he
did heal her with a simple touch. The love between him
and Fearless ran deeper than the valleys, stronger than
the mightiest tree, and wider than the sky.

The medicine woman taught Fearless all she knew.
Quickly, Fearless surpassed her skills and became the
most powerful medicine woman ever to have lived.

Before her death, the medicine woman tasked Bear
with carving a totem of protection for her daughter. A
symbol to all in the region that her daughter would be
protected into eternity.

When Fearless and Bear neared the end of their
earthly lives, Bear carved the totem atop the highest hill.

They went to the ancestors together, dying on the
same night, at the same time. Their bodies were anointed
in bear grease, and a great funeral pyre was erected in
their honor. Black smoke filled the sky for days and
days, and when the fire cooled, the people rubbed the
ashes into Bear's carving to seal Bear and Fearless
together inside the totem forever.

It didn't matter that it was just a story Grandpa had
told her. Helena believed in it. Believed in that kind of
love and devotion. The kind of love that was so powerful that—

"You okay?" A female voice spoke behind her, startling her out of Bear's embrace. She whipped around.
An old SUV idled in the road, the passenger window
down. A woman who looked about the same age as

Helena sat behind the wheel. She wore a thick pair of pink mittens and a pink knit cap with a giant fuzzy ball on the top. With all that pink, she was the epitome of innocence. Not someone who should be stopping to chat with a stranger alongside the road.

Helena had once looked that way. Like she had a whole life in front of her and was excited for the journey.

"Are you okay?" The woman's face wrinkled with concern.

Helena glanced at the old totem, then back at the woman, and cringed at how insane she must've looked.

The woman laughed a sweet sound. "My uncle says that hugs are healing... They make everything better." She lowered her voice and whispered, "He's right, of course. But I tease him about being a big softie." She paused as if waiting for Helena to say something, but when she didn't, the woman started talking again. "My uncle is... Well, if I was going to be technical, he's my great-uncle. Audie McCray. Pastor Audie. He looks exactly like Gandalf. Do you know him?"

Helena's head bobbed up and down on her shoulders.

Pastor Audie. He'd been friends with her grandparents. Despite the fact that Grandma and Grandpa never attended church, they'd all been good friends. He never judged them. Never pushed religion on them. He lived by setting an example of love and acceptance. He'd even testified as a character witness on her behalf during the trial.

"Of course you know him. Everyone around here does. What's your name?"

Helena met the woman's gaze and tried to apologize with her eyes for not speaking.

The woman cocked her head to the side as if trying to understand Helena's silence. "You can't talk?"

Helena gave her a thumbs-up.

A warm smile landed on the woman's face. "I'm Charity." She glanced around. "Did you walk here?"

Helena nodded and tried to tack on a friendly smile, but somehow, it didn't feel right on her face.

"Girlfriend, it is too cold to be out on a nature stroll. Why don't you hop on in, and I'll take you home or wherever you want to go."

It took a while longer than it should for Charity's words to register. And when they did, Helena was horrified. The woman was naive and stupid to be offering a ride to a stranger. Helena was a felon, convicted of murder. Someone Charity should be running from, not offering a ride. It was simple luck the woman had stopped to talk to Helena; what if she'd happened upon a rapist or a serial killer?

If Helena used her voice, she would've admitted she was Helena Grayse—just to scare the woman, so she'd never again offer a ride to a stranger.

Charity leaned over and opened the passenger door. "Hop on in."

Helena walked to the door, waited until Charity looked at her, then pressed down the lock and firmly shut the door.

She turned and walked back the way she'd come.

———⁕———

Thomas walked through the granite garden, looking for an open grave. His mother's grave. Cold air stung his face and seeped in around the collar of his coat.

A chill sliced across his shoulder blades—part cold, part dread.

Trees dotted the landscape, their naked branches spearing the clouds. The sky above and the land below shared the bland, gray color he'd come to associate with winter in Ohio. Grass crunched under his feet and looked as desiccated as the bodies planted beneath it. Nothing was more depressing than a cemetery in winter. Would it look more alive with color? Was the sky really blue, while all he saw was gray? Were the gravestones a motley of different types of granite instead of the same dull color? Was there beauty here while all he witnessed was drab and dreary?

It was so frustrating not being able to see what everyone else saw. As if the world had a secret and wouldn't share it with him. He clenched his hands into fists.

Clng. Clng. Clng. The sound of metal clanging against metal sounded as loud as a church bell in the quiet cemetery.

Across the endless sea of gravestones, Thomas spotted a canopy erected to protect the mourners from the elements. The fabric flapped and snapped in the wind. A metal grommet hitting one of the legs made the endless *clng, clng, clng* noise. The sounds grew in volume, became unnaturally loud. He reached up to cover his ears. But before he could get his hands into place, his vision winked out. Gone. Blackness.

He just stood there. Frozen. Not from fear, but from acceptance. He was blind, and he should be freaking out. But then, blinding himself had been something he'd contemplated in his darkest moments. He'd always thought blindness would grant him an odd sort of relief. No more gray existence, no more seeing the shadow of death. Ignorance really could be bliss, right? The only thing that had kept him from following through was not wanting to be dependent on anyone for anything.

Light flashed in his dark vision like far-off lightning. His sight blinked back on. Everything was the same. But everything had changed.

He still stood in Sundew Cemetery, but it was as if everything around him had faded into the background and a spotlight gleamed on a woman in front of him.

She stood no more than fifty feet away, a beacon of light, a burning flame that he couldn't look away from.

Her body was bundled against the cold, her thick, black coat zipped up over her mouth with the hood pulled down over her forehead. The tiny bit of skin he saw was the palest of—his mind searched for the name of the right color—pale peach. Her skin was pale peach. Pale. Peach.

Holy motherfucking son of a bitch.

He saw color. *Color*. She brought vibrancy to his gray existence. And she carried no shadow of death. Not even a wispy hint. If love at first sight existed, he loved her for these gifts.

At this distance, it should be impossible to see the color of her eyes, but they were gold and shining right at him, locking him in place with their brilliance, their luminescence, and some ethereal quality that made him think of purity and perfection.

Call it instinct, call it pheromones, call it instant visceral attraction—his dick went hard.

"Thomas? Are you all right?" The question he'd been asked too much lately punched him in the head, breaking his attention on her.

Sound clicked back on. He heard the canopy flapping and the metal clanging. Almost as if his body was working in slow motion, he turned his head, absorbing a world that was alive with vitality for the first time. He felt like a kid who'd just learned to name colors. Brown grass. Green canopy. Red scarf.

Audie stood outside the canopy wearing the same getup as last night. Only now, Thomas could see the hat and scarf and mittens were bright red.

Thomas raised his hand in a gesture somewhere between wait-a-minute, a wave, and what-the-hell. Audie smiled, his wrinkled face conveying a wordless understanding. That was why Thomas always liked the guy. No explanations, no empty phrases needed. And it didn't hurt that he looked like Gandalf.

Thomas turned back to the woman, but she no longer stood there. She was walking away, carrying an aura of color with her. The sky above her glowed a sweet, watery shade of blue, the grass under her feet a subtle tan, and the grave she passed was a pinkish granite. *Holy shit*. It was all so beautiful, but then his gaze locked on the erotic sway of her hips.

Without warning, his mind flashed him images of her in his bed and him being mesmerized by her golden eyes, her matching gilded hair, and all that creamy, warm skin surrounding him, holding him tight. Without ever seeing her face, he knew she would be beautiful, so lovely that it would hurt to gaze anywhere but upon her.

There was the *before her* part of his life. Now there was the *after her* part of his life. And he couldn't let her go. He needed her in every sense of the word—emotionally, physically, sexually. He wanted to be underneath her, on top of her, inside her. He wanted to surround her, swallow her, take her into himself and keep her there. *Forever. Always. A-fucking-men.*

He ran after her, opening his mouth to shout her name, but... He didn't know her name. Yet he felt like he *should* know it. And know her. She was his other piece. She completed him. Healed him. Made up for all his deficiencies.

"Thomas? What are you doing?" Pastor Audie yelled. The concern and worry riding along the old man's tone were more effective than diving headfirst into one of the granite markers dotting the cemetery.

What was he doing? Chasing after some random woman in the cemetery who obviously had no reaction to him. If she'd felt even an ounce of the connection he had, she wouldn't be walking away.

He stopped running. But the urge to keep going pushed him forward a few more steps. He grabbed on to a gravestone to keep from following her. His heart rammed against his sternum so hard, it threatened to knock him to the ground. It hurt—physically hurt—to watch her walk away, taking color and beauty with her, leaving him alone inside his gray existence once more. It felt like she'd amputated half of his soul, leaving him with the phantom pain of what could have been. A cold heaviness settled over him. He felt as dead as the stone he clung to.

If he did chase her down, what would he say when he caught up to her? *You bring color to my life. You're the most beautiful thing I've ever seen.* Yeah. He sounded woo-woo-cuckoo.

Ffuucckk... What was wrong with him?

He was about to attend Mom's memorial service, not

get his wood waxed by a random stranger. And that's what she was—a stranger. He didn't even know what she looked like beyond her eyes. As if to prove him wrong, his mind flicked through images it created of what it *wanted* her to look like. And she was glorious. High forehead, lush lips, delicately arched brows, and her eyes. *God, those eyes*. Forever he'd associate the color gold with her. *Stop it. Fucking stop it.*

And she didn't have a shadow of death. Impossible. Everyone had one. From a newborn to someone who'd recently passed. What was it about her that made her so different from everyone else? *Stop it. Stop thinking about her.*

He sucked in a resigned breath, forced the pictures of her out of his brain, and headed toward the canopy covering his mother's grave and his gray, bleak existence.

The coffin dominated the small enclosure. Roses and delicate flowers trailed off the top. Would Mom have thought them pretty? He'd never really known her. Her attention had always landed on his stepfather, his stepbrother, and his sister. Thomas had been the invisible child.

And now that he thought about it, why was he even here? Mom never loved him. His sister had flat-out refused to attend the service. Thomas couldn't blame her—she was still healing from everything she'd been through. He wished he could've stayed away too, but some sick sense of obligation and duty had forced him here.

Only two seats were taken. Pastor Audie sat in front of the coffin, his shadow flitting around him, light and playful. Thomas squinted his eyes, trying to force them to see the color of Audie's hat again, but…nothing.

A gust of wind swept through the tent, and Audie shivered. It was too cold for the guy to keep doing all this outside work. A cold for someone his age could easily turn deadly.

"You warm enough?" Thomas started to unzip his coat. "You can use my coat. I'm always hot anyway."

"Oh, no. You keep it." The old man stood slowly as if to test his balance, then walked to the far side of the coffin where a portable podium had been erected. "Charity, my niece, made me wear long underwear today. And insulated pants. And three sweaters. Dressed me up like a Thanksgiving turkey. Any more clothes, and I won't be able to walk under the weight of them." The man chuckled good-naturedly, then motioned toward the seat he'd vacated.

No way was Thomas sitting next to Malone. He turned toward the other man in the chairs and stopped. Instead of Malone occupying the other seat, Wiley Lanning, Thomas's superintendent, sat there. His shadow carried a hint of gray, was thicker, and rolled like waves of honey. What was his boss doing here? It was nice of him to attend and all, but not what Thomas had expected. They weren't BFFs or anything.

And that was it. No one else. Where were all the people? Where was his low-life bastard of a stepfather? It had been his idea to delay the burial of his wife by a week and a half so he could bury his son and hunt for his son's killer—priorities and all that. But he wouldn't dare blow off his wife's memorial service. That wouldn't look good. And Malone always kept up appearances.

"Am I early?" Thomas aimed the question at Pastor Audie.

"No, son. You're right on time."

"Where is everyone?" Thomas couldn't force himself to move any closer.

Pastor Audie reached inside his coat pocket and held out a folded newspaper. "I'm assuming you didn't read the paper this morning."

Thomas scrunched his face in confusion. "The paper?" Even from the distance between them and reading upside down, he saw the headline.

POSTHUMOUS LETTER OUTLINES SHERIFF'S CRIMES

The words screamed inside Thomas's head. His heart crashed around the cage of his ribs, seeking an escape. The goddamned scar on his face blazed to life, instantly wetting his skin with a sheen of sweat as he grabbed for the paper.

He scanned the article, but only certain words registered.

Murder.

Cover-up.

Sex companion.

Child abuse.

Investigation.

His mother had written a confess-all and sent it to the newspaper and the Bureau of Criminal Investigation where Thomas worked. She'd admitted to murdering his biological father twenty-five years ago.

As a child, Thomas used to dream that his father would show up and rescue him from Malone. But as the years passed, the fantasy had faded and morphed into a diffuse anger at the man who'd abandoned his children. He'd never suspected his father might be dead.

The real kick in the nuts was his mother's accusation

that Robert Malone had helped her cover up the murder—for a price. The price being her children.

Their mother had given Evanee, Thomas's sister, to Malone's son as a sex companion. And granted Malone permission to do as he pleased with Thomas. The selfish bitch had sacrificed her children to keep from going to prison.

The day their mother died, Evanee had glared at him with anger and hurt in her eyes. *Are you blind or stupid or in on it?* she'd asked him. He hadn't exactly known what she'd meant, but he'd had his suspicions.

From as early as he could remember, he'd suspected something was wrong with his family. Something bigger, broader, badder than just Malone hurting him. "I knew. I damn well knew." He shouted the words. Or whispered them. Or didn't speak them at all. But they echoed through his mind, bouncing off the walls of his skull and colliding with one another until what little sanity he possessed went bye-bye. Adios. Ciao.

For one moment, his mind went blessedly blank. He grabbed hold of the nothingness with both fists. Tried to stay in that safe space. But reality wouldn't be denied. It body-slammed him. He turned away from the coffin and coughed, but the foulness of his life wouldn't come out. It had grown roots into his soul.

Thomas dropped the paper. Watched it flutter to the ground. Then raked both hands through his hair, grabbing onto it and pulling.

Maybe his mother had felt better for clearing her conscience, but really, the letter was a final fuck-you to both her children. His mother had once again forced him and his sister into a situation not of their making. The article called what had been done to him and Evanee *a horrific case of child abuse*. And now *everyone* knew, and everyone would see them—him—as a victim. And that just pissed him off.

He stared at the flower-draped coffin. "You bitch." He raised both fists and slammed them down on all those pretty roses. The hard *thunk* of flesh to wood reverberated up and down his arms. He beat the lid as if he could wake up his dead mom and yell at her, then tore what remained of the blooms off the top, shredding them with his rage. Their cloying scent snuck up his nose, and he knew that the smell of roses would always make him angry. His chest heaved, his body shook, and he wanted to hit something human. But his stepbrother was dead. His mother was dead. The only person left was Malone.

"Where is he? Where the fuck is Malone?" He aimed the question at Pastor Audie, who stood there as stoic and calm as a mountain in a thunderstorm. A mountain never got angry at the thunder. Never feared it either. No, the mountain just accepted the storm and all the damage as the cycle of life. That was the thing about Pastor Audie. Total and complete acceptance, no matter what. It was damned hard to keep stoking the fury fire when Thomas was the only one tossing wood on the blaze. And it was damned hard to be angry when he half expected Audie to zap him with his staff for misbehaving.

"Maybe you should sit down." Pastor Audie gestured to the empty seat he'd vacated. The seat next to Superintendent Lanning.

Thomas had forgotten about his boss. "You knew this was in the paper." Thomas's words were an accusation and a question. "Why didn't you tell me?"

"I called. All morning. Your phone kept going to voicemail." Lanning's tone was calm.

"I turned it off after we discussed Jeremy Tucker. Knew you wouldn't call me in today because of..." He pointed at the coffin and the mess littering the ground.

Lanning gave him a sympathetic look. The guy didn't need to say a word. Thomas could see the future in his eyes. And it hurt.

Despite his mother's admission that Malone had abused him, the powers that be would still conduct an investigation. They'd want him to talk about what happened when he was a child and would then label him uncooperative when he couldn't force himself to utter a word about it. Because of his uncooperativeness, they'd search for collusion between him and Malone. After all, both he and Malone were in law enforcement. And how convenient that Malone had called him out on a case *last night*. Right before this article went public. Didn't help that his mother had sent the article to the BCI where *he* consulted. Wouldn't the agents have fun interpreting what that meant? Was his mom seeking his help or trying to put a target on him?

"The only thing I'm going to say about Malone... I'm not involved in any of his shit. I've got nothing but hate for him. Growing up, I knew something wasn't right between Junior and Ev. I didn't know the extent until the day Mom died. And even then, it was mostly a guess. That article confirmed everything I suspected." Reality stung so much worse than ugly speculations.

Lanning nodded as if he understood, but silence ticked by slow and suspicious. "We can't find Robert Malone. Looks like he got wind of the story before it made the paper and took off. You know how that makes him look."

"Guilty." Thomas wanted to be happy that karma was finally searching out Malone, but he couldn't find any joy.

"The BCI has an investigation to conduct at the same time we're searching for Malone. We've got eyes on us over this. The ripple effects are turning into a tsunami. The ghosts of every case Malone touched will haunt the legal system for years. So I'm going to need you to come in this afternoon and answer some questions." Lanning's face went as somber as a soldier facing a suicide mission. "While we investigate…" He trailed off.

Thomas might not be able to see color, but he could see the words his boss didn't speak. Thomas's career—the only reason he kept sucking air—was going to be put on hold, because Malone was the gift that kept on giving. He pulled his wallet from his pocket and yanked out his consultant credential. He stared at his name, then let it go and watched it flutter to the ground. "Fuck this."

"Two weeks. A month. When the investigation is over, everything will go back to the way it always was." Lanning's words were rushed and full of false reassurance.

Thomas knew exactly how the BCI investigators would look at him—through the lens of Malone's behavior, overanalyzing, misinterpreting, and dissecting every single thing Thomas had ever done or not done in his entire life.

And then there was how everyone else would look at him. Before the letter, everyone just thought he was odd—odd-looking and odd-acting. Now, they'd be able to put two and two together and realize the damage done to his face as a child was caused by Malone. Thomas should be happy about that. It was what he'd wanted, but now, all he felt was shame. As if all the dark corners of his life, all the parts he carefully kept hidden, were on public display. And everyone would know that he was partly to blame for never speaking up. For being too damned scared to say a word about it.

He willed time to reverse, willed himself back to childhood so he could've killed Malone and Junior and saved him and his sister a lifetime of abuse. Hindsight sucked ass.

Reality stood right next to him, as cruel and merciless as ever. He clenched his teeth together so tightly, he could hear them grinding. He turned away from the casket.

"Thomas." Pastor Audie's voice stopped him. "We still need to conduct your mother's service."

Foul words filled Thomas's mouth, but he swallowed them down for Audie's sake. "You do whatever you need to do to be right with your God. And I'm going to do what I need to do."

He walked away.

Chapter 3

HELENA STOOD IN THE MIDDLE OF AN EXPANSIVE, ETERNAL WHITE space. No walls, no ceilings, no bars, no locks, and best of all, no people. A gentle breeze whispered over her arms and legs. Warmth heated her skin as if an invisible sun shone upon her. And the sweet, sweet silence felt like a miracle. A deep sense of peace subdued the bad memories that played on repeat in the back of her mind.

Real life could never look so pristine or feel so serene. She had to be dreaming.

Her abdomen suddenly hardened as if she were tensing her muscles, except she wasn't. She reached down to feel her stomach, but what met her fingers wasn't warm flesh. It felt like cold...metal. What was going on? She lifted the simple white smock she wore to look at her skin. A silver shimmer spread over her torso. Each place the shimmer touched hardened the same way her abdomen had.

She dropped the hem of her shirt to watch the shimmer travel down her arm to her hand. She made a fist and felt something strange in the gesture—leashed power. As if she'd suddenly become Superwoman and could punch through steel. Too bad she hadn't had this shimmer thing back in Fairson. She could've cleaned the women's toilets with the Sisters' faces.

Without her brain issuing the order, her mouth opened and words flowed out of her—words spoken *through* her, not *from* her. "You are the warrior." The voice boomed loud with a resonance that rattled her bones. "It is your destiny to teach others how to survive. The armor will protect you from any pain the dream body suffers."

Before she had time to process the words and their meaning, vibrant color flashed against the stark white.

She found herself standing in the middle of a bedroom that looked as though a rainbow had exploded in it. Everywhere were cheerful colors. Bright-yellow walls. A red comforter. Orange pillows. Blue curtains. A green rug. The shades and hues somehow all worked together to create a vivacious space.

But despite the liveliness, a dark menace hung in the air. That place between her shoulder blades itched, goose bumps rose in her hair, and a warning crawled in her gut.

Something bad was about to happen. And she felt readier than she'd ever been.

She whirled around, arms up, fists clenched, expecting to see a Sister, but a young man stood there.

He was average in every way except his eyes. They carried a feral look—the same look a shark gets when it scents blood in the water. "You'll never be anyone else's." Spittle flew from his lips, and he punctuated his words by pointing a hatchet at her.

"Always attack." That strange voice spoke through her again. "Never react. If you are reacting, you are losing." Something else was inside her, controlling her mouth and her body. Fear latched on, but evaporated when her body lunged at the guy, slamming front to front with him, pushing him, trying to make him topple over backward. She drove him back one step, two, three, staying in his space, leaving no room for him to use his weapon. But then he rebounded, plowing forward and shoving her off with a thrusting movement of his shoulder. Momentum knocked her backward. Awkwardness tripped her feet.

She landed—ass, shoulders—then her head *thunked* on the ground. Sparklers of light shot through her vision, but she felt no real pain.

Time did something strange. It stopped completely. Freezing her on the ground with the man locked in a lunge, hatchet raised in the air.

"Use your legs. They are stronger than your arms." Words flowed through her again. What was going on?

Time released her from its grip. Automatically, her legs started kicking.

He launched himself at her, hatchet raised over his head, but she was ready. Her heel struck him in his hip. A zing of dull sensation vibrated up her leg as she connected with the point of his hip bone. The blow twisted him, knocking him back a step, throwing off his aim—which had been toward her face. But he'd already committed to the downward stroke.

Micro moments of time passed while she watched the hatchet descend closer and closer to her thigh. Time grabbed hold of her and tossed her forward a few seconds, skipping completely over him actually hitting her with the blade. For that, she was grateful.

She kicked out with her other leg, connecting with the softness of his kid-makers.

Breath *oomphed* out of him, and he fell to the side in slow motion. His body hit the ground, and she was on top of him. Using her knees, she bashed blows into his ribs and stomach while grappling for control of the hatchet.

His grip on the weapon faltered, and she unexpectedly found it in her hand. Time froze them both again.
"He won't stop until he's incapacitated." That strange
voice came through her again. Time released her once
more. There was a strange pattern to this. Whenever the
voice had something to say, time stopped, then started
again when the voice was done speaking.

The hatchet felt surprisingly light in her hand. She
turned it in her palm and swung it at his temple, hitting
him not with the blade but the flat side. The sound of metal
to bone smacked loudly in the quiet. The man slumped,
unconscious but alive.

She threw herself off him and crawled a few feet away.
In her wake, she left a trail of blood from her thigh.

Out of nowhere, a woman stood over her. Her blond
hair was streaked with perky pink highlights. Her face was
fresh and lovely and wide open in horror. "Who are you?
Why did he attack you in my bedroom?"

"That is how you will survive." The words came through
Helena.

As she watched, the shimmer on her flesh began to
recede, leaving insurmountable exhaustion in its wake.
From a distance, she heard the woman asking more questions, but she was too tired to answer and too weak to
move. Sleep claimed her.

Thomas lurched upright in his bed. Adrenaline scorched
through him. He gasped for breath as if sleep had held
him in a choke hold. Probably another nightmare. It was
a blessing that he couldn't remember his dreams.

He stood, legs quaking beneath him, and stumbled to

the window to press his forehead against the cold glass. He closed his eyes and sucked in a few slow breaths to calm himself.

In the basement, the old-fashioned, completely inefficient boiler clicked on. A radiator downstairs popped. The comforting sounds of his old Victorian eased him.

The invisible terror he'd woken to finally let go of him. He opened his eyes and stared out into the dark.

Black night and white snow contrasted, casting the world in an X-ray glow. In the woods behind his house, no more than a quarter mile away, a tiny patch of light caught his gaze. Faint and flickering the way a campfire does. A campfire?

Why was someone out there in the middle of a wintery night, and more importantly, why were they trespassing in *his* woods? It was cold out. Snow covered the ground. More was fluttering down. There'd be half a foot by morning.

A thought detonated inside his head, the impact so great, he gripped the window molding.

Malone.

It made perfect sense. Malone knew exactly where law enforcement would be searching for him—highways, airports, bus terminals, train stations. All those places would be on alert, but here he was, hiding so close to home—in Thomas's backyard—where no one ever would suspect.

That flickering light outside was an opportunity. A chance to right all the wrongs and bring Malone down.

Thomas shoved away from the window and ran downstairs and through his house to the kitchen.

The lights were out, but the newspaper he'd bought

with that terrible headline—POSTHUMOUS LETTER
OUTLINES SHERIFF'S CRIMES—seemed to glow in the
dark from its spot on the table. He practically had the
article memorized.

In the mudroom, he threw on his winter gear and
sprinted out the back door.

The cold air invigorated him, charging him with
anticipation. He ran past the post his bird feeder was
perched on—needed to refill the thing tomorrow.

Fat flakes of snow meandered out of the sky, taking
their sweet time to hit the ground. The naked trees, their
trunks black in the night, speared toward heaven. In his
stark, gray existence, few things were more beautiful than
snowfall at night. But he didn't stop to savor its majesty.

A calm settled over him. His mind shifted into hyper-
focus; his body became a finely crafted machine built
for racing through the snow, dodging and darting around
the trees, jumping over the fallen limbs. Bushes and
brambles that would've been impossible to walk through
in the spring and summer were mere annoyances that
scraped along his legs. His pajama pants would probably
be full of burrs when he got back—if he got back. No
telling what this confrontation with Malone would bring.

He burst into the small clearing and slid to a halt. A
pup tent frosted with snow sat near a smoldering fire.
Even in black and white, the scene was oddly pictur-
esque. Something he'd expect to see in a magazine
advertising the outdoor life, not in the woods behind his
house at o dark thirty.

"Get out here and face me like a man." His voice
came out sharp and angry. He held his breath, waiting
for a reply.

He scanned the tent for movement. Nothing.

He scanned the snow for footprints. Nothing.

He scanned the edges of the clearing. Nothing.

Years of pent-up rage sizzled along his nerve endings. He clenched his fists, ready, willing, and able to handle whatever happened next.

But nothing happened. Not a single thing.

He walked to the tent. With rock-steady hands, he reached out and began unzipping it. The release of each zipper tooth was as loud as a machine gun in the quiet clearing. Plenty of time for Malone to ready, aim, fire from inside.

There was a line where reckless crossed into suicidal. Thomas suspected he'd jumped it when he ran out of the house without calling for backup and without a weapon. He didn't care.

He inhaled, braced himself as if expecting a blow, and parted the tent flaps.

His mind went empty, as if everything he'd ever known had been suctioned out, leaving a chasm. Yet somewhere in the empty depths, new, unbelievable thoughts began to grow.

Chapter 4

THE. WOMAN. FROM. THE. CEMETERY. EACH WORD SLOWLY bloomed in Thomas's mind, along with the dawning realization that he saw color again.

A warm, radiant blue glowed inside the tent. Orange firelight flickered across the woman's face. A thick, red sleeping bag covered her entire body. She still wore her coat zipped over her mouth, hood up and pulled low over her forehead. Only her nose, a sliver of cheek, and her eyes were visible—gorgeous tawny eyes that reminded him of sunshine, autumn, and Indian summer.

Their gazes collided. A head-on impact of massive proportion—a visceral, raw moment that catapulted him into another era where she was his world and he was hers. A place where nothing mattered except the two of them. They were a lock and key. They could open themselves to power or lock themselves away from pain.

He clamped his eyes closed, cutting off the connection. Surely, he couldn't really be seeing this—or her. He popped his lids open, bracing himself for disappointment. For an empty tent or, worse, Malone. But she still lay there watching him. Just watching.

"Thomas." His name popped out of his mouth without warning. It seemed to hang suspended in the air between them with no reference. "Yeah." His head bobbed on his shoulders. "My name." *Jesus.* He was acting like he'd never talked to a woman before. Well, he'd certainly never spoken to one as beautiful as this one. "Thomas. Thomas Brown. My name." *Jeez*. He sounded about a dozen IQ points below average. "My name is Thomas Brown." At least he'd figured out how to string a coherent sentence together. Finally.

He witnessed his name being taken in, absorbed, and could almost—almost—read her name in her eyes. It was something alluring and regal. An image air-dropped into his mind of her riding him, using him in the best way, while he chanted that elusive name. *Whoa, whoa, whoa*. Where was that thought coming from?

A tiny voice inside his head whispered that he might be losing his shit—he'd just met her. Well, sort of. A louder voice argued that if ever someone had been created for him, it was her. She brought color and texture to his gray world. She carried no shadow. She was his miracle.

During it all, she watched him, never moving, never speaking. His heart walloped against his sternum, propelling him into the tent. "What's wrong?"

He waited for her response, but she just watched him. Shouldn't she be flipping out? He was a strange man, invading her tent in the middle of the night, in the middle of the woods, in the middle of nowhere.

"Can you tell me what happened…where you're hurt?" He studied her face for a response, but not so much as a muscle moved.

Stroke. Spinal injury. Brain damage. His mind listed the most terrible things that could've happened to her since he'd last seen her at the cemetery.

"I'm just going to check you over before I get you out of here." He took off his gloves, untied her coat's hood, then slowly drew down the zipper. Millimeter by millimeter, he revealed her face. High cheekbones, pale porcelain skin, plump, full lips with just a hint of natural rose. Lips that begged to be kissed, as if she were his Sleeping Beauty. Beauty personified. The only beautiful thing he'd ever seen.

She enthralled him, cast a spell over him. She was lovelier than spring blossoms, more captivating than a sunrise, more magnificent than a thunderstorm. It was more than the way she colored his world. It was her. Something about her. Something about him when he was near her. A deep internal sense that she was intended for him.

He pressed his fingers to the warm skin of her neck, searching for a pulse. An electric jolt zipped from where he touched her—up his arm, down his torso, straight to his dick.

He ripped his hand off her and flung himself against the flimsy tent wall, nearly toppling the thing over. His dick didn't need to have anything to do with this situation. So why the hell was the little fucker reacting to this woman as though she was his favorite fetish when she was obviously in distress.

What was wrong with him?

Thomas smacked himself in the forehead to knock some sense back into himself, but knocked a thought loose instead.

Soul mates. *Holy motherfucking shit, they were soul mates*. Only he didn't believe in that crap. Or hadn't believed. Until now. Until her. It felt as if they'd been carved from the same block of wood, and the joining of the two created something expansive and vast. Too large for mere words.

He shook her shoulder like a little kid trying to get a sleeping parent's attention. "Do you feel..." There wasn't a word in existence to describe the sensation between them. "...this thing between us?"

She returned his stare, and he knew without her speaking that she felt it too.

The hood of her coat slipped back off her forehead, and all those thoughts vanished.

Her hair. Oh God, her hair. It was the same color as her eyes. The gold of a wheat field at the end of a summer day—all burnished and full of wonder. He settled his hand over her hair as if it were priceless metal. Damn if it didn't feel precious and silky. He wanted to run those strands over his lips while inhaling the scent of her.

He brushed a clump of hair off her forehead, revealing a jagged wound stretching from just above her eyebrow to her hairline—pink, painful, and fresh. Coarse black thread held the injury together.

All his pansy-assed feelings died as neatly as if they had been chopped off by a butcher's knife. "What happened?" Could that injury be the cause of her paralysis? An urge came over him. An instinctual feeling that he needed to touch her injury, despite how weird that seemed.

Lightly, so as not to hurt her, he settled his fingertips over the thick, black thread. Her eyes locked with his. He tumbled into them. Let waves of warmth stroke him from the inside out. Peace and a sense of deep connection surged through him. She relaxed him in a way he'd never experienced. He wanted beyond wanting to spread his body over hers and simply live out his days staring into her and feeling her body beneath his.

"Are you hurt anywhere else?" His voice was thick and slow.

Her eyes narrowed almost as if she were trying to force words from her gaze since her mouth wouldn't work. And damn if he didn't read her loud and clear. Only the message she conveyed couldn't tell him the whole story.

"I won't let anything else harm you." His voice sounded like Determined and Obstinate got together to make a baby named That's-a-Promise. Way too intense. *Jeez.* And those words weren't even what he'd intended to say. He'd been going for something along the lines of *I'm going to check you over*.

Instead of letting anything crazier pop out his pie-hole, he pulled his hand off her forehead, but it took effort, like pulling two magnets apart. Or maybe that was just in his head, and he needed to get a grip on his mental reins.

He unzipped the sleeping bag to reveal the rest of her body. Her hands were covered with a fat pair of gloves. Her coat was long and bulky and landed half-way down her thighs. Her legs were covered in heavy insulated pants, and she wore a pair of thick socks on her feet. At least she was prepared to be out here in the cold and snow.

He scanned her for any wounds or injuries. Ran his hands over her, feeling nothing other than the gentle curves of a woman hidden beneath all that fabric. No, he was not going to allow his mind to conjure images of what his hands were touching. No, he would not. He would focus on what was most important.

Priority one: Get her help. Call him psychic, but he

saw a trip to the ER in their future. "I'm gonna get you out of here."

He backed out of the tent. There wasn't a nice way to do this. He grabbed her ankles and hauled her limp body out onto his lap, then paused to savor the sensation of her being in his arms. The gentle pressure of her weight against him. The way she leaned in to him. The way she needed him, an intoxicating combination he'd never experienced, and never wanted to let go.

He got to his feet, expecting holding her—hell, holding anyone—to feel awkward, but it was comforting and slightly addicting. The closeness of human contact…amazing.

He turned away from the tent. Vibrant, brilliant colors filled the world around him. A gasp of shock and wonder slipped from his lips. The flickering campfire cast the clearing in a warm light, making the snow shine as if cast in gold leaf. The fire itself flared, fluttering with every shade of orange imaginable. He could've stood there all night just taking in the beauty.

Reluctantly, he kicked snow over the blaze until it went out, then started following his tracks back through the woods.

He glanced down at her. She looked up at him, gratitude in her gaze.

"Hey…" His voice soft and imploring. *Damn.* Didn't even know he possessed the ability to use that tone. "My house is a little ways from here. I'll take you to the hospital and then…"

It was like watching the tide turn, subtle and violent at the same time, those gorgeous, tawny eyes filled with naked terror.

No hospital. She hadn't moved her lips, but he swore he could see her unspoken words.

"You don't want to go? But you're not talking. You're not moving. Something is wrong."

She begged him with her eyes, pleaded with him to not take her to the hospital. Despite all the *logical* arguments that lined up inside his head, he couldn't force her into something she didn't want.

A sigh of absolute resignation and capitulation came out of him. "Listen. I'll give you an hour. If you aren't better by then, I'm taking you to the hospital. No matter how you look at me."

The relief in her expression was enough to assure him that he'd made the right decision. For the moment, anyway.

Whoa… Wait…

What. The. Hell. He'd just had a semi-conversation with her, and she hadn't spoken a word. He *thought* he knew what she wanted just by the way she looked at him?

Either his sanity had cracked down the middle…or for the first time in his life, everything was impossibly right.

As he carried her through the snow, his eyes darted around, taking in the colors he'd been missing. The verdant leaves of a wild cedar. The way snow at night took on a sapphire-blue hue. The world dazzled him. And it was all because of her.

He walked out of the woods into his yard. Without warning, tension grabbed him by the back of the neck. He turned to look back the way they'd come, but saw only trees and snow and his own tracks.

A feral howl pierced the quiet, the sound eerie and too close for safety. His heart clenched, holding tight, refusing to release. The forest was full of coyotes. All year, he heard them yipping and howling at night, but this one sounded…mad and threatening. Like it wasn't happy that Thomas had just walked off with its meal and was going to fight him for her.

Thank Christ, he'd found her when he did and she was safe with him. He wouldn't let anything—man or beast—hurt her. "I've got you."

A coyote was more likely to attack if Thomas turned his back on it. He slowly backed toward his house.

Deep in the woods, a large indistinct shadow glided from one tree to another.

He picked up the pace, careful to keep from tripping over his own damn feet and landing in a heap on the ground. That would be a formal invitation for an attack.

It'd never occurred to him that his yard was fifty miles long until he had to walk across it backward with a rabid coyote stalking them.

───────

The coyote in the woods didn't matter. That movement and sensation were returning to her body didn't matter. What mattered was that he was taking her home.

Home sweet home. Home is where the heart is. No place like home. Never had she believed those phrases more than now.

The moment Thomas poked his head inside the tent, she recognized him as the man she'd seen in the cemetery. And when he'd told her his name…another jolt of recognition.

It had been his name on the paperwork she'd signed three years ago when she sold the house. Having to let go of the place so soon after Grandma and Grandpa died had been another terrible loss. The only bright side was the money. As a felon, no one was going to want to hire her. The cash gave her a cushion until she could find someone willing to take a chance on her.

As he carried her through the back door, the unmistakable scent of home wrapped itself around her—wood and the polish Grandma had used on the woodwork. Helena inhaled, savoring the smell. Tears burned in her sinuses as a lifetime full of memories flooded her mind. But she wouldn't let herself cry. There were always more important things than tears. Things like serendipity and fate.

Prickles of pain permeated Helena's muscles. The sensation similar to the pins and needles of a limb waking up after it had fallen asleep. Had her entire body fallen asleep because she'd fallen asleep at the end of that dream? She wiggled her fingers and toes to reassure herself that movement was coming back online. Yes, it was.

Thomas shifted her in his arms, holding her tighter to him, almost as though he worried someone was going to try to steal her away. She wasn't one of those tiny women who barely made it past five feet. She was five foot eight, and yet he carried her like she weighed nothing. Didn't that make a girl feel all protected and safe? She resisted the urge to wrap her arms around his neck, snuggle in closer, and pretend that this was all that would ever exist. No pain from the past. No worries about her future. Just this. Being held by a good man and feeling truly safe for the first time in years.

She craned her neck, taking in the dark house as he carried her through the kitchen, into the butler's pantry that led to the dining room, then across the grand foyer with its open staircase and into what her grandma had always called the parlor. He settled her on the couch as gently as if she were made of spun sugar, then stepped back and looked at her.

His face was angular and hard, but his eyes were soft and soulful and filled with a sadness she longed to soothe. No one should carry that kind of hurt in their gaze. Especially someone as kind as him. He didn't have to help her. He could've just left her. She would've been all right. Already, she could move again. And that coyote was probably just being protective of its den. Not aggressive.

His features softened. "You're doing better." The words themselves were a statement, but question dominated his tone.

She wiggled her fingers and toes, then lifted her arms and legs in a poor imitation of a marionette.

"Glad to see it." A genuine smile fired on his face. Even though he hadn't turned a light on yet, she witnessed a moment—just a moment—when the sadness left his eyes. But now she realized that he carried more than sadness; he was drowning in pain.

"I should get the light." He started to turn away, to head for the wall switch, but she grabbed his hand with her gloved one. She felt the sting of the injury the Sister had given her across her palm, but it was just an annoyance. She didn't let go of him.

"What's wrong?" Concern wove its way through his tone.

It was silly, but she didn't want him to turn the light on. As crazy as it sounded to herself, she feared that if he flipped the switch, the spell would be broken and she'd wake up outside in the tent all alone. Which was what she'd wanted when she bought her camping gear and pitched her tent out in the grove. But now more than anything, she wanted to be right here, right now. In this house, with him. In the dark.

Thomas knelt, his face level with hers, and stared into her eyes. The way he looked at her... It was like the guy had X-ray vision. She could feel him inside her, shining a light on her truth. All those parts that she'd been careful to keep hidden from the Sisters and Fairson were bared to him. If he'd been anyone else, she'd have felt violated, but there was something special about him.

"I understand." He squeezed her hand.

Pain sliced across her palm. She flinched and yanked her hand away from him, clutching it to her chest, more from reflex than from thinking he'd intended to hurt her.

"Whoa." His eyes widened, and he held up his arms as if she had a gun aimed at him. She knew he didn't mean to hurt her. "I'm sorry. I would never do anything to cause you harm. Never." He spoke the words with a passion and intensity that shouldn't exist.

She offered her gloved hand to him to show that he didn't frighten her. That she trusted him.

"Your hand is injured too?"

Her head jerked up and down on her shoulders. It didn't faze him that she didn't speak out loud. He wasn't like the annoying social worker at prison who'd kept trying to convince her to talk. Or the COs who'd assumed she was either deaf or stupid because she didn't speak. Or the Sisters who'd taunted her ten times worse because she never taunted them back. He understood and accepted her silence in a way no one else ever had.

He took the hand she still offered him. Slowly, delicately, inch by inch, he pulled the heavy glove off. The thick elastic bandage the prison doc had used over the white gauze had brown splotches of dried blood on it.

She wasn't surprised. Camping out was work, but she'd endured the discomfort. Same as she had for the past ten years. The cut on her palm ranked as nothing on the scale of injuries she'd survived from the Sisters.

He cradled her hand in both of his as if it were an offering he was about to make to the gods. "What happened?" He glanced up at the stitches on her forehead, then back down to the bloody bandage, knowing the injuries were related. "Who hurt you?" He searched her face for the answer.

She slammed her eyes closed before he could see the ugly truth inside her. She'd been attacked by the Sisters while she'd been in prison. She was a felon. When he found that out… She didn't want to see the sadness and pain in his eyes transform into revulsion.

Funny how every minute of the day she'd been so conscious of her felon status. Conscious of how every law-abiding citizen would condemn her if they knew she'd been in prison for murder. But somehow from the moment he'd showed up in her tent, she hadn't really thought about him judging her until now.

"Hey." He settled his hand alongside her face. It was all she could do to keep from nestling her cheek against his rough palm. "It's okay. You don't have to tell me." His thumb swiped over her cheekbone so gently, it was like being kissed by a breeze.

She shoved all thoughts of being a felon, of being in Fairson, of the Sisters, down deep inside her. No way

could she let him see those things. Forcing her eyes
open, she still wasn't confident enough to meet his gaze.
She looked everywhere in the room but at him.

A disappointed sigh came from him as he removed
his hand from her cheek. "Okay. Let's see what we're
dealing with."

She ventured as far as looking at the bridge of his
nose.

"Let's get your coat off first."

With her bandaged hand, she grasped the zipper.

He stopped her. "Let me. I don't want you to hurt
yourself."

She let go and watched him unzip her coat. When
was the last time anyone had done anything to care
for her? Grandma. Grandma had made her favorite
breakfast—homemade pancakes with Nutella and
bananas—ten years ago. It had been a last breakfast
before prison.

Thomas stood and helped pull the material off her
arms, then draped the coat over the back of the couch.
He took off his coat and laid it over hers, then pulled
the winter cap off his head. His dark hair pointed in
every direction, messy and adorable in a way that
reminded her of an ornery little boy. "I'm going to run
upstairs and get the first aid kit. I'll be right back." He
caught her gaze for a brief second, and she could see
that he feared she'd run off while he was gone.

She pointed to her stocking feet and wiggled her toes.
With it snowing outside, she wasn't going anywhere.

"You've got a point." He chuckled and walked out
of the parlor, crossed the foyer, and then took the stairs
by twos. She didn't mean to notice the way his pajama

pants rode low on his hips. Or how the Henley he wore stretched across his broad back and clenched around his biceps. But she noticed. Any woman would.

She looked around the parlor and the open room next to it. Two large, squared-off pillars jutted out of the wall—the only indication that it was meant to be another room. Thomas hadn't changed any of the wallpaper. It was still the same pattern—silver background, cherry blossoms, and hummingbirds. It comforted her to know he'd kept the place the same. Maybe that was why seeing him inside this house felt so normal. He belonged here just as much as her grandparents had.

Being back here, it was easy to remember the girl she'd once been, but the memories felt like someone else's. She wasn't that person any more. She couldn't imagine she'd ever felt so light and carefree.

That only made it all the more important to remember who she was. She was no damsel in distress. She knew how to take care of herself. Her breath hitched unexpectedly. He could bandage her wound, but nothing else. Then she'd borrow a pair of boots and get herself back outside to the clearing. Once there, she should pack up camp and give up the idea of staying outdoors this close to home. It was a stupid idea anyway.

He jogged back down the stairs, carrying the standard white plastic first aid kit and an adjustable desk lamp. Her heart went soft and squishy. He could've turned on the large overhead chandelier, but he'd known she didn't want him to do that, so he brought a lamp to see her wound. Wetness stung the backs of her eyes at his consideration and kindness.

He aimed the soft light at her lap, then knelt in front

of her, opened the kit, and held out his hand, waiting for her to make the final move.

Without hesitation, she set her hand in his palm. While he unwound the elastic bandage, she watched him. Head bent over her, his brow furrowed in concentration. The sharp angles and panes of his face made all the more distinct from the shadows. And that's when she saw the damage done to him.

Shiny pink skin spanned his cheek, his temple, and part of his forehead. Not a horrifying disfigurement that made her want to look away. No, the scar was a curiosity. Something she wanted to devote some time to examining. Some time to touching.

The damaged skin looked like a windswept tree of life. Trunk along his temple, roots dangling down his cheek, bare branches spreading across part of his forehead. It was pretty in an exotic sort of way.

She reached out and touched it with her fingers. He froze. Didn't look up. Just continued to stare downward as if he feared her reaction. Obviously, he'd had his own reasons for not wanting to turn on the light.

She settled her palm against his face, just as he'd done to hers. He closed his eyes, his dark lashes casting deep shadows. He rubbed his cheek against her skin, doing what she couldn't allow herself to do. His stubble tingled against her palm, creating a friction and heat that traveled up her arm and down her torso until it settled low in her stomach, warming her in the most delicious of ways. She should move away from him, but it felt too good.

He turned his face and kissed her palm. His mouth on her skin soft and sweet and sinful. A white zing of longing raced to her core. Primal need rose within her. It was all she could do to keep her hips from gently thrusting because damn, she was primed and ready to go.

She pulled her hand off his face before she ended up humping him. What the hell was that about? After some of the shit the Sisters had done to her, she'd assumed sex was gonna be a no-go for her. Guess not. Maybe that was one thing they'd tried to take from her but had failed. Score one for her. She still wanted sex. Not just any sex. She wanted to have sex with him. That would be a solid *screw you* to the Sisters, the past, and all the pain.

He sucked in a slow breath, opened his eyes, but didn't look at her, just continued unwrapping the bandage as if nothing had happened. And on his end, maybe nothing had. It was good that he didn't look at her. He would've seen the steam of embarrassment rising off her.

When he finished removing the bloody bandage, he examined the wound.

The cut running along her lifeline was deep and gaping, with smears of both fresh and dried blood. The prison doc hadn't stitched it. He'd claimed it was just a scratch. In her mind, there was a distinct difference between a scratch and a gash. This was a gash. But she hadn't argued with the guy. She'd wanted out of there as quickly as possible.

Thomas looked up and snagged her gaze before she could look away. "You're not going to want to hear this, but I think you need stitches. A quick trip to the ER, a few stitches, you're out of there. No big thing."

She leaned back and shook her head. *No. No way.*

"Hey, I get it. You don't like hospitals."

No. He didn't get it.

She wasn't setting foot inside a hospital. It was too similar to an institution—a prison. The only difference was there weren't any bars on the doors and windows. But there would still be the same antiseptic stench and people. Doctors and nurses who would remember her because she kept surviving unsurvivable injuries. Not to mention her status as the local murderess. Mrs. Ellis had done a fine job of making sure every man, woman, and child knew Helena had murdered her only son.

Definitely, no hospital.

"Can you look at me?" he asked, resignation dominating his tone.

No. She didn't want him to see the vulnerability that might be shining in her eyes. She stared up at the ceiling, at the antique light fixture that at one point had been converted from gas to electric.

"I... Okay... I understand. You don't want to go to the hospital. I'm with you. I hate those places too. And I'm certainly not a people person. But this cut is too deep to heal normally. I have a friend. He's a doctor. He has everything he'd need to treat this at his home. Will you at least let me take you to him so he can stitch this up?"

A tug of war raged inside her. She should leave as soon as he got done bandaging her hand. She shouldn't stay, and she most certainly shouldn't let him help her anymore. He'd already given her more than she'd dared to hope for. He'd taken her home. And now it was time to say goodbye to this place once and for all. Closure. This was her closure.

But...she flexed her palm, and the wound gaped open, blood rushing into the gash.

"See. It's too deep." He grabbed a gauze pad and pressed it gently to her palm.

Damn it. He was right. She did need stitches. She rubbed the fingers of her other hand together to indicate money. There were a couple hundred bucks stashed back at her camp. Anything more than that, and she'd need to visit the bank.

A smile tipped the corner of his mouth. "You don't need to worry about that. You'll get the friends-and-family discount because you're my friend. First thing in the morning, we'll head over there."

He opened the first aid kit and set to rebandaging her. His touch more gentle than it had a right to be when tenderness was something she hadn't experienced in a decade. She knew how to handle anger, aggression, and apathy, but not this.

Her heart went heavy and light at the same time. Her sinuses burned, and her eyes filled with water. She speed blinked to fan away the wetness. What was wrong with her? Tears hadn't been a part of her life in Fairson, so why would she want to cry now when someone was being nice to her?

A tear reached the tipping point and slid down her cheek. She swiped it away, then realized he was watching her.

The look in his eyes—compassion, caring, kindness—only made it worse. The tears doubled in volume, turning into a geyser. She turned her face away and hid it between her shoulder and the couch while he finished wrapping her hand.

This was not her. She was not a crybaby. She was strong. She'd survived the Sisters and Fairson. She wasn't going to make it out of there alive only to have a mental breakdown on the outside.

He shifted and sat on the couch next to her, his weight dipping the cushion and tipping her toward him. If he touched her... If he hugged her... If he offered her any words of empathy...she would shatter into a million pieces. She didn't need those things right now. She needed oblivion and distraction and a giant screw-you to the Sisters. She knew exactly what she needed.

She turned toward him, wetness still on her cheeks, and shoved him off the couch.

Chapter 5

HER HANDS RAMMED INTO HIS CHEST, KNOCKING HIM sideways off the couch. Thomas landed ass first on the hardwood floor.

Before his brain had a chance to catch up with what had just happened, she landed on top of him, straddling his body, lifting her hands like she meant to—

Instinct raised his arms to shield his face. But no blow ever came. Instead, she lightly, gently wrapped her fingers around his wrists and tried to tug them away. He resisted. Humiliation burned a bright and steady blaze across his flesh.

Fucking shit. Not facing her was only gonna made it worse.

He submitted to her, allowed her to breach his defenses. The only saving grace was the dim light from the lamp on the end table. Maybe she wouldn't notice that he'd turned embarrassment's favorite color.

Concern for him carved a deep wrinkle across her forehead. *Great*. Why couldn't a portal to hell open right now so he could jump in? That would be better than having to admit that he'd acted like an abused dog. "I… uh…don't do so well with… You know…"

She stared at him for a long time, then tenderly touched the scarred side of his face with her fingertips. He didn't want to meet her eyes, but he was helpless against her. He saw the question she didn't speak aloud.

"Yeah. I'm…jumpy"—that was better than calling himself a pussy—"since that happened."

She wanted to know more. He could see her curiosity but wasn't going to tell her anything else. It would only make him sound childish—in need of growing up and getting over it. He turned his head to the side so she could no longer see the scar.

And that's when he felt her fingers on the bottom of his Henley, tugging the material up, up, up.

His gaze snapped to her. He couldn't look away. She was a beacon in the dark, a promise of salvation. But what the fuck was she doing? He stretched out his arms and lifted so she could pull the shirt over his head.

Was she… Did she want to… Was there any way to mistake her intentions here? His mind searched for any and every possible meaning behind her taking his shirt off. All he could come up with was that *she* wanted *him*.

Her golden eyes were warm and her mouth slightly open as she took him in. The only words he could find tumbling around inside his head to describe how she looked at him were a combination of approval, awe, and adoration that no one had ever given him until now.

What little pride he had pumped up a few notches under her perusal. With both hands, she traced the cleft between his pecs, then the hollow of muscle that ran down his stomach. Her touch was cool and carnal.

Goose bumps erupted on his skin. His dick went from zero to boner in record time. The way her inner thighs hugged his hips, she had to feel it. She rubbed herself against him. Fireworks of pleasure burst through him. Oh yeah, she felt it.

Her eyes widened, then slid half-closed. A moaning gasp, brimming with desire, escaped her lips. Whenever she chose to talk to him, he just knew her voice was going to be sex and satin to his ears.

He wanted to spend an eternity studying her, memorizing each detail of her features. Even with the cut on her forehead, she was beautiful. His kind of beautiful. A whole world of beautiful.

But…there was still wetness on her cheeks. No matter how much he wanted this, he wouldn't do it with those tears on her face.

"Hey." His voice came out a rough and ragged thing. Slowly, her eyes found his. Goddamn, whenever she looked at him—really looked at him—it was as if she saw beyond the surface to his deep-down dirty core. And somehow liked him anyway. Her head tilted to the side, and her brow furrowed.

"I can't do this with grief on your cheeks." Slowly, he reached up and grasped the sides of her head, letting his fingers slide into her hair, and then used his thumbs to wipe at the wetness on her skin. She closed her eyes the way a child does when she's tolerating her parent cleaning an injury. He could see that now. She was injured. Not just physically. Emotionally.

And this—her legs wrapped around his body, making it clear what she wanted, being on top, taking the lead—was her way of coping. She wanted to fuck the pain away. And he would let her use him to do it. Maybe he was a shit for letting this go any further. But he wouldn't stop her. Not because he was Mr. Altruistic and willing to sacrifice his body for her mental health. No, he would let her take this as far as she wanted because he wanted the connection with her. He wanted to bury himself balls deep inside her and never leave.

When her cheeks were dry, he whispered. "I'm going to kiss you now." He hadn't realized how badly he wanted a simple kiss until he spoke the words aloud.

Her eyes popped open as though she was afraid, but she submitted to the gentle pressure of his hands still in her hair. As the distance between them closed, her gaze never left his. A wary trust shone in her eyes. He knew that look. It said she would agree to this as long as he didn't hurt her, yet she was still expecting the pain. And he was going to do everything in his power to *never* cause her harm. Only pleasure.

In that impossible last moment, right before their lips touched, something hot, magnetic, and powerful roused inside him. Something dormant about to awaken and forever change him.

Her lips touched his. A spark of electricity jumped between them, startling them both, but neither moved away, and neither closed their eyes.

She tasted of winter and snow. Surprise flared in her eyes. Her warm, wet tongue found his, and he lost himself in the sensations of her. He wanted to keep looking at her, but she was too much. She overwhelmed all his senses. He smelled her clean, natural scent. Tasted her sweetness. Felt every inch of her body that touched him.

Nothing else existed. No world. No problems. No past. No future. The only thing that remained was her. She surrounded him. Owned him. Through all the years of suffering, he'd been biding his time, waiting for her. The reason he hadn't ended himself decades ago? Some innate knowledge that she was out there in the world, and eventually, they would meet.

A need born from something more powerful than himself moved his hands out of her hair and onto her waist. She wore such bulky clothing that her true form was visually hidden, but he could feel her through the layers. Felt the bones of her hips and the hollow of her stomach underneath his hands. He slid his fingers up under her shirt, craving her skin the way the devil lusts for sin.

The first ripple of marred flesh met his fingers, then another and another. What was... Before his brain finished asking the question, it had already supplied him with the answer. Scars. She was badly scarred.

She grabbed his wrists, her grip firm and unyielding. She used her injured hand in a way that had to hurt and would probably cause it to bleed again. Leaving no room for argument, she guided him away from her body, pressing his wrists to the floor on either side of his head. She stared into his eyes. She didn't want him to touch her. No, it was more than not wanting his touch. It was fear. She was *afraid* of him touching her.

He lay completely submissive to her, not fighting the way she held him. "Hey. It's okay. You've got a scar. I've got a scar. It's no big—"

She let go of his wrists to settle both hands over his mouth and shook her head. He wanted to argue with her. Wanted to convince her that no matter what resided underneath her clothing, she was beautiful. Gorgeous in a way that was meant just for him. Call him delusional, but he believed in that more than he believed in any higher power. Scars were nothing compared to the shadow of death that surrounded some people.

Without removing her hands from his mouth, she bent over him and looked into his eyes. Her long, golden hair fell around them like a stage curtain. The ends of it tickled his palms, still lying where she'd placed them. She stared deep inside him and let him do the same with her. She was asking for his promise not to touch her and questioning if she could trust him.

She finally took her hands off his mouth.

Slowly, so she could see his intentions, he reached up and cupped her face with both his hands—the only kind of touch she found acceptable. "I won't do anything you don't want me to do. I would never hurt you. And I would never judge you by the scars you carry. I promise."

Her eyes searched his, looking for deception, but he had none.

Gently, she grasped his wrists and moved them to the floor, just above his ears once again. She leaned over him. For a split second, he thought she meant to kiss him, but instead she shoved her nose against the side of his neck—a gesture both sweet and intimate. Goose bumps pebbled over his skin. Her hair fanned out across his chest, so appealing and pleasant, he wanted to stroke the strands against his skin, but he wouldn't move from the position in which she'd placed him.

She inhaled deeply as if she enjoyed the scent of him. He turned his face into her hair and did the same, smelling all the secrets he longed to discover.

Her lips against his neck were a cherished treasure as she kissed and nipped and licked him. His dick yearned for the same treatment.

More than anything, he wanted to grab her, roll over on top of her, and mark her as his. But he lay still, trembling under the weight of his promise to not touch her.

She sat back, taking all the pleasure with her. He opened his mouth to promise again and again and again that he wouldn't touch; he just wanted—no, needed—her to continue. She ripped the zipper of her insulated pants down, then shifted off him long enough to get one leg out—her actions speaking louder than the words trying to come out of his mouth.

Call him a perv—he would have to own it—he strained to see that lovely cleft of skin between her thighs, but her shirt was long and covered her too well.

And then she yanked at his pajama pants. He lifted his hips so she could pull them down. Holy shit, this was really gonna happen.

When she'd freed his erection, she stopped. For half a moment, he thought she was looking at him with revulsion, but then she reached for him—her hand scalding and cooling against his skin.

Her touch devoured him, vanquishing the ability to think and leaving him only able to feel. Feel everything. Her fingers on him, tracing the bulging vein that ran up his shaft, leaving heat and pressure and the urge—oh God, the unbearable urge—to push himself inside her. His balls burned; his dick throbbed. The pleasure and agony too much to bear. He thrust his hips at her in a primal gesture of desperate need.

And then a miracle occurred. She straddled him again, lifting herself as she wrapped her hand around his dick and positioned herself above him. Her hand on him one of the wonders of nature…until millimeter by millimeter, she sank down.

Color and light and sound winked out of existence. He was lost in sensation. Her warmth, her wetness, her tightness. There weren't any words in existence to describe the nirvana of being inside her. He felt enlightened, as if she were a deity who'd granted him a priceless gift. Herself.

"Oh, Hell… Hell… Hel—" He couldn't contain the words flowing out him. "Helen." The name slipped out of him unconsciously.

She froze.

Oh shit, what had he done? He clawed his way out of the ecstasy and back to logic, barely. "Oh God. I'm sorry. I don't know why I said that. I don't even know anyone named Helen."

A small, curious smile brightened her face as she pointed at herself and nodded.

His brain—absent blood flow—took longer than it should to understand. "Your name is Helen?" Incredulity filled his tone.

The smile that fired on her face was one of pure angelic beauty. It lit up his soul like a sunrise.

She sat back on his hips, and he slid impossibly deeper inside her. That was her answer. Her name was Helen, and it had just bubbled up from the muck of his mind as if he'd known it all along. How had that—

She raised herself, the friction of her sliding against him too wonderful to allow thought. He clenched his hands into fists to keep from touching her, his arms shaking with the need. But he'd amputate both limbs before he'd break a promise to her.

A guttural sound of pain and pleasure burst out of him, and he arched his spine, the intensity almost too much. She groaned, and together, they made a perfect song of sex.

She rode him, pumping, grinding, setting a rhythm and pace that blinded him in the beauty of her using his body. This was for her. And he'd be damned certain she got what she needed.

Her pace quickened, her thrusts harder and messier. His control slipped, and he bucked against her, hips slamming into her with a wild frenzy. And then she seated herself so deeply upon him that he swore he touched heaven. She flung her head back on her shoulders, moaning her bliss while her hands kneaded his pecs. Her body clenched around him, her orgasm giving him permission to let go.

"Helen. Helen. Helen." He chanted her name in time with his thrusts. A tiny part of his mind remembered that he'd imagined this moment back in the tent. How could that be?

Something immense and powerful and awe-inspiring crashed over him. Everything he'd thought he knew about life and love was torn apart, then somehow pieced back together in a new order that made him strong and powerful and made him feel fucking indestructible. That's the effect being with her had on him.

She watched his orgasm, a self-satisfied grin tickling the corners of her mouth. When he'd spent every ounce of himself, she draped herself across his chest, her breath coming in long gulps of warm air directly over his heart.

As if the bonds on his hands had finally been broken,

he wrapped his arms around her, holding her tightly to him. Her body seemed so small and fragile, but she carried a quiet strength inside her. Yeah, she might be injured, but she wasn't weak.

He rubbed his hands up and down her back in soothing circles. She squirmed and snuggled tighter against him, like a kitten seeking warmth and safety. Through the fabric of her shirt, he felt the rough ridges of scarred skin, but he kept up the comforting caress. If she knew he could feel her scars, she would become frightened. The last thing he wanted.

She relaxed against him and sighed a sleepy, contented sound that would've had his lips tilting upward at satisfying this gorgeous woman, but all he could think about were the scars. He couldn't risk deviating from his strokes to map out each one, but they were extensive. Almost as though someone had taken a cat-o'-nine-tails to her. But then there were other places, hollows where the skin had sunken in instead of puckering out. *Fucking. Christ.* What had happened to her?

A car accident? A fire? Then a thought slammed into him so violently, it knocked his mental world off-kilter. Had *someone* done this to her? Was that why she didn't talk? Because he knew she had the ability to speak. The way she groaned and sighed—he could hear her voice behind those sounds. Had someone hurt her badly enough to steal her voice?

His brain stopped functioning. Something hot and angry pumped through his veins. A rage so potent, he could taste it in his mouth, smell it in the air. He wanted to kill whoever had harmed her. Rip them into pieces and then beat them with their own body parts.

He'd stopped rubbing her back and was now tracing the lines of her scars with his fingers. Which only fueled his anger. He forced his hands to stillness before he shook her awake and demanded to know who had hurt her so he could hunt them down and perform some anger management on them.

Bloodthirsty and possessive seemed to be his new norm when it came to her. He didn't mind. Yeah, he'd just met her, but she didn't *feel* like a stranger. She felt familiar and… What was the word he wanted? *Destined*.

Destined? Did he dare to believe that she could be meant for him? It was too fucking late for that question. He *knew* she was supposed to be his. But he wasn't sure she felt the same way. She might be seeking comfort of the one-night-stand variety. Well, then it was gonna be his job to convince her to stay with him without seeming like a psycho stalker.

The wood floor was cold and uncomfortable against his back and ass cheeks. And yet he'd lay here holding her for two eternities and a forever. Logic and rationality were too weak to make him end his time with her. He'd hold her until she didn't want to be held any longer.

But right here, right now, he would memorize everything about her. The way her hair felt like a soft breeze against his chest, her soft inhales and warm exhales, her breasts pressed against his chest through her shirt as she slept. The way it felt to have his arms around her, holding her tightly to him. And he'd never forget for as long as he lived what it felt like to be inside her.

He'd sacrifice his life to keep this one moment alive.

⁓⁓

Outside, an anemic dawn had just begun its attempt at dragging in an unenthusiastic new day. Or maybe Thomas was just reluctant for the night to end. Over the past hours, he'd come to terms with the fact that an eternity of holding Helen would never be enough. He was that far gone.

She lay on top of him, in the exact position she'd fallen asleep. He'd expected to be uncomfortable, but he wasn't. Holding her all night pleased him in an unexpected way. The steady inhale and exhale of her breath relaxed him. The weight and warmth of her better than a heated blanket.

As he held her, he looked around his living room, seeing it for the first time. The old Victorian wallpaper was subtly colored with pink blossoms and ruby-throated hummingbirds. The rich brown of the crown molding and baseboards were a perfect accent. He'd loved this place from the moment he walked in the front door, seeing it in only black and white. Now he loved it a little more.

Helen jerked violently in her sleep. The first time she'd done that, it'd startled him. Almost as if his body had a mirror response to hers. But after the third time, he'd gotten used to it.

He tightened his arms around her. "Shh… It's okay. I've got you. You're safe." Thomas whispered the words to the top of her head resting on his chest. He kissed her hair, and her body relaxed and drifted off again. What horrors visited her dreams? He wanted to go all medieval knight and slay her dragons.

Dawn had finally slipped into day when she stirred against him, sighing a sound so full of contentment that he grabbed on to the melody and refused to let it go. He wanted to luxuriate in her satisfaction, but he was a damn coward. He slammed his eyes closed, breathed slow and deep, and pretended to be asleep.

She sat up, pushing herself off his chest. His arms around her resisted the movement, but he let her go. Without her body against his, he felt hollow and empty. A strange panic and hysteria hovered at the edge of his conscious mind, ready to swarm over him.

She was still nude from the waist down. His chest was bare, and his dick felt like a tree trunk jutting out from his body. Hopefully, she'd just think he had morning wood. Really, the thing had been ready for reentry for hours.

He could feel her assessing the situation as she moved off him. Did she regret what they'd done? They hadn't used protection. Not that he even had any rubbers lying around. Sex for him was an anomaly, not something he prepared for. He wasn't worried about himself. He was clean. All his concern was for her and her reaction to their bareback ride. Regret was something he didn't want to see on her face.

Pretending to be asleep was way better than confronting her disappointment.

A whisper of sensation against his damaged cheek derailed those thoughts. His brain went into hyperdrive, trying to figure out what it was feeling. Her fingers. She traced the outline of the scar with all the leisure of a child drawing on the sand. He couldn't have moved even if he wanted to. He absorbed her touch, savored it.

Yesterday, life had seemed so out of control and awful, but now he couldn't even remember why. All he could feel, all that mattered were her fingers on his face. *Goddamn*. It felt so right, so damned destined. *Destined*. That word again.

A sigh laced with some intangible sadness came from her, and then she took her touch away.

He heard the whisper of her picking up her pants. His eyes yearned to open and see her long legs, the roundness of her ass, and the beautiful place at the apex of her thighs that he'd only visited and longed to stay. But he was wary of her reaction. Would his gaze on her cause fear?

There was no whisper of fabric from her sliding her pants on. No. She padded across the living room, through the foyer, and then silently up the stairs.

When her footfalls sounded in the upstairs hallway, he rolled over and looked at the staircase. Damn, she was a stealthy thing. The old oak floors were over a hundred years old and squeaked and groaned with every one of his steps, but not with her.

He stood, yanked his pants over his hips, careful not to decapitate his dick, and tiptoed to the staircase. He looked upstairs, listening. What was she doing? Trying to rob him? Was that her game? Act all damsel in distress, satisfy him sexually, then steal from him?

His heart thwacked one hard hit against his chest wall as if to knock some sense back into him. *Damn*. The sucker seemed to have a mind of its own about her and wasn't afraid to beat some common sense into him.

A whine and thump of pipes rang through the old house. He'd recognize those sounds anywhere. She was in the guest bathroom and had just turned on the shower. *Hmm...*

At the top of the stairs was a door to the right—his

bedroom. Farther down the hall on the left was a bedroom door. On the other side of the bedroom, behind
another door, was the bathroom. Not easily visible, yet
that's where she'd headed. Hell, he couldn't remember
if he'd put towels or soap in there when he moved in. *Oh
well. Too late now.* He was just glad she hadn't snuck
out the back door.

He turned away from the stairs and headed to the
kitchen. Dull winter light shone through the leaded-glass
windows, but still, his home fascinated him. The deep,
rich brown of the polished oak floors. The bright pops
of pink in the wallpaper. He felt like Dorothy when she
landed in Munchkinland. He wanted to marvel at every
glint and glimmer of color.

In the kitchen, he opened the cupboard. A rainbow
met his gaze. He marveled at the cans and boxes and
tubs as if they were priceless artwork. He reached for the
coffee tub. It was red. Fucking red. He never would've
guessed red. A huge smile tugged at the skin on his
cheek. She'd changed him. Healed all his wounds.

He put on a pot of coffee, set out two mugs—one dark
blue and one dark green. He'd never realized they were
different colors. Before her, they'd both looked black
to him. The carton of creamer had purple writing on it.
Purple. He held the carton up to his eyes, staring at the
gorgeous color. Everything was so lovely. He wanted to
spend hours just looking through his cupboards, but she
was upstairs taking a shower, and he didn't want to seem
like a total oddball when she came down.

Should he make breakfast? Have it waiting for her?
Was that too much for the morning after? Too familiar?
Hopefully, she'd still agree to let him take her to Dr.

Stone's and get stitched up. Whatever she decided, she didn't have any shoes.

He went into the living room, nabbed his coat off the couch, and shrugged it on. It would be a quick trip to the woods to get her boots. If he was lucky, he'd be back before she finished with her shower.

He headed out the kitchen door, shutting it firmly behind him, then marveled at the color of his house. A subtle, calming shade of yellow, trimmed in pristine white. *Holy shit.* He'd thought it had been pure white with a black door, but now he saw that his door was a dark walnut color. Seeing his home in full-color glory warmed him from the inside out. This is what everyone else saw, that he hadn't been able to until Helen. Her presence vanquished the damage done to his brain and his eye.

Reluctantly, he turned away from the house and headed down the porch steps.

Birds hopped and fluttered around his feeder. Red ones. Blue ones. Brown ones. Their colors all so vivid. He'd never been interested in birds until he'd moved here and discovered that a bird feeder had been mounted on a post in the backyard. It made him sound eighty years old, but he enjoyed feeding the birds and watching them while they ate.

The world flicked to black and white again, almost like someone had flipped a switch. "What the hell?" He turned and looked at the house. Solid white, with a black door again.

He wanted to throw himself down in the snow and scream at the loss. He swallowed the urge and tried to find some rationality. Okay. So he'd seen color for a while. That was better than nothing. Maybe seeing color was going to be glitchy. Something that winked on and off randomly.

Or maybe it was something that only happened when he was near her. Both times he'd seen color had been within her presence. It was a theory he couldn't wait to test.

He headed toward the woods. Six inches of snow covered the ground and had distorted his tracks from last night. A thick wad of clouds obscured the sky in a color that resided somewhere between lonely and melancholy. A few stray flakes of snow meandered hesitantly toward the ground. All around him the world was quiet and…sad.

Ping.

The soft sound seemed so out of place.

Ping.

His cell phone. He should just let the thing go to voicemail, but he couldn't. Maybe there was an update on Malone's case. He yanked the phone out of his pocket and looked at the screen.

Evanee calling

He slid the answer icon over and held the phone to his ear.

"Hi, Ev."

"Oh, good. You're awake." His sister's voice was light and carefree. So different from yesterday's phone conversation when he'd read the article to her and heard the soft sounds of her crying on the other end of the line. But today, it sounded like the shit their mom had pulled hadn't dimmed the brightness Evanee had found with Lathan. "I was worried I was calling too early."

He snorted. "I haven't even been to bed yet. What's up?"

"You worked all night?" Concern dominated her tone.

He paused, not knowing how to answer the question. He didn't want to lie to his sister, but saying *I slept with a woman I found in the woods* just sounded weird. "Nah. Just couldn't sleep."

Cold air snapped against his face and burned his hand holding the phone. Maybe he should've bundled up a bit more.

"Well, I'm calling with good news." Evanee's voice squealed a bit on the last words. He opened his mouth, but she rushed on. "We're getting married." Happiness overflowed in her voice. A sound he was grateful to hear. She deserved all the joy she could get.

"Congratulations. You know I'm happy for you. Lathan's a great guy." Without Lathan, Evanee would've been lost forever.

"I know. He's the best. The best. And I want you here. Tonight. At seven."

"Wait. You're getting married tonight?"

"Yes! Yes! Yes! Isn't that the most awesome word?" She laughed. "Yes. Tonight. There's no sense in waiting. I don't want anything fancy. Just our friends and you."

A month ago, they didn't even talk. Weren't at all close. Didn't really know each other. It had taken a helluva lot of tragedy to bring them together, and both were determined to keep their sibling relationship alive. "I wouldn't miss it."

"Yay! Okay. I've got to make some other phone calls. And find a dress! See you tonight!"

She disconnected the call, taking the energy of her

enthusiasm with her. He was happy for her. Evanee had come out the other side of her nightmare happier than seemed possible. But happiness to him meant... His brain conjured up a picture of Helen. Her golden hair and matching golden eyes. She was sunshine on a cloudy day. It was easy to picture himself feeling for Helen the same way Evanee felt about Lathan.

Show the hermit a little affection, and he turned into a stalker. For Helen's sake, he needed to try to take things a bit slow. She'd freak out if he came at her with words like *destined*. Yeah. Best to keep that word to himself.

He realized he was standing halfway across his yard, just staring at his phone.

Helen was probably close to getting out of the shower, and how fucking weird would it seem when she came downstairs to find he'd vanished? Creepy. That's how it would seem. Why didn't he think to leave her a note?

He started jogging toward her camp, his feet crunching loud and obscene while the rest of the world seemed so silent. He entered the woods, glimpsing her tent up ahead.

Against the stark white, the trees were black, branches raised in supplication as if pleading for spring days. Normally, the forest seemed peaceful and serene after a snow, but not now for some reason.

He wasn't worried about the coyote. They were nocturnal. The thing was probably holed up somewhere in a warm den, snoozing the day away. Yet a prickle of foreboding wound around his guts.

He jogged into the clearing and froze.

A horror surrounded him. An abomination of destruction and rage.

Nothing was as they'd left it.

All was destroyed.

Her quaint pup tent had been shredded, strips of it dancing on the light breeze. Her sleeping bag had been savagely ripped apart, stuffing hanging out of it in fat piles that reminded him of guts. The neat fire circle was obliterated as if it had never existed.

Debris littered the area. Food was torn open and spread over the ground. Arms ripped off a shirt. A leg ripped off a pair of pants. A busted lantern. A cheap camp stove broken and dented as if it had been the victim of violent fury.

All of it destroyed.

This wasn't the work of a coyote. Animals weren't capable of such insanity. It hadn't been a coyote in the woods last night. Someone had been after her.

Amid the destruction were footprints in the snow. He strode the perimeter of her camp looking for tracks. Found them at the back edge, leading deeper into the woods.

He glanced back through the trees toward his house, barely visible through the branches. All seemed well. She was probably getting out of the shower, heading downstairs to get some coffee. If the worst that happened was her wondering where he'd gone, he could live with that. Right now, he needed to follow these prints to see where they led.

He lifted the collar of his coat to shield his ears from the cold, then shoved his hands into his pockets and followed the trail. *Should've fucking bundled up.*

While he followed the footprints, his mind asked questions. Why was she sleeping out here in the woods in winter? Was she trying to hide from someone? All that camping gear cost money—why not just get a hotel room? She was a gorgeous woman. Maybe she was hiding from an abusive boyfriend. Her body was covered in scars. Had she endured years of abuse?

The footprints guided him along the edge of the woods in a direction that seemed to run parallel to his house but then shifted, and Thomas realized he'd been walking in an almost perfect semicircle that led right back to his place. All the questions in his mind stopped with a terrible realization: these footprints weren't old and distorted like the ones he'd followed from his house back to her camp. These were fresh.

His heart ceased beating. His lungs refused to suck air. From nearly a quarter mile off, he spotted the roof of his Victorian through the trees dotting the landscape.

Helen was there all alone. Unaware of the danger headed her way.

"Helen!" Her name came out in a primal scream of sound. He started running, slipped, fell, went down on all fours, but was back up and sprinting toward home. "Helen!" He yelled her name again as if she could hear him.

Time shattered into a million pieces. Seconds, minutes, hours, days, weeks, months, years, decades, and centuries were all strewn about like flakes of glitter.

He ran harder than he'd ever run but got locked into an odd suspended animation. His body seemed to move at the speed of light and in slow motion at the same time. He fought time's hold on him. Fought to get to Helen. To protect her. He didn't know what had happened to her in the past, but he knew she'd been hurt deeper than most people could survive. She didn't deserve any more pain.

Ppgglll… A gunshot from inside his house.

His heart fell out of his chest and landed in the snow. He didn't stop to retrieve it; he just kept running. If something happened to Helen, he wouldn't need his heart anyway.

Chapter 6

In the vanity mirror of her old bathroom, Helena caught sight of her naked torso and wished she hadn't. She'd known her body looked bad. But it was so much worse than she'd imagined.

Water rained from the showerhead, ringing against the old claw-foot tub, a sound that should've comforted her for its familiarity, but it didn't. Not now. Not staring at the disaster that was her body.

Her skin bore witness to the brutality she'd suffered at the hands of the Sisters. Thick scars. Jagged scars. Smooth scars. Sunken-in hollows. Disfiguring and ghastly to look upon. The top of her left breast had a fat, puckered mark from one of the Sisters trying to bury a screwdriver in her heart.

Dizziness came over her. The world distorted, fading out of focus until the only thing visible was the mess of her flesh. Every damaged piece of skin flamed to life, burning and itching in an I-won't-ever-let-you-forget of epic proportions.

She turned and looked over her shoulder at her back in the mirror.

The ability to breathe stopped. Both sides bore dozens, maybe hundreds, of scars from the gang shanking she'd endured. The raised, angry skin looked like a grotesque pair of fleshy wings had slipped down her shoulders to rest in the middle of her back.

The night of the gang shanking was one of her worst memories. She'd struggled and fought the Sisters' hold on her until she couldn't fight any more. After that, it had been about endurance.

It wasn't until they'd left her alone, with only her blood to keep her warm, that she'd felt her consciousness fade and embraced death with wide, open arms.

She should've died.

She should've died after the first wounds.

She should've died after they left her lying there until morning.

But life was so much crueler than death.

She'd awakened in the hospital after that one. Cuffed to the bed. Every nurse, every doctor pretended to be unafraid of her. All of them failed. Because of course the CO stationed with her had told everyone why she was in Fairson. Murder.

Hospitals were just a different type of prison.

A sob launched out her throat, slamming her back to reality. She clamped her hand over her mouth, not wanting Thomas to hear.

She was not going to cry. Not again. But another sob threatened to erupt. This time, she understood it was about more than the Sisters. It was about Fairson and being a felon and about how the wounds of her past would never heal.

Thomas would eventually find out she was a felon. Not just any felon. Convicted of murder. That was condemnation enough, but when he found out that she'd grown up in this house... That was too much of a coincidence for him to dismiss. He'd probably be frightened of her. Think she was plotting his death to get her home back.

She turned away from the mirror and got into the tub, closing the shower curtain around her. Water stung the cut on her forehead, and she realized too late that she'd forgotten to unbandage her hand. Oh well. She'd rebandage herself after the shower, and if she was lucky, she'd be able to sneak back to her camp, pack up, and leave for a hotel before Thomas woke.

A fresh, unused bar of soap sat in the soap holder. There wasn't a washrag, but that didn't matter. She lathered her body and even used the soap in her hair. When she finally felt clean, she just stood there, steeling herself for leaving this house and leaving Thomas. She wasn't sure which upset her more.

So what if he'd been kind? Kindness had limits.

So what if she trusted him? Trust could be broken.

A floorboard squeaked right outside the shower. Ice-cold betrayal streaked through her entire body despite the warm water raining over her. And right here was an example of trust being broken. She'd trusted him to understand her need for privacy. Not try to sneak in some shower sexcapades. She hadn't locked the bathroom door. She hadn't even shut it. Did he think that was an invitation?

She opened her mouth to tell him to go away, but hesitated. He didn't deserve her voice if he was going to—

The shower curtain was yanked back so violently, the material ripped.

Adrenaline tore through her. She startled and turned and tried to cover the awfulness of her body with her hands. Indignation and hurt were naked on her face, but she didn't bother to hide them.

A gun. Pointed at her heart.

A gun? Why would he have a gun on her? Had he found out about her? In slow motion, her gaze traveled up the dark-blue coat sleeve—why was he wearing a coat? Up his shoulder and on up his wrinkled neck... wrinkled neck? This wasn't Thomas.

Finally, she looked at the person's face.

A woman. An older woman.

Recognition was a nuclear bomb in her brain. Everything inside her felt weightless, as if she'd just been thrown out of her reality and was waiting for the crash landing.

Mrs. Ellis.

Rory's mom.

Once upon a time, Helena had loved this woman. Mrs. Ellis had been cool. Fun. Perky. Beautiful. Time had not been kind to her. Her face bore deep grooves of sadness. Her hair used to be rich, reddish brown and always fashionably styled. Nothing like the faded gray, shaggy mess that currently topped her head. Her once-trim body, plump.

But the thing that hadn't changed was the anger and grief radiating off her. The same anger and grief she'd worn every day since Rory's death.

Flashes of thoughts and feelings from the past came over Helena.

No one listening. Everyone blaming.

Truth denied. Lies believed.

Guilty. Guilty. Guilty.

Hatred sparked in the woman's eyes. Even the Sisters had never looked at Helena with such single-minded malice.

"It's not fair"—Mrs. Ellis's chin trembled as she spoke—"that Rory died and you lived."

None of this was fair.

It wasn't fair that Rory died.

It wasn't fair that she'd been convicted.

It wasn't fair that the Sisters decided to hate her.

Life didn't care about fairness.

Helena should have been frightened. She was standing there naked with a gun aimed at her chest. But she felt disconnected. As if none of this mattered. If Mrs. Ellis shot her, would that be so bad? Hadn't she wished for death hundreds—no, thousands—of times over the past decade? Hadn't she wished that each attack by the Sisters would be the one she couldn't bounce back from?

Maybe this was as it should be. She'd gotten to visit Rory's and her grandparents' graves. She'd gotten to see the house, spend time here. She'd had great sex with a good man.

Oh God. Thomas. Had Mrs. Ellis hurt him? Helena looked beyond Mrs. Ellis and out the open door into the bedroom. Empty.

Thomas. Wherever you are, don't come in here. Keep yourself safe. She sent the thoughts as if they were a psychic email and hoped he would get them.

"A parent isn't supposed to bury their child. You know why? Because they carry most of your heart inside theirs." Mrs. Ellis beat her chest with her fist, thumping her breastbone loudly. "Every day, I live only half a life. The other half is in the ground. Because of you." Her words were a wail of heartache.

I didn't do it. Helena screamed the words in her head.

The same words she'd screamed a million times during
the trial. And just like back then, no one—except her
grandparents—believed her.

"The Sisters were supposed to take you out on your
first night in Fairson."

Take you out on your first night in Fairson.

Almost as if it was set on delay, Helena's brain
plugged into what the woman had just said. A deep hurt
resonated through her body, heating her face. Mrs. Ellis
knew the Sisters? Knew they'd tried over and over to
kill her?

"I wanted you punished." Mrs. Ellis spoke the last
word through teeth gritted so hard, Helena could hear
them grinding. "I want to see what they did to you."

Helena hesitated to remove the shield of her own
arms and hands. But what did it really matter? Mrs. Ellis
was so lost in her suffering that nothing Helena could
say or do would ever change the woman's opinion of
her. She dropped her arms and stood up straighter. Let
the woman look at the damage her hatred had bought.

Mrs. Ellis's eyes widened as they roamed over
Helena's body, taking in all the destruction. "Turn
around." Her voice straddled some elusive line between
satisfaction and hatred.

Helena turned in a circle, warm water hitting the cold
side of her body. Then she faced Mrs. Ellis again.

"Good." Tears welled in the older woman's eyes,
then slipped down her cheeks. Grief came off her in
typhoon-sized waves, threatening to drown Helena. "All
these years, I always thought the Sisters must be pansies
for not killing you that first week, let alone over the past
ten years. But now I see they tried. Boy, did they try." A

terrible smile stayed on her lips. "When Arnold would get home from work, the first thing he'd do was tell me about your day."

Arnold? Wasn't CO Holbrook's first name Arnold? So Mrs. Ellis and CO Holbrook were…together? And responsible for the past ten years of her suffering? She should feel outraged, wronged, kicked-while-she-was-already-down, but there was a place beyond those emotions…a place where none of the past mattered, because the future would never exist and the present was about to end.

"There were days you went on about your life as though you hadn't killed Rory. And there were days you should've died. Arnold couldn't believe that you just kept on surviving. Twice over the years, he made certain you'd die. But you didn't." She sucked in a resigned breath. "The past ten years of your life taught me one thing: You want something done right, do it yourself."

In slow motion, Helena watched Mrs. Ellis squeeze the trigger.

The gun went off. The sound thunderous. The impact devastating.

Helena's body slammed back against the wall. Why didn't she feel anything? As if answering her question, pain exploded in her chest, a deadly mushroom cloud that devoured all sensation, leaving nothing except abject agony.

Her legs folded beneath her. She fell, banging her temple against the rim of the tub on her way down. Lights and colors glittered in front of her eyes, but she didn't feel anything beyond the misery in her chest.

She stared at the white porcelain. Her bathtub was

going to be the last thing she saw on earth. It reminded her of that white place in her dreams. If these were her last seconds alive, she wanted to remember the good things. She thought of her grandparents. The way Grandpa always smelled of pipe smoke even though he swore he'd quit smoking. The way wrinkles and age spots didn't dim Grandma's beauty, because love always shone in her eyes.

Best of all, she remembered Thomas as she'd last seen him. So innocent in sleep. There was goodness in life. And she'd found it in him right before she died.

Thoughts became harder to think, fraying and dissolving before she could form them. The end really was near. She could feel it this time. Feel death's warm arms wrap around her and lift her from the tub. Holding her, hugging her, comforting her, taking all the pain away.

Thomas burst through the back door on a dead run. Each footfall a jackhammer of sound. Stealth didn't matter as much as getting to Helen.

He didn't remember running through the house and up the stairs, but suddenly, he burst into the bathroom she'd been using. He skidded to a halt. Helen lay in the bathtub, curled on her side. Water rained over her nakedness. She wasn't moving. Didn't seem to be breathing. And somehow, he was seeing in color again—a garish river of scarlet gushed from the massive wound in her chest, pooling as it waited to slip down the drain.

His organs, his muscles, and his bones all pressed against the barrier of his flesh, trying to force him to go to her, gather her into his arms, and save her. He took a step toward her, but almost as if his brain decided to feed him information one small bite at a time, he noticed the woman standing over Helen.

In all the scenarios he'd imagined, none of them contained a woman as the perpetrator.

Gray dominated her fading auburn hair. Frown lines bracketed her mouth, and deep grooves furrowed her forehead. At one point in her life, she had probably been pretty, but time wasn't an equal-opportunity ager.

Even though he only saw her in profile, a look of pure, unadulterated satisfaction lit her face and charged the atmosphere with her glee. That's when he noticed what he didn't see.

The woman carried no shadow of death. What was going on that all of a sudden, he'd met two people who had no shadow? Almost as if the universe were answering his question, the air around the woman wavered and morphed into a thick, slate-colored fog that vibrated with her excitement.

As if his presence in the room wasn't all that important, the woman slowly turned her head to look at him.

There was the gun in her hand. It was no pretty and petite ladies' pistol. No, her gun was large and lethal and promised total termination of life. The woman's gaze roamed his face. "She won't hurt you anymore." Her words were so inconceivable, so inexcusable that he had no response other than the truth.

"She's never hurt me." His tone carried accusation and condemnation.

The woman looked at him with genuine concern, as if he were Helen's abused lover and suffered from Stockholm syndrome. "Oh, honey. I just saved your life," she said as if trying to explain something serious to a small child.

"You shot Helen." His tone carried aggression.

"I saved you." Each word came out with the conviction of a true believer.

He was done talking. Helen needed help, medical attention, him. He started to reach in the tub for her.

"Don't you touch her." For the first time since he'd entered the room, the woman raised the gun at him. It didn't matter. Nothing was going to prevent him from getting to Helen.

A sound erupted from deep inside him, part growl, part shout. He charged the woman, shoving her and her gun away from the tub. As if he possessed superhuman strength, she slammed into the wall with impossible force. The gun clattered out of her hand, and she slumped to the floor, unconscious.

Good.

He scooped up the weapon, shoved it in his coat pocket, then went to Helen.

Her face was an abominable shade of blue and gray and devoid of life. Water rained over her, swirling the blood leaking from her chest in mesmerizing streams. The wound was massive. Destructive. Deadly. Something no one could survive.

Despair emptied him out. He became a shell of skin with nothing on the inside.

He reached for her, but even though he stood as close to the tub as he could get, she seemed so far away, as if miles and miles stretched between them. Water rained over his head, drizzling down inside his coat, but he barely noticed.

His hands didn't seem like they belonged to him as

he scooped her out of the tub. Her skin was slick and slippery. Her body limp and lifeless. "Helen." His voice contained a vast desolation. Her head lolled awkwardly to the side, and wet strands of hair clung to her face in fat tentacles. Ribbons of blood leaked from the gaping wound over her heart, sliding over and around her breast, pooling in the bend of her stomach.

A sick sense of dread filled all his empty places. The wound should be gushing, not dribbling. He was too late. She'd lost too much blood.

No. No. No. Goddamn it. She couldn't be dead. He wouldn't let her die. Not now. Not when he'd just found her. Helen needed to be alive. Even though they'd just met, he couldn't live in a world without her in it. Didn't matter if they were together or not, she just needed to be alive. That would be enough for him.

His legs folded beneath him. He sat on the floor, leaned against the old tub, and held her. He grabbed her chin and shook her head gently, "Helen. Oh God. Helen, wake up." This was wrong. So wrong. None of this should be happening. Not now.

Never taking his eyes off her, he reached into his coat pocket for his phone and then dialed the number he called the most. Work. He pinched the phone between his ear and shoulder while it rang.

"No news yet," Lanning said when he picked up the call.

Thomas opened his mouth. Only one word came out. "Helen." His brain had clogged up, allowing only a trickle of thought at a time.

"What?" Confusion dominated Lanning's tone.

"Helen." It was just a name to Lanning, but to

Thomas, she was everything. "Helen's been shot. I need an ambulance. The police." He let the phone drop and distantly heard Lanning shouting.

Nothing in his whole life seemed as important as Helen. "You've got to fight." A lump of some unnamed emotion rose in his throat. He struggled to swallow it back down. "You hear me? You have to fight to stay here with me. I know we just met. But you and me—there's something between us. I knew it the moment I saw you. And you need to stay so we can explore this thing. Because it feels powerful. It feels destined. Like we are supposed to be together."

His voice hitched, and he struggled to keep talking around the fear and grief bubbling up inside him. "Just listen to my voice." He smoothed wet hair from her face. Chilled skin met his fingertips. She was too cold. The tang of her blood sickening in the damp air. "Follow my voice. Don't let it go."

Thomas shifted Helen's body until she was settled in the crook of his left arm. Blood pooled on her stomach, seeping into his coat.

Without any reason or rationality, he pressed his hand over the bullet hole. A zap of static electricity blazed through him at the contact. Her body jolted, and then his hand suctioned to her chest.

Everything changed.

Inside his torso, a cool and pleasant sensation gathered, then rolled down his arm to his hand and poured into her. His eyes rolled back in his head under the waves of bliss pouring from him into her. *Holy shit*. Maybe he was losing his grip on reality, but some vital part of him—his essence, his strength, his soul—flowed into her. The ultimate act of giving. And it felt amazing. "You feel this? You feel me inside you? Making you better?" He sounded crazy. He'd worry about his sanity later.

Underneath her delicate eyelids, her eyes rolled. For the first time since he'd picked her up, he noticed the subtle rise and fall of her chest. Blood no longer trickled from the wound. He stared at his hand mashed against her chest. Were his eyes playing tricks on him? Making him see what he wanted to see instead of reality?

Did it really matter what was happening as long as Helen seemed to be improving? Everything inside him that had been so devastated perked up as if spring had arrived.

She wasn't dead. He knew that now. Knew it as surely as he knew he was alive. He slumped back against the tub and sucked in a giant breath.

"You're going to be all right. I'm with you. I'm inside you. I'm a part of you now." His gaze traveled beyond his hand over her heart to her body. All the horror he thought was behind them reignited.

Her chest and stomach were covered in scars. Her body told a story of misery unimagined, of incomprehensible suffering. And from last night, he knew there were more on her back that he couldn't see.

"Oh, Helen." He hugged her tighter to him. What on earth had done that to her? "This is it. After this, all your pain is over. I won't let anything hurt you ever again." He kissed her forehead, sealing the deal.

In the distance, sirens sounded—a reassurance that everything was going to be okay. He just needed to keep his hand on her. Keep himself flowing into her.

Downstairs, his front door burst inward and pounded

against the wall, the sound shaking the house. Far off, he could still hear the sirens—that wasn't the police or paramedics down there.

He ripped his hand off her chest, pain stabbing through his palm as if *it* had been shot. An anguished gasp escaped his lips. He flapped his hand to ease the terrible sensation. But there was something more important than his discomfort. Her safety. He shifted her in his arms so her back mostly leaned against his chest and covered her injury with his other hand. Immediately, the pain vanished, and he felt the sensation of the most vital parts of himself pouring into her.

He reached into his coat pocket and found the woman's gun.

Footsteps pounded up the stairs, down the hallway, toward the bedroom and the bathroom they sat in.

Thomas aimed the gun at the open doorway. Blood dripped from his fingers, but his grip was firm and steady.

If anyone tried to harm her, he'd commit murder.

Gun first, Kent Knight swept into the bedroom, looking around like he expected an ambush. His shadow was like a thick, white fog on a spring morning. The kind Thomas liked because it carried no malice.

Kent froze when he saw Thomas and Helen. "Hey, man, I'm a friendly." Kent was a BCI agent, but Thomas didn't *know* the guy. He could be working with the woman. They could be partners.

When Thomas didn't say anything, just kept his gun aimed at Kent's center mass, the guy lowered his weapon to the floor. Then he straightened and held his hands in the air.

"Why are you here?" Thomas spoke slow and clear and didn't bother to hide the suspicion in his tone.

"Lanning called." Kent raised his hands a bit higher.

"Why would he call you?"

"Because I live closer to you than anyone else. Told me to get my ass over here. It was life and death. Someone had been shot."

Kent met him stare for stare. The man's dark-blond hair, square face, and hard jaw all gave him the appearance of someone trustworthy. Looks could be deceiving. Thomas knew that better than anyone—Malone looked like Mr. Hometown-Nice-Guy-Sheriff. But what Thomas did trust was the shadow. The shadow was light-colored and felt harmless.

"How'd you know we were up here?" He couldn't help asking.

Kent heaved an impatient sigh. "I followed the wet footprints that led up the steps."

Thomas lowered the weapon and set it on the floor next to him.

"What happened?" Kent scooped up his own gun, reholstered it, and walked into the bathroom.

"She"—Thomas canted his head in the direction of the woman still passed out against the wall—"shot Helen. I was out back when it happened. I don't even know who she is or why she'd try to hurt Helen."

Kent turned and ran out of the room.

"Where you going?" Thomas yelled at his back. What use was the guy if he took off the moment he knew what was going on?

But then Kent was back, holding a wad of clothes he must've found in Thomas's bedroom. He shoved the clothes over Thomas's hand on Helen's wound. "Here. Let me."

There was no way in hell Thomas was letting go of her. He could still feel himself flowing into her. Healing her.

"You've got to stop the bleeding." Urgency hardened Kent's tone.

Thomas didn't listen.

"Listen, man, it needs pressure."

"No. She needs me." The words came out in a snarl of sound. He clutched Helen closer. Kent backed off, hands in the air as though Thomas had the gun on him again.

The only thing that mattered was that sensation of himself entering Helen. The logical part of his brain realized how fucked up it sounded that he thought he was healing her by touching her. The other part of him recognized the unbelievable, unexplainable, unimaginable truth of it all.

The sirens that had seemed so far away a minute ago pulled into his driveway, then cut off midwail. That's when Thomas noticed that Kent had moved to the woman slumped on the floor and was checking her over. "She's alive. Looks like she just got conked on the head."

Thomas stared down at Helen's pale face. "You make sure every charge in the book gets slapped on her."

"I'll see to it." Kent walked to the bathroom door and then paused. "This doesn't have anything to do with Malone, does it?"

"Not a damn thing."

"I didn't think so, but I had to ask. I'm gonna go show the boys in." Kent headed out of the bathroom.

As soon as he was gone, Thomas whispered to Helen.

"You're gonna hate this, but there's no getting around it this time. You're going to the hospital." He paused, waiting for some reaction from her. But she kept breathing, and her heart kept beating, and that was enough for him. "But don't worry. I'll be with you the whole time. You don't have anything to be afraid of. I promise."

With his free hand, he arranged the wad of clothes Kent had brought in over Helen's body. If she hadn't wanted him to see her scars, she wouldn't want anyone else to see them either.

Footsteps sounded on the staircase, then treaded down the hallway toward them.

"She's in there." Kent said from in the bedroom.

Two EMTs entered the bathroom. Thomas didn't look at them; he just kept his attention on Helen. Her color was better, and he knew in the way-down-deep parts of himself that she was going to be all right.

"Dddaaammmnn…" One of the EMTs stretched the word out long and low.

Thomas's attention snapped up to the guy. What the fuck was he…

The guy had his gaze glued to Helen's face. "That's Helena Grayse."

Thomas knew that name. Everyone in Sundew, Ohio, knew the name.

He looked back down at Helen. She looked so fragile and damaged. Nothing like a murderer.

Chapter 7

WORRY SHIVERED THROUGH THOMAS'S GUTS. HE STARED at his reflection in the mirror. The lighting in the little alcove bathroom of Helen's hospital room did no favors for the scar on his face. The thing looked better in black and white. At least in a monochromatic world, he'd been able to fool himself into believing the damage wasn't that bad. In full color, the shiny pink skin shocked him. But his face was the least of his concerns.

Helen wasn't waking up. Her vitals, her blood work, X-rays, MRIs, and some test where they looked at her brain waves—all normal. The diagnosis—sleeping. She was sleeping. And he had a hard time believing it.

He bent down and splashed cold water against his face.

Nobody slept that deeply. But then none of this situation resided on the normal scale. How on earth had she been shot in the chest, lost so much blood, then ended up not even needing stitches? The answer tickled his mind. He'd healed her. But that sounded illogical and utterly impossible.

He dried his face without looking at it in the mirror again, then left the bathroom.

A man in a cheap, baggy suit leaned over Helen, his shadow looming dark and dangerous as a storm.

In two long strides, Thomas was at her bedside. The

man's shadow reached out, invading Thomas's space. Heat radiated from the mass… Was it really the fires of hell he could feel in the presence of a bad shadow? All he knew for certain was that the guy wasn't a good fellow.

With both hands, he shoved the man away from her. As the guy stumbled back a few steps, Thomas inserted himself in front of Helen. The asshole would have to get through him before he ever got close to Helen again. "Stay the fuck away from her." The words were heavy with the threat of mortal danger.

The guy's expression morphed into something vicious, and Thomas instantly recognized him.

Hal Haskins. Childhood bully extraordinaire. Hal's hair had receded from his forehead, and he carried extra weight in the middle that made him look like he was ending his second trimester, but he stood there like the king of the hospital—entitlement and attitude radiating off him. It didn't help that he'd grown up to be one of Malone's boys.

"Boy. You need to be careful. I'm Hal Haskins with the—"

"Boy?" Thomas crossed his arms over his chest. "You're calling me 'boy'? Seriously? That might work as a humiliation tactic if you were twenty years older, but since we're the same age, it makes you sound like an idiot."

Hal paused, stared at him, then the light bulb in his brain fired up. "Tommy!" A joviality brimming with bad intentions seeped into his tone. "Tommy Tree Face. I didn't make the connection that you were Thomas Brown until now."

Tommy Tree Face. The childhood nickname didn't

hurt. Even the memories of Hal and his friends holding him down and spitting in his face until he cried didn't hurt. What did hurt was remembering how it felt to be absolutely powerless. Something he'd finally gotten over when he got big enough, strong enough, and fast enough to defend himself. "You're almost thirty. Name-calling as an adult makes you desperate and pathetic."

"Aww... No." Hal held his hands up in a show of innocence. "I didn't mean anything by it. It's just a nickname." His gaze flicked over Helen. "So, wow. That's Helena Grayse. I expected her to look more... you know...white-trash-skank-bitch-hoe. She's actually kinda hot."

Thomas shifted where he stood, blocking Helen's face from Hal's sight. "I don't care if you are the damn pope riding in on a unicorn, you *will* treat her with the respect she deserves." He packed a ton of promise into that sentence.

Hal's features wrinkled as if Thomas's words were a bug he wanted to flick off his arm, but his lips carried a smarmy smile. "Oh, I am. In case you don't know, she's a felon convicted of murder. She doesn't deserve respect." He reached into his suitcoat pocket and withdrew a notebook. "I need to get your statement about what happened. Let's step outside so we can talk."

"No." The word shot out of Thomas's mouth, hitting its mark when it reached Hal.

The man cocked his head to the side as if working to translate the meaning of *no*. "Okay. I guess we can talk here. I just thought you wouldn't want to disturb—"

"No." Thomas wasn't wasting his time on one of Malone's good ole boys.

That I'm-going-to-pretend-to-be-nice-just-so-you'll-let-me-get-close-enough-to-pound-on-you smile from when they were kids found its way to Hal's lips. "It's not exactly policy, but seeing as how we're old friends, I could get your statement over a few cold ones."

Did Hal seriously think Thomas would want to spend time with him? "I'm gonna spell this out for you, since you seem to be having trouble translating the meaning of the word *no*. I don't want to talk *to you* about what happened."

Hal's face paled, then pinked up, then turned an unattractive shade of red. He looked like a toddler about to throw himself on the floor and have a tantrum worthy of an ass-whipping. "You don't want to talk to me about what happened, then I'm gonna think you're hiding something."

"Don't threaten me and think it'll work."

"All right." In a leisurely movement, Hal unclipped a pair of handcuffs from his belt. "I can have you arrested for obstructing an investigation."

"Rreeaallly?" Maybe he shouldn't antagonize the guy. Thomas gestured a come-and-get-me motion with his hand. "Try it… Try to arrest me."

Hal stepped forward on the verge of giving it the good-ole-boy try.

Bring it. Thomas was ready. He'd been ready for decades. It would be fun for Hal to be on the receiving end for once.

A sharp knock on the door drew their attention. Kent stood there, a fat file folder under his arm. "I was just looking for you." He aimed his words at Hal and moved into the room, coming to stand next to Thomas, the two of them creating a barrier between Hal and Helen.

Thomas didn't know Kent very well, but the guy was depositing trust into Thomas's account.

"What do you want?" Hal's tone was designed to talk down to Kent, which only highlighted the bully's defensiveness.

Kent looked down at his shirtsleeve, picked at an imaginary piece of lint, then casually let the invisible material fall from his fingers. "From here on out, BCI will be handling the investigation." He spoke with a nonchalance that had to infuriate Hal.

Thomas laughed. Out loud. In the guy's face. Seeing Hal put in his place was the only shiny spot on this shitty day.

"Wait. What?" Hal's voice rose a few decibels too high for proper hospital etiquette. "This is our case. You have no jurisdiction here."

"*Was* your case. Now it's ours. Easy come. Easy go. I suggest you step outside and call your sheriff to ask him." Kent theatrically tapped his chin with a finger. "Oh shoot. I forgot. You don't have a sheriff anymore. He ran off because he's being investigated for dozens of crimes. And everyone who worked under him will be investigated too. Including you. That's why it's our case now."

Thomas smiled a big, goofy grin that felt weird on his face but oh so right. Yep. Kent was turning out to be a good guy.

Hal opened his mouth to say something else but then clamped his lips closed. At least the guy was smart enough to know that his behavior was gonna be under the microscope. He turned and left the room. Kent hung back for a few seconds, then followed him.

Thomas sat on the edge of Helen's bed. "Wake up. Come on. Show me those beautiful eyes." He shook her shoulder. Nothing.

His gaze fastened on the clock over Helen's hospital bed. It was 5:45 p.m. Each *tick-tock* was a countdown to the moment he needed to leave for his sister's wedding. He couldn't miss it. They were each other's only family, and he couldn't—wouldn't—let her down on her special day. Especially after everything she'd been through.

He'd only be gone an hour, two at the most. So why the hell did he feel as if leaving Helen was flat fucking wrong? Maybe because there was a selfish reason why he didn't want to leave her. In the bustle of her being whisked away in the ambulance, of her having to go through tests, he'd discovered something astounding: When he was near her, he saw color. When he wasn't around her, he had the same monochromatic existence as always. Not to mention simply being in her presence made him feel whole. It was more than seeing color; it was her filling up all his empty places. Her bringing him to life after he'd been dead inside for years.

He reached out and stroked her hair, the strands soothing underneath his fingers. The cut across her forehead that had looked so pink and angry yesterday was healed, leaving only a thin, pink scar. For it to have mended so quickly was as impossible as the gunshot in her chest not needing stitches.

He settled his hand over hers. Her skin cool and soothing—a breeze on a hot summer evening. Just touching her made him different, better, stronger.

Wake up. Wake up. Wake up.

When she remained asleep, he turned over her hand

and examined the place where the deep, bloody gash had resided. Gone. Just another scar. He shook his head, having trouble assimilating the message his eyes sent. She was healed. The entire situation was a mystery. One he didn't want to examine too closely. Fear of looking a gift horse in the mouth and all that.

He raised her hand to his lips and kissed the tops of her knuckles. "Helen…come on… I need you to wake up. I need to look in your eyes. I need to see *you* to know that you're okay." As stupid as it sounded, he held his breath, waiting for her to wake up. She didn't.

Kent walked back into the room and shut the door behind him. "I just talked with the charge nurse and hospital security, informing them that Hal Haskins is not permitted in this room." He moved around to the other side of Helen's bed. "Still no change?" True concern dominated his tone.

"Not yet. The doctor was in a bit ago. Said everything was normal and that she's just sleeping."

Kent whistled a low sound. "She went through something today. Maybe it's her body's way of dealing."

Yeah. Maybe. Or maybe it was something more. Like what had happened last night when she hadn't been able to move. He should've mentioned that to the doctor. Why hadn't he thought about it until now?

"I've got some updates. You want to talk in here, or do you want to step out into the hallway?"

"Here's fine." As pussy as it made him sound, he didn't want to let her out of his sight. He moved across the room, out of Helen's earshot.

Kent held a thick folder out to him. "What's this?" Thomas flipped open the folder and began leafing through the copied pages. Newspaper articles pulled from the internet. Court documents. Transcripts. Police reports. All about Helena Grayse.

"I thought you said this had nothing to do with Malone." The look Kent gave him was innocuous, but the guy's tone carried suspicion, curiosity, and wariness.

"It doesn't." Thomas fired back.

"How much do you know about Helena Grayse?" Kent asked and leaned against the wall next to the door.

"'Bout the same as anybody." He rattled off the random bits that stuck in his memory. "That she was emotionally stunted because her grandparents had homeschooled her and had supposedly sheltered her from social interactions with anyone her own age. At trial, all her character witnesses had been her grandparents' elderly friends. The court of public opinion condemned her as odd. Odd enough to have committed a murder. Supposedly, she killed her boyfriend—the only person her own age she'd ever interacted with—when he tried to break up with her, because she couldn't handle rejection."

"Yeah. Those are the highlights. But you left out the part about Malone."

Thomas's gaze snapped to Kent. "Malone's involved?" The name tasted sour on his tongue. "What does he have to do with Helen?" Thomas searched his mind for any link. Came up empty-handed.

"Look whose name is on all the police reports." Kent pointed toward the folder. In neat, almost girlish writing was the signature—Robert Malone. "The highlights: Malone witnessed her getting out of Rory Ellis's car and thought she was acting suspicious. He checked on Rory. Found him dead. The rest of the evidence against her is slim-shady, circumstantial, and let's-make-a-leap. It's damn clear the only reason she was convicted was because of Malone and his testimony against her. There was no reason for the jurors not to eat every word he fed them." He paused only long enough to draw in a breath. "You realize that every case Malone has ever testified in is going to file an appeal. Helena's won't be the only one."

The stone in Thomas's heart grew into a boulder. "That man has ruined too many lives." *Mine. My sister's. My mother's. And now Helen's.*

He glanced at her sleeping peacefully, face devoid of worry and pain. The woman she would've been—if Malone had never touched her life—so close to the surface, he could almost see her. Almost. Not quite. Because he knew what lay beneath that hospital smock. Scars.

"You saw…" He paused, not sure how to say it. "All her scars."

Kent's mouth pinched tight. "Yeah."

"They're from…prison?" His heart was full of tears for what she'd endured.

Kent sucked in a large breath as if what he was about to say was going to take some serious air. "I put a call in to Fairson. Haven't heard back. Not sure if they will talk to me without a lawyer and a warrant." He met and held Thomas's gaze. "Elaine Ellis—the lady who shot Helena—has Arnold Holbrook living with her. He's a corrections officer at Fairson. He was downstairs with her in the ER but pulled the attorney card for both of them when I identified myself."

"She's been arrested, right?"

"Yeah. But she'll bond out either today or tomorrow. No record of violence. First offense. It won't matter that she tested positive for gunshot residue or that the gun had been fired. There's been no bullet found and no bullet wound on Helen. You know how this is going to turn out."

Thomas did, and it chafed his balls. "She shot Helen and is going to get away with it."

"There's *no evidence* of Helena being shot."

Kent was right. There was no use arguing about it. "I don't want that woman even thinking about Helen. If she gets anywhere near her…" He trailed off, smart enough to realize he shouldn't be making a threat in front of an officer of the law.

"Helena's gonna need an attorney. Someone to help her get a restraining order. And someone who's willing to pursue a wrongful conviction case."

A lot of unpleasantness lay in front of Helen, but hopefully none of it would be as bad as what lay behind her.

Thomas glanced at the clock. *Damn.* He had to leave right now, or he wasn't going to have time to shower off Helen's blood before the wedding—and he wasn't going to ruin Evanee's big moment by looking like he'd just come from the scene of a slaughter. "Can you do me a favor?"

"Depends."

Thomas shouldn't have expected anything less. They barely knew each other. "I need to leave for a few hours. My sister's getting married tonight, and I have to be there."

A genuine smile fired on Kent's face. "That's good news. With everything going on, I'm glad to hear she's not letting it get to her."

"Me too. Can you stay with Helen until I get back? She hates hospitals."

Kent checked his phone. "I can stay a half hour. I've got a meeting with Lanning to update him on everything."

Thirty minutes was better than nothing. "Stay as long as you can. And if she wakes up, tell her not to freak out, that I'll be right back." Thomas shook Kent's hand. "Thanks, man. For everything. For showing up today. And for taking care of Hal. We appreciate it."

We. Somewhere along the line, he'd gone from being a *he* to a *we* and didn't mind it one bit.

Thomas went to her. He bent over, staring at the quiet beauty of her while she slept. His heart expanded, and a strange tingle took up residence inside his chest. It was a feeling he'd never felt before but one he instantly recognized. *Love.* He brushed a kiss against her mouth, then whispered in her ear. "I have to leave for a little while, but I'll be back. I promise." Even as he said the words, worry formed a stone in his gut.

Chapter 8

THOMAS STOOD ALONE ON THE PORCH OF LATHAN'S cabin, staring out over the black-and-white world. Sounds of love and laughter drifted out to him from the postwedding celebration, but instead of the merriment making him happy, his insides shivered and his palms were sweaty.

Leaving Helen alone in that hospital was the same as leaving his heart in the care of strangers. The flat-out truth: He was better with her. He needed her. An hour away from her felt like an endurance test. Every moment here, while she was there, felt wrong. He turned in the direction of the hospital. If only he could see through the night and across the miles into her room.

He didn't want to go back inside. But after a few more minutes of solitude, he'd plaster a smile on his face, go back in there, bid the bride and groom farewell, then drive like he was in NASCAR to get back to Helen.

The cabin door opened, and Lathan and Evanee stepped out into the chilly night air. Ev was radiant in a simple white gown. And Lathan almost looked tame in the suit coat and button-down shirt he wore.

Thomas forced a smile across his face that felt more like a grimace. He really was happy for them. They deserved all the joy they could get.

Ev put her hand on Lathan's cheek and whispered something to him. He glanced at Thomas, nodded, then shed the jacket he wore and draped it over her shoulders. He crossed his arms and leaned against the doorframe, watching her as she moved across the porch toward Thomas. After everything she'd been through, Thomas couldn't blame the guy for not letting her out of his sight.

He felt the same way about Helen.

Ev's brow furrowed in concern.

After he'd left the hospital, Thomas had rushed home, showered, shaved, and changed into a dress shirt, tie, and suit coat, but he knew he looked like he'd just come from an all-nighter at the keg house. Lack of sleep and soul-deep worry did that to a person.

"What's wrong?" Ev asked as she moved closer to him.

The list of things not going right was endless. Their mom destroyed their lives by marrying Malone. Malone was still out there. The whole world now knew Thomas had been Malone's victim. He couldn't work until Malone's case was closed. Helen had been shot and wasn't waking up. And that was just the highlights reel.

"I'm happy for you." He tried for a real smile, but it slipped away before it fully caught on.

Ev's gaze raked over his face, skimming the scar. "What's wrong?" She repeated the question, and her tone said she wasn't going to let it go.

He looked out across the snow-covered lawn and into the dark woods that surrounded Lathan's house. It took him a while to figure out what to say, because so much was wrong, and only one thing felt right. Helen.

Words rushed out of him. Words that surprised him. "I hate him. I hate Malone. I hate him for what he did to you." His voice got tangled in his throat. He could barely speak. "I hate him for what he did to me." *I hate him for what he did to Helen.*

He felt Ev's gaze on his face but couldn't look at her. She was silent a moment, then stepped closer to him, put her arm around his waist, and leaned her head against his shoulder.

"Damn it. I'm sorry. This is your wedding day. I shouldn't be bringing this shit up now. I don't even know why I said it."

"What did he do to you?" she whispered into the night. The only knowledge she had was from their mom's article.

Terrible memories crowded his sanity, all looking for some airtime. But years of conditioning, years of silence clamped his lips closed. He hadn't been able to talk yesterday when Lanning formally questioned him, and he sure as hell couldn't speak about it now.

He couldn't speak at all.

In that way, he and Helen were alike. Sometimes silence was its own answer.

"Oh, Thomas. I didn't know." Evanee responded as if he'd just told her everything, when he hadn't said a word. She turned in to him and gave him a hug.

He stood there not sure how to react, then hugged her back, the little boy inside him clinging to the comfort his big sister offered.

"I was so caught up in trying to survive Junior that I didn't realize you were being hurt too." Regret settled heavily in her tone.

"I feel the same way. I knew something wasn't right. I should've seen what was going on. Should've stopped it." He matched her regret and raised her one.

"You were a kid. You couldn't have known. Mom

forced us both into an awful situation. We can't change the past, but we can choose not to let it have any more power over us."

Her words made sense on a logical level, but Thomas wasn't feeling very logical about Malone. Unable to find his voice, he nodded his understanding. But the one thing he knew on every level: Helen was the key to a future he'd never dared to dream about. She was a balm to all his wounds. Healed him mind, body, and soul in a way that shouldn't have been possible.

Just as Ev and Lathan and what they'd survived seemed impossible.

"Ev...I need to ask you something."

She pulled back from him and moved to stand shoulder to shoulder at the railing, staring out over the dark yard again. "Anything."

"When you were taken... Well... Everyone talked about you and Lathan having a...connection, a bond, something that linked you together. I thought they were spouting some New Age bullshit. I didn't believe that kind of thing could exist. But now..." God, he was making a mess out of this. He just needed to shut the fuck up and get back to the hospital.

"It's real." She looked back at Lathan standing in the doorway, doing a great impression of being a bodyguard. "I know how crazy it sounds, but it's real. It's the reason Lathan's alive. You know Junior shot him." Her voice faded to a whisper. "In the heart. He should've died. But I healed him."

Thomas whipped around to face Ev. There wasn't even a hint of joking. She was serious.

Helen had been shot in the heart too. And he'd

suspected from the moment he'd placed his hand over her heart that he was healing her too. How else could he explain the gunshot wound requiring only a bandage by the time they'd gotten her to the hospital?

A million questions lined up in his brain. "How did you know you were connected? How does this thing between you work? How is it even real?" Impatience raced his sentences.

Ev stared at Lathan, love naked on her face. "It's woo-woo-hocus-pocus. It doesn't make sense in any logical way. It's something deep inside…intuitive. Almost a sense of inevitability and…destiny."

Destiny. The same word he'd been thinking.

"A deep sense of knowing." She sighed and turned away from Lathan, looking at Thomas again, taking in his haggard appearance. "Why do you ask?"

"I met someone. It feels"—he restrained himself from using the word *destined*—"more than normal…"

"Do you have an ability?"

An ability? What was she talking about? Oh…wait… He'd never thought of being able to see the shadow of death as an ability. More like a hindrance that he'd figured out how to use for good.

"I have…" He'd never uttered the words out loud. "I see the shadow of death." He cringed, waiting for her to react with disbelief. When she seemed to be waiting for more, he went on. "Everyone is born with a shadow of death. Some look light and lovely, and some are foul and dark. I can connect with a dead person's shadow and see their life. I know… It sounds crazy."

She waved her hand in the air as if dismissing his words. "I believe you."

He froze, not sure he'd heard her correctly. She believed him? Without explanation? Without a million questions?

She turned and motioned for Lathan. The guy shoved off from his spot leaning against the doorway and came to her, wrapping his arm around her waist and hugging her tightly to his side. Ev slid her hand up and placed it on his cheek, covering the tattoo blazoned there.

"I believe you because Lathan has an ability too."

"Whoa…" Lathan raked him with a gaze.

"Thomas, tell him what you told me."

When he told Lathan about the shadow of death, he expected the guy to give him some narrow-eyed suspicious look, but Lathan nodded his head slowly as if taking in and processing everything Thomas had just said without question.

He'd expected doubt, skepticism, disbelief. Not total acceptance of…his ability. But Ev said Lathan had an ability. Thomas opened his mouth to ask Lathan about his ability, but Ev cut him off and spoke to her husband. "He's met *her*." The way Ev said *her* carried a meaning Thomas couldn't translate.

Helen. Helen. Helen. His head bobbed up and down on his shoulders.

Ev smiled her crooked grin. "We come in pairs. Xander and Isleen were the first pair." Thomas wasn't surprised. Xander also consulted for the Bureau of Criminal Investigation, and the couple had both helped to search for Ev when she'd been kidnapped. All you had to do was be in the same room with them to see how much they adored each other. "Then there's Lathan and me. So… who is she? Where is she? Why isn't she with you?" Ev peppered him questions.

A part of him wanted to keep Helen hidden from the world. His secret. Not because he was ashamed of her or her past. But because he didn't want to expose her to people's judgment. He sucked in a slow breath before he spoke her name. "Helena Grayse."

"The murderer?" Shock raised Ev's voice, the sound echoing in the night.

Anger tightened the muscles between Thomas's shoulder blades. "Just so we're clear"—his volume was a little louder than he'd intended—"she's innocent." And he'd prove it to the world. Helen had suffered through her years in Fairson. The least she deserved was a public exoneration. "Malone was the entire reason she was convicted. His testimony alone put her in prison."

"If Malone was involved, she most likely *is* innocent. Poor girl." Ev's voice filled with compassion.

"Where is she?" Lathan's tone was gruff. "Why aren't you with her?"

"She's…" Might as well spit it out. "She's in the hospital. She got shot…in the heart."

Evanee inhaled a shocked breath. Lathan's arm around her tightened.

"I"—Thomas hesitated to say the words out loud— "healed her." The words felt weird in his mouth and sounded even weirder to his ears, but felt so right in his soul.

"Of course you did." Lathan's words were spoken matter-of-factly. "Then why aren't you there with her now? You should be with her." Lathan's voice edged toward aggression.

"I didn't want to miss the wedding."

"You don't know how this works, do you?" Lathan fired at him.

"I don't even know what this is," Thomas shot back.

"You know that bear totem out on old Route 40?" Lathan gestured with his head in the direction of the highway.

The subject change left Thomas's brain with a severe case of whiplash. "Yeah."

"It all started there for me. At that totem. There's a story behind it that explains all of this." Individually, all of Lathan's words made sense. It was when Thomas tried to add them up that he had problems. How could he and Helen be linked to an old bear carving?

"It's the story of Fearless and Bear. Our best guess is that all of us couples are like a reincarnation of them," Evanee offered as if that would help him understand. "Let me go get Dr. Stone from inside. He's the one who explained all of this to us. He can explain it to you."

"It's simple." Lathan pinned him with a look more serious than death. "You want your woman safe? You want her unharmed and healthy? You don't fucking leave her side. You keep touching her at all times. Touching. That's the only way you are both protected. Nothing—I mean nothing—can hurt either of you when you're touching. And if she's in the hospital, that means she's hurt. You need to be there to finish healing her. She needs you."

The man's words were confirmation and permission. Confirmation of everything Thomas had felt and permission to leave. His sister and Lathan understood his need to be with Helen.

"I've got to go." He sprinted past Ev and Lathan.

"Don't leave her," Ev yelled after him. "I'll tell Dr. Stone to stop by your place tomorrow."

Thomas raised his hand to acknowledge her words as he ran to his truck. He was only twenty minutes away from the hospital, but twenty minutes seemed like forever. Terrible things could happen in twenty minutes.

———

Helena lurched awake, heart beating like a gong while she gasped for air as if she'd been holding her breath. A dizzy, disconnected feeling swarmed over her.

She focused on a random point on the wall and stared at it while forcing her breathing to ease. Slow breath in. Slow breath out. The edges of panic began to recede.

Her gaze slid across the wall and found a TV playing the evening news on mute. Words scrolled along the bottom of the screen. Closed captioning. On the wall next to her, a long window was covered with vertical blinds. She looked in the other direction and saw an open doorway, but all she could see was a hallway.

A woman in scrubs walked past. Scrubs? Adrenaline shot through her. She was not in the hospital. But even as denial tried to latch on, she heard those familiar sounds. Moaning, quiet conversations, the beep of machines. How did she get here? Had the Sisters attacked her again? No. She'd been released from Fairson. She remembered that much.

Memories came to her from a great distance. Being in her grandparents'—no Thomas's—house. Him taking care of her. Being gentle and kind to her. Oh, and... they'd had sex. Incredible sex. A flush of warmth settled between her legs.

The last thing in her memory file was Mrs. Ellis shooting her. Helen closed her eyes as the scene replayed on the back of her eyelids. Somehow, she'd gotten here, but she didn't know how. And where was Thomas? Had Mrs. Ellis hurt him too? Doubtful. The woman's hatred was targeted on Helena alone. But if Thomas wasn't here… Mrs. Ellis must've told him her true identity. A heavy weight settled over her like a blanket made of lead.

She needed to get the hell out of here. Get back to her camp. Gather her stuff. And get the hell out of this town.

A woman on the TV caught Helena's attention. She had pink streaks in her hair and lay in a hospital bed with a thick, white bandage around her thigh. She looked familiar to Helena. Someone she'd gone to school with? Someone she'd seen at Fairson?

She read the words scrolling across the bottom of the screen.

I'D SEEN IT ALL HAPPENING BEFORE. ALMOST LIKE I'D DREAMED THAT HE WAS GOING TO ATTACK ME, AND I KNEW EXACTLY WHAT I NEEDED TO DO TO SURVIVE.

Helena looked away from the words and back to the woman's face. A memory hit her in a thunderclap of clarity. That woman was the one from her dream, the one who'd stood there watching Helena after she'd won the fight with Hatchet Guy. Which couldn't be possible, because if it was, then that would make her dream…real.

Chapter 9

THOMAS'S MIND REFUSED—FLAT-OUT FUCKING REFUSED—TO believe the message his eyes sent. Helen's hospital bed was empty. Not only was it empty, but it was made, the room had been cleaned, and any indications that she'd been there were gone. All of it confirmed the worst of his fears.

No. Goddamn it. No. He grabbed a handful of hair and yanked. In his peripheral vision, the walls expanded and contracted with his heartbeat. He couldn't look away from that empty bed.

"Where is she?" he bellowed to no one and everyone.

"Sir. Please."

He whirled around. A woman stood in the doorway of Helen's room, wearing a set of scrubs with an ID badge clipped to her collar. A white shadow floated around her. "Keep your voice down. Patients are trying to"—her gaze landed on the scar on Thomas's face—"sleep." The word fell flat between them as she backed up a step.

His appearance intimidated her. His attitude frightened her. He couldn't blame her.

He gestured toward the empty bed. "Where. Is. She?" He made a half-assed attempt at keeping his volume under control, barely succeeding.

"I can't discuss a patient's care with you." She spouted something about HIPAA and hospital policy, but Thomas wasn't listening.

"Tell me what happened to her. She's my…" He trailed

off, uncertain what to call Helen. *Girlfriend* seemed too juvenile. But they weren't engaged or married.

"Oh, she's your wife." A strange sense of relief rinsed the nurse's features of anxiety. Thomas nodded, not bothering to correct the woman. "She left against medical advice." Her words came out in a rush of placating noise. "We tried to get her to wait until morning, but she refused."

Of course Helen refused. She hated hospitals. He just hadn't counted on her hating them badly enough to leave before he got back. "What did she wear? She had no clothes here. No shoes. No coat."

The woman shrugged an I-don't-know gesture.

"You let her walk out of here in the middle of winter, wearing nothing but a hospital smock?" He was shouting again. Fuck his volume.

"I wasn't here. I just came on shift. I'm sure they gave her something to wear." She took another step back.

He stalked toward her, knowing he was frightening her—and not caring. Nothing mattered except finding Helen. "When did she leave?"

"I came on forty-five minutes ago. She was gone before I got here."

He jabbed a finger at her. "You better hope I find her unharmed. Or else..." He couldn't find words to express his wrath. He wasn't being fair to this woman. None of this was her fault; she just happened to be the person in front of him.

He brushed by her, jogging toward the stairs. Didn't have it in him to wait for the elevator. He banged through the doorway, the sound echoing through the stairwell as he took the steps at a full-on run.

Where would she go? Did she have friends or family? There was so much about her that he knew simply because she was Helena Grayse, but there were also a hell of a lot of gaps. He pulled out his cell phone and dialed Kent.

"Yeah," Kent answered, sounding distracted.

Thomas burst through the doorway at the bottom of the stairwell. "Helen is gone." He ran across the empty waiting room to the exit doors.

"What do you mean gone?" The sound of Kent's full attention hit him.

"I mean she's not at the hospital. Her bed's made, room cleaned as if she'd never been there. No goodbye. Nothing." Outside the hospital, Thomas scanned the parking lot and searched the road in front of the facility, looking for her. The interstate was less than a mile away. What if she'd hitched a ride on one of those long-haul semis? She could be anywhere by now. He couldn't allow himself to think about that.

A heaviness settled across his shoulders.

He realized Kent had been talking and he'd zoned out. Whatever the guy had been saying didn't matter. "Elaine Ellis is still in custody, right? What about Holbrook? You know his location?" The idea of that woman or her husband hurting Helen again…

"Give me a moment. Hold the line and I'll check." Kent's connection clicked.

Thomas climbed into his truck, started it, and pulled up to the road. Should he drive around looking for her? Check out the rest stop near the interstate to make sure she wasn't trying to hitch a ride? Or should he drive through town?

"Goddamn it!" He slapped the steering wheel.

The line clicked again. "Elaine Ellis is still in the county jail. Holbrook answered their house phone when I called there just now." Kent's voice sounded impossibly calm. "I think you should just go home."

"Go home!" The words roared out of Thomas. "You can't expect me to do nothing. She's out here. She doesn't have any winter clothes with her. She doesn't have any money on her. She could freeze to death, and you want me to just go home?"

"Shut your shit and listen to me." Kent's voice sounded every bit the authoritarian FBI agent. "You obviously didn't hear what I said a minute ago."

Thomas clamped his lips closed. There was nothing Kent could say that—

"She grew up in *your* house. Lived there with her grandparents her whole life. So maybe she'd go home. Makes sense... That's where you found her last night."

Thomas sat back in his seat. "Whoa..." His mind flashed back to the Realtor telling him an elderly couple had lived there, and their only surviving heir couldn't afford the upkeep on the place. He'd never bothered to pay attention to whose name was on the paperwork.

Well, that explained why she was camping in the woods behind his house. Maybe she wanted to be close to home. He couldn't blame her. She'd been so young—only eighteen—when she'd been arrested and convicted.

"Thanks, man." He disconnected the call before Kent had a chance to reply. Wings of hope fluttered in Thomas's chest. He slammed his foot on the gas, the truck whipping into the road. *Please let her be there. Please let her be there. Please let her be there.* If he lost her…he wouldn't be able to survive. She'd given him a taste of something he couldn't live without. Her.

——∿∿——

Helena stood in the clearing staring at the destruction. Her little camp had been destroyed. *Obliterated* was more accurate. As if a bomb had gone off and all that was left were pieces of her life. All her worldly possessions had been contained in the pack she'd carried here. She didn't have anything of importance beyond a ziplock bag that contained a few pictures of Grandma and Grandpa, her ID, her debit card, and some cash.

Mrs. Ellis had done this. That feeling of baby spiders hatching in Helena's gut when she'd been walking to the Bear yesterday… The woman had probably been following her the entire time.

Helena rubbed the spot over her heart where Mrs. Ellis had shot her. Or tried to shoot her. Obviously, something had gone wrong, because she was still alive and only had a bandage and some bruises to show for being shot at point-blank range.

Her teeth chattered, the sound loud and obnoxious in her head. Her face had moved beyond the sensation of cold to numbness. Her muscles tensed and strained to retain their warmth, making her feel in the throes of a full-body charley horse.

In hindsight, it wasn't the smartest idea—okay, it was downright dumb—to leave the hospital wearing a pilfered pair of scrubs, the blanket from her room, and a mismatched pair of tennis shoes and some clothes she'd found in the lost-and-found bin.

But she couldn't stay there. Freezing to death had

been preferable to seeing Thomas again. He had to know her true identity. No more being *just Helen* to him. Now he'd look at her with the same fear and contempt people reserved for Helena Grayse.

The frigid temperatures nipped at her skin, making an already miserable situation downright unbearable. It would've been nice to have her coat and gloves from inside Thomas's house, but she wasn't about to knock on the door and ask for them. Hypothermia sounded better than humiliation. Pride goeth before a fall.

She picked through the wreckage around her, searching for the ziplock bag. It had to be here. Had to be. It was her only salvation in this horrible situation. She sorted through the remains, stacking the trashed items in one pile and the only slightly damaged items in another, all the while looking for her most prized possession. Underneath a shredded pair of underwear, she found the ziplock bag and let out a tiny squeak of triumph.

Her pictures of Grandma and Grandpa had survived, along with the rest of the contents. A major miracle. She hugged the bag to her chest. Now that she had her debit card and money, she would walk back to town and get a room for the night. Tomorrow was a new day.

She turned to head out of the camp. The shadowed form of a man stood among the trees watching her. Even though she couldn't see his face or his eyes, she knew it was Thomas. Her body felt his presence.

Her heart warmed pleasantly, heating her from the inside out. The cold didn't seem so cold, and the mess around her didn't seem so messy. Simply being near him made her world a better place. She took a step toward him, but then her brain sounded the self-preservation alarm. He knew who she was. He had to know. Mrs. Ellis would've told him and everyone else with ears.

Something inside Helena broke. She felt the snap of it inside her chest and realized it might've been her heart. Without meaning to, she'd fallen for the fantasy of what-might-have-been.

Seeing condemnation in his gaze was something her soul couldn't tolerate. It made her a coward, it made her weak, but she ran, sprinting through the maze of barren trees—arms pumping, legs churning while she fisted the bag tightly in her hand. The contents were the only thing she could rely on. Nothing else.

If there was any mercy in the world, he'd let her go. Grant her the dignity of avoidance.

"Stop," he shouted, his footsteps falling into rhythm behind her. He was chasing her. Holy hell, he was chasing her. Maybe he wanted to catch her and have her arrested for trespassing. She was playing into everyone's bias against felons. Out of prison less than forty-eight hours, and she'd already broken the law.

The only solution was to keep running. She wasn't going to stop. She was going to escape everything. Him. This town. This state. She was going to keep running until she found a place where no one had ever heard of Helena Grayse. And even then, she might still keep running.

She tripped over a branch hidden beneath the snow. Her arms windmilled to keep her upright, but balance lost the battle with momentum, and she fell facedown into the snow. Before she could move, he was on top of her, flipping her over.

For some reason, her mind flashed back to Hatchet Guy. She raised her hands to defend herself against his blows, while at the same time, her brain tried to convince her that the man looming over her was Thomas, not Hatchet Guy. A small part of her preferred Hatchet Guy. He'd only harmed her body in a dream, but Thomas had the capacity to decimate her heart in real life.

"Helen." Her name came out sounding like an anguished plea. "I'm not going to hurt you."

Oh God. He'd called her Helen. Not Helena. By some miracle, he didn't know she was Helena Grayse.

She dropped her arms from their defensive position. Even though it was dark, starlight reflected off the snow, providing enough illumination for her to see him. His face was ravaged with some emotion she couldn't name. The scar on his cheek blazed bright, somehow looking painful. There were no words to utter, so she cupped his damaged cheek.

He sucked in a breath as if her touch pained him, but when she tried to withdraw, he grabbed her wrist and held it in place. He *wanted* her skin on his.

Their eyes met. The impact devastating and healing at the same time. She tumbled into his gaze like a free fall. Enjoying the freedom, fearing the fall. And then he broke the connection and let go of her wrist and grabbed her by the shoulders. "Why did you run from me? I would never hurt you." Truth twined through each of his words. "I was worried out of my head when you weren't at the hospital." He shook her, emphasizing his words. "You know how stupid it was for you leave there without a coat, or gloves, or boots?"

She nodded, couldn't help it. Her body had been screaming that same message thirty seconds after she'd walked out the hospital doors.

"Why would you do that? You could've frozen to death out here."

Not thinking, she shrugged.

He grabbed her face in his hands. His fingers warm and rough and perfect against her skin.

The world fell away, leaving only him and her. He stared into her. Warming her from the inside out. She no longer felt the coldness of the snow against her backside. All she could feel was him. Inside her. Around her. Over her. He was the air she breathed. The heartbeat in her chest. He was her whole world. And she never wanted this impossible moment to end. She wanted to stay right here. Right now. Forever.

"Don't you do that." His tone was deep. His volume soft. "Don't you ever act as if your life doesn't matter. It matters." His thumbs brushed over her cheekbones, sending pleasurable tingling along her nerve endings. "It matters to me."

Her ears heard his words, but her brain had a hard time translating them.

"Yes, you." Again, he seemed to be answering the question she didn't ask. "You matter to me." He spoke with heartbreaking sincerity. "How could you think otherwise?"

Because I'm Helena Grayse. She slammed her eyes closed.

"Stop that." The irritation in his tone startled her eyes open. "Stop hiding from me." His expression was tense, but one thing didn't change—his kind eyes. "Good God. You've got to be freezing to death." He moved away from her and stood, then grabbed her hands and pulled her to standing. He took off his coat and placed it over

her shoulders. The inside warmth soothed her cold skin,
and his scent rose up, surrounding her like a hug. He
helped her thread her arms through the sleeves and then
zipped the coat up under her chin.

The backs of her eyes burned, and she felt the beginning of tears forming. *Damn it.* She wasn't going to
cry every time he was nice to her. That was just stupid.
Stupid. Stupid.

"Come on. Let's get you back to the house and get
you warmed up." He held out his hand in invitation,
giving her the opportunity to decide her fate.

Her feet shackled her in place. She shouldn't go with
him. She should follow her plan and go find a room for
the night. She squeezed her hand holding the ziplock
bag, just to make sure she hadn't dropped it. The more
time she spent with him, the harder it was gonna be
when he found out her identify. All he had to do was
peek at her ID card.

Logic dictated she walk away. Her soul told her to stay.

She reached out to him. He turned her hand over and
examined the gash that had been there just yesterday but
had since healed. She'd always been a fast healer, but
even for her, that was record time.

His gaze flicked up to her eyes, and he smiled, an
upturning of the lips that contained satisfaction and truth
and happiness. The scar on his cheek completed him,
making him more breathtaking, in the same way that
a flower's delicate imperfections only made it lovelier.

Together, they trudged through the snow toward the
house. Winter didn't seem quite so cold with him holding her hand. His skin against hers infused her with a
heat that traveled up her arm, across her shoulders, and

down into her belly, causing warm tingles of arousal to stir.

She glanced at him out of the corner of her eye to see if she affected him the same way he affected her. He didn't seem fazed by the chill temperatures. Not at all. In fact, he acted as if they were out for a stroll on a pleasant spring evening.

"I'm sorry I wasn't at the hospital when you woke." He glanced at her, then back through the woods in the direction they were traveling. "Tonight was my sister's wedding, and I couldn't miss it. Evanee's been through some bad times, and this meant a lot to her."

They broke through the forest and started across the lawn, following a line of tracks that led to his back door.

"I told her—my sister and her husband—about you. They were excited." The corner of his mouth tilted upward.

Her mouth went dry, and a stone lodged itself in her throat. Denial looked exactly like this. It looked like a woman and man holding hands while they walked in the snow. It looked like everything was all right on the surface. But underneath…it was all a lie. A lie that had started with him accidentally calling her Helen. A lie she'd perpetuated because she'd never corrected him.

She thought about yanking her hand from his and running, but he would catch her and demand to know the reason. *Ugh*… How did she go from her plan of getting a hotel room for the night to deciding to go back home with him? She was powerless to resist temptation.

At the house, once again, the smell of home enveloped her, folding around her and flashing her lovely memories of Grandma and Grandpa. She trailed behind him as he led her through the dark familiar rooms, then up the stairs and into his bedroom.

Oh... Maybe he was just horny. Maybe he wanted sex. Maybe she'd been reading his actions as caring when they'd really been self-serving. Her heart went heavy, but her girlie parts went *rah-rah-sis-boom-bah*. But then he kept walking, guiding her into the master bathroom.

"Have a seat." He gestured to the closed toilet lid. As if her body couldn't disobey him, she sat.

He bent over the claw-foot tub and turned the water on. The familiar bump of old pipes sounded, and she couldn't help the smile that bloomed on her face. Other people loved a familiar song. She loved the music of old plumbing.

When he was satisfied with the temperature, he stepped back and looked at her. "Come on, let's get this off you." He unzipped the coat and helped her take it off, then unlaced the mismatched pair of tennis shoes, removing them from her feet. "You're shaking so bad, you look like you're having a seizure."

Her entire body trembled. She hadn't realized she was cold until he'd let go of her.

He leaned over her, and before she knew what he was doing, he picked her up. "I know you're self-conscious about your scars."

Tension rammed through every muscle, and she almost leaped out of his arms, but he tightened his grip, pinning her to him.

"But I'm not going to argue with you about it." He bent and settled her in the tub—clothing and all.

The water scalded her. She hissed and clung to his neck, trying to crawl up him and out of the fire.

"Easy. The water is barely lukewarm. Just give it a second. You'll see."

His words were magic, because her skin adjusted, and the blaze faded to a burn, then a warmth. Slowly, she released her grip on his neck, and he let go of her.

"I'll be back in a moment." He left the room. She stared after him, but then turned her attention to the water filling the tub. Already, her body had adapted to the temperature. She reached for the faucet, turning the cold down and the hot up.

She sank into the water, letting the heat absorb into her. As with the rest of the house, he hadn't changed anything. The claw-foot tub, the sink, the toilet were all the same. The walls were still the pale green they'd been her entire life.

She recalled bath time in this tub, splashing and laughing and playing with suds and bubbles. Grandma grinning and giggling. This house—every room of it—contained memories of her life and the people she loved.

She couldn't help herself. She grabbed the shampoo bottle from the side of the tub and squirted some in the water, then swished it around, creating a frothy mess of bubbles. It made her heart happy.

Thomas chuckled when he walked back into the room. "This has got to be the first time anyone's ever had a bubble bath while fully dressed." He held a steaming mug out to her.

Her soaked shirtsleeves weighed down her arms as she reached for it. She held the cup to her face and inhaled the aroma of a strong cup of coffee laced with cream. Tentatively, she took a first sip. Dark and delicious and smooth, it tasted better than the weak prison-issue java she'd been forced to drink.

A sigh of pure pleasure slipped from her lips as she leaned back in the tub, holding the mug to her face to let its heat and glorious smell waft over her.

"I brought you some clothes of mine to wear, since it looks like everything out back got destroyed." He laid a sweatshirt and a pair of track pants on the edge of the sink, then sat on the closed toilet seat next to the tub, watching her drink the coffee. "So what was your plan? Grab your stuff and go?"

Yes. She focused on the cup, refusing to look at him.

"After everything, you were just going to vanish?" His volume was barely above a whisper. "Helen." The way he said her name was a caress of vowels and consonants that pulled her gaze to him. "I know…"

Who you are… Her brain automatically filled in the rest. Her heart seized like a rusted bolt.

"I know you've been through some really bad shit. I know it left scars…inside and out. But…" He reached down and stroked his hand over her wet hair, then let his fingers trail down her cheek. She couldn't look away from him. Instead, she clung to his words like a lifeline she didn't deserve.

"But…you're beautiful to me. Inside and out." Truth shone in his eyes.

Under another set of circumstances, those words would've been the most wondrous thing anyone had ever said to her. But in this reality, they injured her, because they weren't meant for her. They were meant for Helen, not Helena Grayse.

He didn't know that she'd been convicted of murder. He didn't know that she'd spent the past ten years in Fairson. He didn't know that she was damaged beyond repair. He didn't know her.

Oh God. She wanted to run. To get away from the look of kindness and affection on his face. But there was no escape when she was fully clothed and neck-deep in a bubble bath. She sat her cup on the edge of the tub, then sank underneath the surface, letting the water close over her face and drown the tears that might've snuck out.

She stayed underwater, letting the absolute stillness settle into her soul. When she needed air, she surfaced, only allowing her mouth and nose above water. She preferred to keep her eyes closed and her ears submerged so she could pretend to be floating alone on an ocean.

Time passed. She didn't know how much, but enough that she felt strong enough to handle those words he'd thrown at her.

She emerged out of the water, wiping the suds off her face, then opened her eyes.

He was gone.

Thomas sat on the edge of the bed, staring at the closed bathroom door as if the key to understanding Helen was written upon the wood.

From the moment he'd met her, everything he'd done had been for her—with the exception of going to the wedding. But even there, she'd dominated his thoughts, and talking to Evanee and Lathan had been enlightening, to say the least.

He had never hurt her, done his damnedest to save

her, and was determined to protect her. But she shut him out. He accepted that she wasn't willing to talk. But her refusal to look at him, listen to him… How much more of herself was she going to keep from him? He didn't want an empty shell that looked like her. He wanted her. All of her. And more than anything, he wanted her to want him.

He gripped the comb in his hand. He'd meant to set it in there with the clothes but had forgotten.

Sloshing, splashing sounds came from the other side of the door. It sounded as though she'd taken off the sodden clothing, wringing out each piece. His mind conjured an image of her sitting in the water, bare breasts dewy and glistening while teardrops of water rolled off her nipples. His dick liked the pictures and went full-on baseball bat in his pants. But then he remembered the scars she bore on her body. Evidence of the immense pain she'd endured in Fairson. The reason she had trouble coping.

Not only was she adjusting to life outside prison, but she had ten years of trauma to process. He couldn't fathom the hell she'd been through, and yet he was pouting because she was coping the best way she knew… Yeah, total asshole move.

He sat there, ears tuned to every sound coming from behind the door. And then the water began draining, and a few minutes later, she stepped into the bedroom. In the glow of the bedside lamp, her skin shone healthy and pink. Her hair was a ratty, tangled, endearing mess that dangled over one shoulder. His clothes swallowed her body, but she could wear a barrel and still look magnificent to him.

He should say something, but profound words were as elusive as fog. Instead, he held up the comb and scooted back on the bed, motioning for her to sit between his spread legs. "Let me take care of your hair."

An adorable little wrinkle formed between her brows, but then a ghost of a smile slid over her lips. She moved closer and sat in front of him. He closed his thighs tight around her. Almost as though his legs were a fortress wall surrounding her, keeping her safe. And, well…it just felt right to be touching her. "I've never combed a woman's hair before. Is there a right way or a wrong way?"

She shook her head and flipped the mass over her shoulder so it hung halfway down her back. In the lamplight, the wet strands looked more bronze than gold. Slowly, he reached out and touched it. Cool and silky and perfect. He held it to his nose and inhaled. The smell of his shampoo mixed with her body's unique chemistry to form a scent that might as well have been a pheromone with the way his damn dick reacted.

He shifted back so the thing didn't poke her in the ass.

Gently, he separated a section of hair and began at the top, sliding the comb through the strands, teasing out the tangles. There was something oddly relaxing, almost meditative about the task. He didn't need to think about anything other than the slip and slide of the comb. She set both hands on his thighs, her touch light and gentle. Her head hung forward, and the tension eased out of her shoulders. She was enjoying this as much as he was.

It didn't take long for the snarls of hair to submit to the comb. "All done." He tossed the comb onto the nightstand, then leaned forward, pressing his front to her back, and wrapped his arms loosely around her. She sighed, her body warm and compliant against his. Her hands found his arms where they wound around her, and she held on to him, reciprocating in the only way she could.

"You had a long, terrible day. Let's get some rest." Slowly, lovingly, he guided them both down to the bed. Her wet hair fanned out across the pillow, the beautiful strands tickling his cheek and chin.

He reached beyond her to the bedside lamp and turned it off. The only light the faint silver glow of stars on the snow outside. He wrapped his arm around her waist again, and this time, she grabbed his hand and laced their fingers together. His heart swelled, and his face tingled from the giant smile on his lips.

She wiggled and snuggled in his embrace, warm and contented. Holding her felt so right.

Tomorrow, he'd talk to Evanee and Lathan to find out about this thing between him and Helen. Then figure out a way to explain it to Helen that didn't make him sound like an escapee from the asylum.

But that was tomorrow.

Tonight, he had her in his arms and in his bed, and that was miracle enough for today.

"I'm so glad you came home," he whispered against her temple and closed his eyes, feeling exhaustion settle into him.

"Me too." The words were sleepy and so quiet, they were more of a breath, but he heard them, latched on to them, and was never letting them go.

Helen had finally spoken.

Chapter 10

Above her, below her, all around her was clean and pristine whiteness. The beauty of it intoxicating, but the memory of the last time she'd seen it sobering. This might be a dream, but it fell more into the category of a waking nightmare.

She looked around the space, searching for someone or something. She was alone, but not alone. Something invisible, intangible was with her.

Suddenly, the shimmer started on her stomach. Just like last time, it spread through her body, coating her in its power and protection. She flexed her fists, loving how strong it made her feel, but hating that she had no choice in it happening to her.

"You are the warrior. It is your destiny to teach others how to survive." The words came out of her mouth but weren't in her voice. They were deeper, more resonant, and the same words that had been spoken at the beginning of her last dream.

"Why is this happening? What's going on?" she asked the endless white around her. Or maybe she needed to speak to the shimmer—maybe it was what controlled the voice.

As if to answer to her question, the dreamscape dimmed and faded until nothing surrounded her except utter and complete blackness. A black so dense, it suffocated. She thrust her hands out blindly and encountered... Wires? Metal? What was it? She traced her fingers over it, discovering a mesh of some sort. Her hand followed the mesh, up over her head, then down the other side. Fingers dancing, she mapped out the dimension of her space. She was completely enclosed inside the area. Large enough to sit in, too small to lie down in.

And then her brain sent her a mental image—a cage. She was in a cage.

Her heart pumped icy fear through her body. Behind her blind eyes, colors burst and faded like fireworks on the Fourth of July.

All her other senses roared online as if their power button had just been hit. The stench overwhelmed her. She'd thought being forced to bunk in the same room as forty-nine other women, many of whom didn't care about personal hygiene, had been bad? That had been perfume compared to the foulness assaulting her nose.

Piss. Shit. The odor of unwashed bodies. And something tangy and metallic that threatened to shove her stomach up her throat. She clamped her hand over her nose and tried to breathe through her mouth, but that was worse, because then she could taste the squalor in the air.

The floor—no, it was damp concrete—chilled her ass cheeks. Wait... Her hands skimmed over her torso, her hips, feeling nothing but skin. She didn't have a stitch of clothing on, but something thick and heavy ringed her neck. Dull spikes were embedded in the material. She traced it all the way around her neck to what felt like a handle.

A collar. The kind some gangsta-wannabe would put on his attack dog. A terror unlike any she'd ever experienced bit down on her.

A soft sigh off to her right snagged her attention and

pinched her heart. She stared through the darkness, willing herself to have night vision. But nope. Of course not.

Was her captor watching her? Was that him sighing? Or was there someone else here in the dark too? Another person in a cage just like her?

"Hello," she whispered.

"Shh..." A harried sound came from in front of her.

"What's going on?" She breathed the words, trying to make them as soft as possible and yet still audible enough to be heard.

"If he hears you, he'll take you. Hurt you again. You want that? Then be quiet." The whispered words came from behind. She whipped around but saw more of nothing.

"Where am I?" she asked, blatantly ignoring the warning to be silent.

"Oh jeez. Your frickin' mind snapped." Another voice sighed into the dark. "You're one of the Hell Hounds' bitches. Remember? Now stop talking, or one of them will hear."

The words froze everything inside her. She couldn't even move. Oh God. She wasn't alone. There were at least four other women here with her.

When she woke up, she was going to be able to escape this. But these other women... They were trapped here. This wasn't a nightmare to them. It was their reality. The brakes on her mind screeched to a halt. Was she really thinking that these women were in reality, but she was in a dream? After what she'd seen on the TV in the hospital? Yes, she was.

Anger warmed her. Anger fueled her. Anger was going to free her. "Come on, you asshole!" She screamed the words as loud as she could. "Come and get me!" She grabbed onto the mesh and rattled it.

A collective gasp sounded from all around her. Her guts leaped. Holy hell, there had to be at least twenty other women in the room. Somewhere across the dark space, a woman sobbed quietly.

"Come and get me! Come on! You a bunch of chicken-shit cowards?" The words flowed from deep down inside, burning the whole way up like hard liquor burns the whole way down.

A scrape of metal. A bang. And then orange light as the door was thrown wide.

A sea of cages. Large dog crates, set side by side throughout the room with narrow pathways leading down the aisles and up the rows. A waste trough ran through the center of the space. They were in a kennel, but instead of dogs, each crate contained a frightened woman. Their eyes wide, all turned on her.

Her stomach shriveled to the size of a raisin. *Oh shit.*

In the doorway, a man stood silhouetted. A big man. "Which one of you bitches is barking?"

The room full of caged women went obscenely still.

"Me." The word came out as a squeak of sound so quiet, she barely heard it. She cleared her throat and tried again. "Me." In case he hadn't heard her, she rattled her cage for emphasis.

The moment Big Man's gaze landed on her, her stomach expanded from raisin size to watermelon size, threatening to explode out of her in a volcanic eruption. His tiny, fathomless eyes were set in a red bulbous face, draped with a scraggly beard that hung partway down his chest.

He plowed through the rows of cages, irritability and eagerness putting a spring into his hulking steps.

"Bitch forgot her lessons on submission. I got no problems being your teacher. And when the rest of the Hounds arrive, they'll reinforce your learnin'."

He used a fat key to unlock her cage and reached inside. It took everything inside her to not scramble away from his grasping hand. He snagged her by the collar, by that handle, and dragged her out.

Not giving her a chance to stand, he towed her along behind him down the row of cages. Most of the women huddled in the farthest corner of their cages; only the most daring watched.

One of the women reached her fingers through the wire mesh and trailed them over Helena's thigh, then down her leg and ankle, as he pulled her past. But the woman in that cage wasn't a woman. She was a girl barely into her teens. Dark hair, matted and snarled, hung limply over bony legs that she hugged to her chest. Her skin was splotchy with filth and dirt. Her face so thin, she looked skeletal. But her eyes—with their appalling combination of sad and haunted—were what Helena would never forget.

Big Man dragged her forever until he dropped his hold on her and she collapsed. Her gaze darted around the room. Empty tables with chairs stacked on them. Neon signs. Kegs of beer stacked against one wall as decoration. She was in a bar?

Before she could move, he nabbed her wrists and duct-taped them together in front of her. A few years back, she'd happened upon a video in the Fairson library about how to escape duct tape. It was so damned easy, she hadn't believed it, but now—maybe, just maybe that video was going to save her life and the lives of all the women in that kennel.

He wore a ripped and faded Hell Hounds shirt, the material straining against his protruding belly. He might be big. He might be strong. But she was determined.

"You'll learn to keep your eyes on the floor, bitch."

And you'll learn I'm nobody's bitch.

"Kneel," he commanded in a voice that sounded very much like a master talking to his slave.

Best to let him think he'd sufficiently tamed her, since that's what he was used to. Submission. She complied with his wishes.

His hand went to his belt. His intentions obvious.

But her mind was on that girl. A girl. In a cage. A girl who should've been out laughing with her friends, enjoying life. Not wearing a face destroyed by despair.

She would save that girl. She would save them all.

She clasped her hands together in a double fist and punched upward into Big Guy's ball sac. He leaped into the air. For such a heavy fellow, he had some hang time before he fell over backward, clutching his nads like he was worried they'd fall off and roll away.

She raised her duct-taped wrists above her head. With all the force she possessed, she slammed her wrists down while pulling her hands apart. For a moment, she thought the video had been wrong, because she still felt the tape against her skin, but then she realized the tightness of the bond was gone. She was free.

She scrambled to her feet, tape dangling off her, and nabbed the nearest chair off a table.

His arm flung out, trying to grab her, while his other hand cupped himself. She hefted the chair over her head and slammed it down on his face. The *thunk* of wood to bone sounded in her gut. But she raised the thing again, hitting him over and over, losing herself in the satisfying rhythm of bashing his face in. Only when the chair broke did she stop.

He lay there unconscious, his face a deformed mass of blood and flesh.

She knelt next to him. Her fingers trembled as she searched his pants pocket for the keys. The metal felt cold and slimy against her fingers, but she pulled it out and stood.

Behind the bar, a cordless phone hung on the wall. She snagged it off the cradle and held it to her ear. The soft hum of the dial tone gave her heart wings. She punched in 911 but couldn't risk waiting for a response. Underneath the phone was a giant stack of brand-new Hell Hounds T-shirts. She slid one over her head, hefted the stack in her arms, and ran back to the kennel.

She threw the door open, letting it bang against the wall with an echoing sound as if to get all their attention. "The police are coming. They're coming. You're safe now."

For a few heartbeats, there was no sound, but then the room erupted into cheers and crying. She rushed to the girl's cage first. Her fingers were clumsy as she fumbled with the heavy key and lock, but she got it open. She flung the door back, reached inside, and helped the girl out. She stood on wobbly, shaking legs, staring in disbelief. Helena didn't hesitate. She unfastened the collar around the girl's neck, letting it drop at her feet. Then she helped the girl pull the shirt over her head and thread her arms through the sleeves.

When the girl was dressed, Helena grabbed her by

the shoulders and looked into her eyes. "I need you to help me." She shoved the stack of shirts at the girl, who clutched them to her.

Helena unlocked the women's cages while the girl unfastened their collars and helped them put on a shirt. The girl had even started tossing in hugs and words of comfort by the time they freed the last woman.

Together as one, all the women left the kennel, following Helena to the bar, past Big Guy's unconscious body and then to the door with a red EXIT sign. She twisted the knob, pulled it open, and stepped out into a beautiful sunny morning. The air was cool and crisp and incredibly fresh. The sunshine against her skin felt like heaven.

The sound of approaching sirens reached them. Her heart sang hallelujah inside her chest.

She turned and looked back at all the women, but a woman she didn't remember freeing stood in front of them. Her face filthy, her arms covered in bruises and her legs smeared with abrasions. Helena had just taught her how to escape.

In that moment, she recognized the differences between the last dream and this one. No voice had paused time to tell her what to do. It had all been on her. The thought both scared her and exhilarated her.

The shimmer faded from her flesh, leaving a profound weariness in its wake. Her legs folded beneath her, and the last thing she saw before she fell into sleep's deep embrace was the woman standing over her, mouthing the words *thank you*.

—∿—

Thomas's heart punched against his sternum, jolting him awake. His eyes popped open to a blinding white light. The shroud of sleep, still heavy on him, made thinking difficult. The only thing he knew was that something was wrong. He could feel it in the way his innards trembled.

In an instant, he took in his surroundings. His bedroom. Sunshine blazing bright outside, casting its cheerful light in the space. Late morning had to be snuggling up to early afternoon. His gaze darted around the room, roaming the corners and doorways. No boogeyman. No Mrs. Ellis with a gun. No one. Just him and Helen's body twined around his.

He inhaled in a shuddering breath to calm himself. Today was going to be a better day than yesterday. She wasn't going to get shot. She wasn't going to go missing. Hell, she wasn't going to leave his sight if he had anything to say about it.

His arm was threaded underneath her neck so she could use his shoulder as a pillow, while his other wrapped her waist, holding her tight. She lay on her side cuddled into him, her legs tangled with his, her knee only a few inches from his morning chub that was acutely aware of her nearness and straining against his pants to get closer. Everything about her curves pressed against his angles was a masterpiece wrought in living flesh.

He'd never felt more comfortable in his whole life. Days could pass, years could pass, and as long as he could hold her like this... Well, this was all he needed. She was food and water and oxygen—everything essential. Now more than ever, he realized he'd only lived half a life until he'd spotted her in the cemetery.

A strangled, gasping sound came from Helen. She

lurched in her sleep. Her muscles went rigid, then slack. Her torso thrust up off the bed in an image he would've sworn he'd seen in *The Exorcist*. Some force, some evil abusing her body.

She slammed back down against the mattress. The headboard cracked against the wall, loud as a gunshot.

"Jesusgod, Helen." Thomas threw himself on top of her, trying to contain her body's flailing, wild movements. The instant his weight settled on her, she stilled. "Helen." He lifted off her enough to see her face, to shake her shoulder. No response. Nothing.

Shit, shit, shit. He straddled her and grabbed her face in his hands. "Open your eyes. I need you to open your eyes."

Almost as though she was obeying his command, her eyelids fluttered, then eased open.

He bent low over her, touching noses with her. "I'm here. I'm here."

Up close with the sunshine filtering through the windows, her eyes looked like a strange combination of gold and silver. A color radiant and resplendent in its uniqueness.

Their gazes locked, and he felt the connection as surely as if it were a physical touch. He tumbled into her, seeing her fear and confusion. She didn't understand what was happening any more than he did.

"Can you move?" Even as he asked the question, he witnessed the answer. He was a goddamned dumbass for not mentioning this to her doctor yesterday. "You're going to be okay." He packed as much assurance as he could into his voice and wished like hell he could believe himself.

Tears formed in her beautiful eyes and then sprinted into her hairline as if they were trying to hide. His heart went warm and soft. "Hey, none of that. There's nothing to be frightened about. I know exactly what to do."

Awww…shit. Did he just say that out loud? *What the fuck?* He didn't know what to do beyond holding her, rocking her, and praying that someone or something was listening.

Trying to not appear concerned—for her sake—he lay down alongside her on the bed. "Just so you know…" He tried to put a little lightness in his voice. "I'm a fast learner. I'm not even going to suggest taking you to the hospital."

Her facial expression didn't change, but gratitude filled her gaze. She didn't look away from him—she locked on to him, staring hard as if he carried the key to release her paralysis. He felt a bit sick at her faith in him. But then a voice whispered something in the back of his mind. And he realized what he was hearing were Lathan's words from last night.

It's simple. You want your woman safe? You want her unharmed and healthy? You don't fucking leave her side. You keep touching her at all times. Touching. That's the only way you are both protected. Nothing—I mean nothing—can hurt either of you when you're touching. And if she's in the hospital, that means she's hurt. You need to be there to finish healing her. She needs you.

The answer she sought from him was suddenly there. There was no logical reason for knowing how to make her better; he just knew. And she was gonna be pissed.

"You know I'd never hurt you." He stared into her eyes, showing her the truth inside him. A truth that was

more than simply not hurting her—it was loving her.
Could he really be thinking love? *Fuck, yes*. And if she
could see into him the way he could see into her, then
she saw it written across his heart. "I know how to make
you better."

Her eyes went wide and willing. Well, at least she'd
be willing until he touched her.

"I swear to you, I won't hurt you." His damn hand
shook as it found the bottom of her long sweatshirt and
slipped inside. The first touch of his fingers to her flesh
sent a jolt of something hot and electric and strangely
satisfying through him.

Her breath hitched. Her eyes widened in surprise and
betrayal.

"Shh… It's okay." And then his fingers found the
ripple of the scars marring her stomach. He settled his
palm there against the worst of it. A rush of something
powerful and unnamable surged through him, converg-
ing in his shoulder, then sliding down his arm. It felt like
cool, refreshing water pouring from him into her, but it
was dry. The sensation soothed and comforted him, and
he knew it was helping her. "It's working. You feel it,
don't you?"

Then he looked at her. Those tears she hated to cry,
hated for him to see, sluiced down her cheeks, and she
couldn't do a damned thing to stop them. She couldn't
turn her face away, she couldn't slip under the water, she
couldn't avoid him seeing her pain. And it about killed
him. He felt like the world's biggest asshole because
those tears were caused by him touching her.

He might be physically healing her, but every second
of him touching her scars carved a deeper emotional

wound. For a split second, he almost pulled his hand away, but didn't. He would rather see her up and moving and angry than paralyzed.

"Awww… Helen." His voice sounded thick. His hand stroked over her stomach, feeling the ridges of damaged flesh. "Your scars are part of your packaging, not who you are on the inside. When I touch you, I don't feel damaged skin. I feel the warm, vital essence of *you*. You are more than any mere disfigurement ever could be. You are everything. My everything." The words didn't come from his heart; they came from his soul.

She blinked once, twice, three times, while more of those terrible tears he'd caused slipped from her eyes. And then she clenched her hands into fists and released. Clenched and released.

It was working. Movement was returning to her. He got the distinct impression that she was imagining punching him, and he couldn't half blame her. The other half of him knew the emotional damage needed healing, and maybe, just maybe this was the pain of him lancing those festering wounds to get the infection out.

Slowly, she bent and straightened her knees. Did the same with her arms, then sat up and leaned forward as if she wanted to touch her toes, then reclined back.

"I can't believe how fast this worked. It took less than a minute." *Damn*. He really could heal her.

She twisted out of his arms. He fought the urge to keep hold of her but didn't want to take away her control. Part of her mending the mental pain would be her finding her power again.

Using the bedpost to ensure her balance, she stood. When she was upright and steady, she turned and nailed with him a glare so full of rage that he raised his hands in a gesture of innocence.

"I'm not sorry that you're up and moving. So you can quit with the wishing-me-dead look."

He saw the truth of his words hit her and then bounce off the shield of self-preservation she'd built around herself. Without a glance, she walked out of the room. He expected her to go downstairs, but she surprised him by heading down the hallway to the spare bedroom and the same bathroom where she'd been shot.

He leaped out of bed and went after her. "Helen. Wait." The bathroom door slammed. "I haven't had a chance to clean up in there." He pictured the room as he'd last seen it. Blood in the tub, blood on the floor. All of it Helen's. The last damned thing she needed was a reminder of what had happened in there. He stood in the bedroom listening, waiting, and realized this was too familiar to what he'd gone through last night, waiting outside his bathroom door for her to emerge.

Was this going to be the pattern of their relationship? Her always avoiding him? Him always waiting for that magic moment when she might choose to engage with him? Part of him wanted to just walk away—give her a taste of her own medicine and all that, but he couldn't injure her in that way.

She wasn't avoiding him out of spite. She ran from anything that hit her emotional sore spots and limped off to lick her wounds in private. It was the only way she knew how to heal herself. What she didn't understand yet was that he could help her heal—mind and body and soul.

Chapter 11

HELENA LEANED AGAINST THE CLOSED BATHROOM DOOR AS if she expected Thomas to try to break it down. But he wouldn't. He was too calm and kind to act that way. Even when he'd touched her scars, he'd reassured her that he wouldn't hurt her, because he'd known she'd freak out. Which she was doing right now.

She was overreacting. Knew it. Couldn't help it. His touch on her scars felt like he'd ripped her wide open, then reached inside to tinker around. What had she done? Run off in the middle of him putting all her pieces back together.

A cascade of tears streamed down her face. She swiped them away.

And that's when she saw all the blood in the bathroom. Her blood. *Oh God*. It was all over the bathtub, all over the floor. The room looked like a slaughterhouse. A scream threatened to erupt from inside her. She needed to get herself under control. She needed to stop crying. What she really needed to do was leave.

Her shirt and pants from the day before were stacked in a neat pile on the back of the toilet tank. Maybe if she weren't surrounded by Thomas, his clothes, his house, she could think straight about getting out of here.

In seconds, she stripped and put on her own shirt and pants. The garments felt cold and too tight against her skin, but she ignored the sensation. She opened the door.

He stood there, his beautiful scarred face full of concern for her that she didn't deserve.

She thrust his clothes at his chest. When he didn't take them, she let them drop on the floor and marched past him, down the hallway and down the staircase. He followed her, but she pretended to not notice.

In the living room, she found her coat on the back of the couch. Exactly where he'd laid it after taking it off her a lifetime ago. The material felt heavy and too bulky as she put it on and zipped it up. She reached for her gloves, but he grabbed her by the shoulders. She refused to look at him. No way was she going to let him talk her out of leaving this time.

"Look at me, damn it." His tone was gruff and guttural.

She tried to shrug out of his grip, but his hands were immovable. Not hard. Not hurting. Just immovable.

"I'm not letting you go until you look at me. You owe me that much." A plea hid inside his tone.

If she caught a glimpse of his eyes, her resolve might crumble. But if she didn't look at him, she suspected he'd stand there holding on to her until they were both old and feeble. Maybe that's what he wanted. Maybe that's what she wanted.

She inhaled a slow breath, hoping to find some willpower in the air, but nope—none to be found. Reluctantly, she shifted her gaze up his chest, over the hard line of his jaw, over his stubble-covered cheeks. Over his beautiful scar, before circling back around to finally meet his eyes.

Something inside clicked, locking them together. He opened his mouth. Nothing came out. He closed his mouth. Then opened it again. "I know you can feel this connection." His midnight-blue eyes blazed with little silver flecks that reminded her of stars on a moonless night. "I'm not… I'm not right unless I'm with you. You make me better. And I know I can take away your pain."

His words made her heart weep for them both. Him because she wasn't the person he thought she was. Her because she desperately wanted to be his Helen. Not Helena Grayse.

Bing bong bung. The front doorbell chime echoed through the house. She startled from the unexpectedness of it. His hands, still on her shoulders, tightened, and he brought her in closer to him as if protecting her from the sound.

That doorbell had always been an annoying sound, but hearing it for the first time in a decade almost made her smile. Almost.

His eyes on hers didn't falter.

Bing bong bung.

"You remember my doctor friend? The one who was going to stitch up your hand?" He waited for the light of recognition to go off inside her. "I think that's him. Please stay. I want you to meet him." Those last words were a fisherman's net tangling around her heart.

But she couldn't stay. She tried to shake her head but found herself nodding instead. How did that happen?

A smile flared across his lips, lighting up his whole face, making him and his scar achingly handsome. *Oh God…* That upward twist of his lips transformed everything about him. Took away the residual pain he carried and gave her a glimpse of the ornery little boy he kept hidden inside. She wanted to weep for the pain she was going to cause this man. He didn't know that every minute he spent with her, she was hurting him. Driving the stake of her betrayal a bit deeper into his heart.

"Thank you." He bent down and brushed a quick kiss on her lips. He let go of her shoulders and reached to lace his fingers with hers. "Come on."

Before her brain could talk some sense into her body, she found herself standing next to him, holding his hand while he opened the heavy oak door. Helen grasped his hand even tighter, holding on as if he were a life preserver in a stormy sea. What if the doctor recognized her as Helena Grayse? *Oh God*. What if he turned out to be one of the many docs who had treated her while she was still an inmate at Fairson and chained to the hospital bed?

A man who looked to be in his sixties stood there. Wrinkles lined his forehead and fanned out from his eyes. He smiled when their eyes met, and his friendliness only made her want to step away from him.

"Come on in." She and Thomas moved to let the doctor in the house. "Dr. Stone, I'd like you to meet Helen."

A boulder lodged itself in the back of her throat. Guilt. Every moment she perpetuated the lie of being Helen was a moment she was playing Thomas for the fool. She could bear his anger when he found out, but she didn't want him to feel like an idiot—especially in front of his friend.

But what was she going to do…blurt out the truth right now? In front of both of them? She wasn't even sure if she could force the words from her lips. It had been so long since she'd actually spoken to anyone.

Dr. Stone aimed his full attention on her. A large, engaging smile fired on his face.

"It is such a pleasure to meet you." His words rang true, but there was an aura of sadness about him. Dr. Stone came forward with his hand outstretched for her to shake. She looked at Thomas and knew she had a what-the-hell-do-I-do look on her face. He lifted his chin in a minute gesture of encouragement. Call it trying to make him proud, but she dropped his hand and awkwardly grasped Dr. Stone's. His grip was firm and full of warmth.

A gorgeous smile beamed on Thomas's face while he closed the door. At least she was able to give him this moment of happiness before she tore it all away.

Dr. Stone let her go, and she shifted closer to Thomas. He wrapped his arm around her, hauling her in to him. It was all she could do to not turn in to his chest and hide. Dear Lord, what was wrong with her that she couldn't even interact normally with one of his friends?

The doctor looked around the foyer, took in the open staircase to his right, the wide-open dining room in front of them, and the double parlors to his left. "They don't build them like this anymore."

"I know. I looked at a lot of newer homes before this one." Thomas motioned for Dr. Stone to go into the parlor. "But I walked in the front door of his place and said, 'This is the one.' It was love at first sight." Thomas looked down at Helen. Heat burst across her face. "I haven't changed a thing. The old girl has good bones and was well preserved before I bought her."

It was silly, but a weird sort of pride of place surged through her. He loved this place as much as she did.

Dr. Stone sat on the love seat, and they sat on the couch across from him. Thomas wrapped his arm around her back, holding her tight to him. Something about his arm around her soothed the anxiety of meeting someone new.

"Helen is very quiet, but I always know what she's thinking." Thomas's words were aimed at Dr. Stone, but his gaze fell on her.

At least he got the awkward part of her not talking out of the way.

"I'm not interrupting, am I?" Dr. Stone looked at the coat Helena still wore. "Were you getting ready to go somewhere?"

She should plaster a happy smile on her face, nod, wave, and walk away. She had her coat on. It would make sense for her to leave now. And maybe Thomas wouldn't try to stop her in front of Dr. Stone. But no matter how much she knew she should, she couldn't.

When neither she nor Thomas responded to his question, Dr. Stone rested his full attention on her. "So Evanee tells me that you two have a special connection. Can you tell me about it?"

Evanee? That was Thomas's sister's name. And she'd told Dr. Stone that they had a special connection? That didn't make any sense. She looked at Thomas to see if he knew what was going on.

He cleared his throat. His arm, still slung around her, pulled her in closer as if she were his anchor in a raging ocean. "I'm not exactly sure what's going on, but something is happening. I think… No, I know…" He looked at her. She felt herself tumbling into his eyes. "I healed her."

His words rocked her back on the couch. That's why he had his arm around her—so she wouldn't fall over.

He looked at her. "I know it sounds weird, but think

about it. You were shot in the chest. In the heart." His gaze flicked down to the wound, then back up. "You should've died. You would've died. But I healed you. You walked out on the other side of that gunshot wound with a bandage."

His voice sounded like it came at her from a long tunnel—tinny and muted.

"And just a bit ago, I healed you again." He sounded so sure of himself, but his words frightened her. Not only for what they meant, but because she desperately wanted to believe him.

When he'd touched her scars, she had gotten the feeling back in her body, but wasn't that just coincidence or an example of being motivated by anger? Her vision swung side to side. It took her a moment to realize she was shaking her head.

"You can deny it all you want, but it happened. You experienced it." The intensity in his expression didn't waver.

Truth and possibility warred inside her.

Truth: Her wound from being shot was miniscule.

Truth: The paralysis had faded almost instantly when Thomas had touched her scars.

Truth: People *couldn't* heal each other just by a touch. It wasn't possible.

"I know what you're thinking." Dr. Stone's tone was slow and soothing as if he were talking to a confused child. "You're thinking he's either gone crazy or you're crazy for wanting to believe him. Because you sense deep inside that something about all this feels right."

It took effort, but Helena pulled her gaze from Thomas to look at Dr. Stone.

"It doesn't seem real. It doesn't seem possible. But look inside yourself. Look at how you feel with him. It's different than anything you've ever felt. You can't deny the connection. It's there. It's strong. It's a living thing."

So much of what Dr. Stone said about Thomas felt true, but how could she believe in something that defied logic?

"We both need more information." Thomas's tone lacked disbelief, and there should at least be a little.

Dr. Stone looked directly at her. "You've been having vivid dreams, haven't you? Dreams that started right after you met him."

She startled. How did he know the dream with Hatchet Guy happened right after she'd seen Thomas in the cemetery? She'd told no one about her dreams. She nodded slowly, not understanding how her dreams were related to Thomas or the weirdness that seemed to be swirling in the room.

The doctor scooted forward until he was on the edge of his seat. "But the dreams you're having are more than just vivid. They're *real* in a way, aren't they?"

His words weren't complicated. They were simple English, yet she turned them over and over in her mind. Because holy hell, how did he know?

"Can you tell me what they're about?" There was no mistaking the eagerness in his voice.

She pointed at Thomas's TV. Even if she was speaking, she wasn't sure she could form words to convey what happened in her dream and what she'd seen on the TV at the hospital.

Thomas pulled his cell phone from his pocket, tapped on the screen, and handed it to her. She saw a keypad and typed in A girl on the TV survived an attack. And then handed it back to Thomas. He read her words aloud.

Dr. Stone's eyes widened. "Wait..." He reached inside his jacket pocket and pulled out his phone and began scrolling. "I think I saw the story this morning, but things like this are so commonplace that I just dismissed it. Got it!" He shouted the words triumphantly. And then he read aloud the entire news story that Helen had seen on the TV.

When he finished, she pointed at his phone and gave a thumbs-up.

"Helen, my question for you is how did you experience the dream on your end?"

She typed into the phone. A voice in my dream told me that I'm the warrior. I fought the guy and showed her how to survive. She handed the phone back. Dr. Stone read the screen, then studied her words.

A part of her realized how completely bizarre she must seem, but he took her seriously. It was refreshing that he spoke to her as if she was a normal person. Most people were uncomfortable with her silence and either ignored her or thought she must be stupid.

"You fought the perpetrator." Dr. Stone wasn't asking; he was confirming. "You showed the woman from this story what to do."

She dipped her chin in acknowledgment.

Dr. Stone pinned Helena with a stare. "I think you might be having a form of mutual dreaming. But I'd need more information."

"Mutual dreaming? What's that?" Thomas asked the question that had formed in Helena's mind.

"It's when you and another person are sharing a

dream at the same time. From the news article, it reads as if the victim might've been inside Helen's dream watching what was happening, learning how to survive."

Her head bobbed up and down on her shoulders. "You've already figured that out. Very good. The sooner you realize your dreams have power, the better."

Dreams had power? Her brain seemed to be having trouble processing the conversation. Probably because a mental shift of epic proportions was going to be needed to accommodate all this new information.

"Have you had any more of these dreams?"

In a haze of knowledge overload, she raised one finger.

"Two total," he confirmed, waiting for her to nod her head, "I'm going to need to know about that other dream. It's all part of the research."

"Research? What research?" Thomas's arm around her tensed as he spoke.

"Oh…" The doctor sat back in his seat and steepled his fingers. "I should've started back at the beginning. My apologies." He took in a deep breath, then let it out as he talked. "Back in the seventies, Gale Walker"— his voice hitched on the name—"and I started the Ohio Institute of Oneirology, the OIO for short."

"O…what?" Thomas asked.

"Oneirology, the study of dreams. Back then, the prevailing view was that dreams were meaningless, a waste product produced by the brain while sleeping. Gale and I didn't agree and began researching dreams from every possible angle. We've been on the cutting edge of dream research ever since. Only now is science beginning to look at the possibility that dreams are meaningful. Dreams impact creativity, mood, learning, and a host of other things essential to our survival. These are effects the OIO has known about for decades.

"Since the beginning of time, people have made claims of having psychic dreams. When studied with the rigors of science, these assertions have almost always fallen apart. Or have been hoaxes. But we discovered Gale was skilled at mutual dreaming. We conducted meticulous studies proving her ability, but the scientific community scoffed at us, disbelieving our research. But we have proven that psychic dreams do exist."

Helena felt like making the gesture for time-out so she could sit and think about everything the doctor had said. Psychic dreams. What the heck was going on?

Dr. Stone's words bounced around her brain, not finding a place to call home. It all seemed so bizarre. So science-fictiony. Not possible.

But the doctor wasn't finished. "Do you have a seizure after these dreams? It's quite common."

No. No way.

"Ah...hell. I think she does." Thomas turned to her, and their eyes met. "Her body was flailing wildly, then she couldn't move after waking up."

"She couldn't move?" Concern dominated Dr. Stone's voice.

"It's happened to her twice that I've seen. She wakes up and is paralyzed." Thomas tattled on her.

"Well, that's a bit different. Sounds like hypnopompic sleep paralysis. The brain paralyzes the body during rapid eye movement—REM—sleep so that dreams aren't physically acted out. In hypnopompic sleep paralysis, the person wakes before the REM cycle is complete. Therefore, the body is still paralyzed."

Every word coming out of Dr. Stone's mouth blew her mind a bit more.

"This all makes a weird sort of sense to me." Thomas's words carried a note of hesitancy. "What I don't get is why this is happening."

"I don't have all the answers, but I do have some of them." Dr. Stone reached inside his coat pocket and withdrew a battered old book. "It's linked to the bear totem out on old Route 40."

Helen's attention snapped to the doctor. The Bear. The story of the medicine woman and her enduring love for her dead warrior and kidnapped child. And how that love created Bear to protect Fearless. *Holy...*

"Sadly, the common denominator seems to be pain." Dr. Stone spoke the words so nonchalantly that she thought she might not have heard him correctly. He opened the book and turned the page. "I'll venture a guess that life hasn't been good to either of you. That you've both had more than your fair share of suffering and powerlessness. How much more powerless can you get than being in prison?"

He kept talking, but Helena was incapable of listening. For a moment, just a moment, nothing changed. But then, as if the detonator had been set on a timer, the implications of his words exploded in Helena's mind.

How much more powerless can you get than being in prison? In prison.

Dr. Stone knew she was Helena Grayse.

She whipped around in her seat to see Thomas's reaction. But he just stared at her with the same kind eyes he always had for her.

He knew. And it wasn't new information to him.

But now that *he* knew, *she* was the one who couldn't live with it.

Chapter 12

A RUSH OF HOT SHAME ZINGED FROM THE TOP OF Helena's head down to her toes. Sweat instantly soaked her skin. Her heart curled in on itself like a pill bug in the presence of a threat. The back of her throat ached, or maybe it closed up—she couldn't swallow or breathe. The room warped and wavered as if she were looking at it through a fun-house mirror.

Raw panic propelled her to her feet, her body locked in fight-or-flight mode. She turned to run, but Thomas nabbed her by the arm. Her legs pedaled, and she yanked against him like a recalcitrant child.

"Helen. Stop." Thomas's tone was calm, meant to soothe. "It's all right."

But she couldn't stop. The urge to escape consumed her. She tugged against his grip.

"I'm not letting you go this time. You need to stop running." The determination in his voice scared her almost as badly as the Sisters had.

She whirled and shoved him. He lost his balance and fell back on the couch, taking her with him. She belly flopped on top of him and lay there stunned.

"It's okay." His words of assurance had the opposite effect. It wasn't okay. She wasn't okay. She was never going to be okay.

Something deep, dark, and ugly bubbled up inside

her. She turned wild. A rabid animal cornered, fighting for the right to survive.

She attacked. Punching. Shoving. Needing him to release her so she could outrun the pain before it swallowed her.

A distant part of her mind registered the sounds of shouting. But the only voice that had any clarity was Thomas's. "Don't touch her. Just leave. Leave."

He yanked her to him, wrapping both arms around her in a bear hug that pinned her fists to her sides. Her legs took up the fight, but he shifted and rolled. She went weightless. Falling. She braced for impact, but Thomas caught her body with one arm, while his other braced against the floor. He lowered her gently, then settled himself on top of her. His chest at her head, his legs off to the side.

She bucked, trying to dislodge him, but he was too heavy.

"Helen." His voice was impossibly undisturbed. "Calm down."

She didn't want calm. She wanted anger and violence. That's what she understood. Not kindness and acceptance.

Rage and retribution rose inside her.

She opened her mouth and bit him through his shirt. The sweet, metallic tang of blood hit her taste buds.

He grunted, a sound she was familiar with. One she'd made too many times over the past decade. The sound of pain being endured.

His anguish obliterated the irrational state she'd been stuck in.

She went absolutely limp, all the fight gone. She panted against his chest, hearing the counterrhythm of his heartbeat. She could still taste his blood in her mouth. And smell it on his shirt. Her insides hollowed out, and she felt sick in her soul.

How could she have done that to him? He'd only ever tried to help her. Even when he'd known she were Helena Grayse, he'd *accepted* her. Not treated her differently. Not acted scared or suspicious of her. Yet she'd tried to run from him. Fled from his acceptance as if it was more painful than his rejection ever could've been.

She was an animal now. Fairson had turned her into a feral beast not fit for polite society.

Gently, she nuzzled her cheek against the place she'd bitten him, hoping to soothe the hurt in some way.

Thomas believed he'd healed her. Now more than anything, she wanted to heal him. She pressed her lips to the injury, clenched her eyes closed, and concentrated on infusing her kiss with the hope of mending all the damage she'd caused.

He didn't say anything but shifted, allowing her the freedom to use her hands. She rubbed his sides, his back, trying to comfort him, all the while never taking her mouth off him. And then her fingers caught in the hem of his shirt, and it felt right and natural to let her hand slip under the material to stroke his warm skin. His flesh felt perfect against hers. Like a kiss, a hug, and a bath.

Her girlie parts warmed and went tingly—an itch she wanted to scratch. She was a greedy girl who wanted more. She tugged his shirt up to his shoulders.

"Helen…" He moved so his face loomed over hers.

The scar blazed with beauty. To her, it looked like a windswept tree, the kind of image she'd expect to see in an art gallery or in the pages of a magazine. It was captivating in a way nothing else could be. She wanted to stare at it, to lose herself in imagining being someplace where that tree really existed.

His midnight-blue eyes showed twinkles of starlight in their depths. "I want to. Really do. But not like this. The next time, it's not going to be you fucking me. It's going to be me making love to you."

His words slapped one cheek with the sting of rejection while caressing the other cheek with the promise of love.

He moved off her and stood. It was insane, but she felt vulnerable and unprotected without him on top of her. He reached out to her, his hand steady. She grabbed on to him, and instantly, the unease that had been creeping in vanished. He hauled her to her feet but didn't let go of her, and she was glad. Something about touching him made her feel almost normal. Was he *healing* her mind when they touched?

Over his heart, she saw where she'd bitten him. Her teeth had scored indentations in the fabric of his shirt, and a few drops of blood showed through the material. Why had she done that to him? Him, of all people.

Shame kept her from meeting his eyes.

"Come on. Let's go upstairs." His voice carried all the dread of a prisoner awaiting execution.

Her cheeks blazed with heat. *Oh God…* She'd been the one to put that tone in his voice. He bore the weight of his own pain. She'd seen it in his eyes the first time she met him, and for her to have caused him more suffering felt like an unforgivable sin. Like ripping the wings off a butterfly.

He squeezed her hand. She hadn't realized he still held it. Something about that little action told her they would be okay.

He kept hold of her as he led her upstairs. She searched her mind for an apology. *I'm sorry* was all she could find floating around in the ether between her ears. But *I'm sorry* wasn't nearly big enough or strong enough.

For the first time in a long time, she realized she was afraid.

Afraid of everything.

Afraid of the past and the future. Afraid of rejection and acceptance. Afraid of living and dying.

The only thing she wasn't afraid of was him.

At his bedroom doorway, he dropped her hand. She froze. Unable to move. As if the reassurance of his touch was all that kept her going.

His eyes were full of anguish. Guilt swelled inside her. She'd put that look on his face. She'd done that to him. She wanted to die.

"It's okay." His voice sounded firm and solid, so at odds with how he looked. He motioned for her to enter the room ahead of him.

She forced her feet to move. Behind her, she heard the door close. The scrape of old metal on metal was loud in the room. The lock. He was locking her in. Another prison.

Blinding terror whipped her around. But Thomas stood there with her, holding the skeleton key. All her fear evaporated.

He put the key in his pants pocket, then met her gaze. "You're not going to run away from this." Each of his words was a blow to her defenses. "We're going to stay in here until you deal with..." He paused as if he couldn't find the word he wanted. "Everything." Compassion warred with terrible determination on his face.

Her body began trembling, and she shook her head.

He took a slow step toward her as if he worried any sudden movements would cause her to bolt. He wasn't wrong. Her legs twitched with the urge to run, to escape.

"Why—" His one word sped at her like a bullet.

Why? Which *why* did he want the answer to? Why had she gone to prison? Why had she murdered Rory? Why did she attack him? Why did she bite him?

"—do you keep running from caring and kindness? Especially after everything you've been through." His tone was soft and serious, his gaze locked on her as if he expected to see an answer, but she couldn't even understand the words he'd spoken.

Her ears heard him, but her mind got tripped up on the translation. Where was the criticism, condemnation, accusation? She needed those things. Not this.

He took another slow step toward her, stopping when he was inside her space, mere inches separating them. She was too tired to fight or resist anymore. Too exhausted to carry the burden of what she'd been through. She wanted to set it down and walk away, but she didn't know how.

"You've been through some shit, and you're having a hard time realizing it's over." He slid his hands around the back of her neck and used his thumbs to

tilt her chin upward. His touch sent pleasant, warm
tingles through her body, calming the alarm bells in
her psyche. Slowly, he lowered his head to her. Was he
going to kiss her? Right now? Her girlie parts cheered:
Rah-rah-sis-boom-bah.

But he stopped when his forehead rested against hers,
and all she could see was him. He filled every inch of
her vision, making it impossible to look anywhere but at
him. In that moment, he was her world. Nothing existed
except him.

His scar heated her forehead where it touched her.
His breath fanned across her face, sweet and warm. His
eyes bored into her.

"It's. Over. Leave it in the past where it belongs,
because in this moment, you're in my house. You're
with me. You're. Safe." His lips brushed against her
mouth as he spoke. "You're. Safe."

She inhaled the words as if they were oxygen. She
closed her eyes and concentrated on his voice, his hands
on her neck, on the meaning of what he said. Desire to
believe him warred with the ugliness in her soul.

"Look at me. I want to see you." His voice brimmed
with some emotion she couldn't name.

She couldn't resist him. His eyes were the night sky,
and she longed to sail among the stars.

"You have nothing to be ashamed of. Nothing. The
scars on your body are evidence of other people's shame,
not yours. They don't define you unless you let them.
They don't own you unless you let them. They can't
change you unless you let them. This self-condemnation
you've got, this fear you have... You're letting them
win. You're letting every single person who hurt you

have control over you, and they aren't even here. You're the one who's hurting yourself."

A tornado of terrible memories scooped her up, whirled her around until she was dizzy, and then set her back down. Here. With Thomas.

He was right.

As much as she hated to admit it to herself, she was the one destroying her life. She might be out of Fairson, but she was treating herself with the same loathing Mrs. Ellis reserved only for her. *Oh God...* And how many times had she yearned for violence and cruelty instead of comfort? Somewhere along the line, she'd let Mrs. Ellis, Fairson, and the Sisters into her mind. Adopted their views of her. Like if she thought of herself as terribly as they did, all the pain wouldn't be so bad. *Wrong. Wrong. Wrong.* It hurt worse.

Her lips trembled, and tears rushed into her eyes. She slammed them shut.

"Don't shut me out every time you want to cry. You think your tears make you weak?"

Yes. I'm weak. So weak.

"They're what make you strong." The word *strong* resonated through her. "Your tears prove you're capable of feeling. You can't experience joy if you can't experience sorrow."

His words made a strange sort of sense to her. As though she had to feel everything—the good and the bad—or be numb. And numb would make her like the Sisters. Incapable of mercy or compassion or empathy. She never wanted to be like them.

Like forcing a rusted bolt, it took elbow grease and effort, but she pried her eyes open and stared at him as her tears welled, then hit the tipping point and slipped down her cheeks. His acceptance gave her the courage to expose her pain to him. With a simple word or an action, he could decimate her right now. It scared her to trust him that much, but it thrilled her too. Because on the other side of this suffering was a different, better version of herself. She could see that now. She wanted to live in that woman's skin.

"Right there. That's what I'm talking about. I see that crazy mix of defiance and vulnerability. I see *you*. It's the most gorgeous thing I've ever seen."

His words nestled into her heart. He knew everything—the things he didn't know, he probably guessed—and instead of telling her to leave, instead of looking at her with revulsion, instead of looking at her with pity, he looked at her with affection.

A sob burst out of her, the sound startling for its abruptness. Behind it, an army containing ten years of suppressed emotion was about to break through the last of her defenses. A wild, panicked, I-need-to-run feeling came over her, but before she could react or move, he gathered her in to him, holding her tight. So tight. Holding her together when she'd been about to fly apart. "Just let it all out. All of it."

His words were a permission she hadn't realized she needed. She flew the white flag, surrendering to the pain, allowing herself to weep for all she'd lost, and then let her tears wash away the destruction. She clung to him—the only safe place—as the battle for her soul and sanity raged. And then it was over, and she hiccupped against his shirt as she tried to catch her breath.

His hands stroked her back, and his lips pressed gentle

kisses against the top of her head. And she was different. It was hard to describe. She felt lighter, cleaner, and stronger than she ever had.

Abruptly, he stepped away from her. She cried out at the suddenness of his departure, reaching out to him, still needing the intimacy—the safety—of being inside his arms. It had been easy to imagine no past and no future while surrounded by him.

"Shh… It's okay." He reached for the coat she still wore, unzipped it, and tugged it from her shoulders. It fell to the floor. He grabbed both her hands in his, brought them up to his mouth, and kissed them as if he were an old-fashioned knight rescuing a damsel in distress. Then he looked deep inside her, and this time, she didn't hide anything from him. She let him see everything.

His chiseled features were so masculine and beautiful to her. His scar a work of art that decorated his face instead of detracting from his appearance. He opened his mouth as if to say something but paused. Swallowed, then spoke. "You need to show me all of you."

She almost argued with him that she *was* showing him all her dark and dirty places, but then she understood what he meant. He wanted to see her body.

She froze, couldn't move. Her fragile self-acceptance threatened to shatter. It was too much. Too overwhelming. Too soon.

He settled his hands on her waist, his touch firm and light at the same time. "This isn't for me. It's for you." He took in a slow breath, never looking away from her. "On our first night, as I rubbed your back, I felt all the damage done. And when I pulled you out of that tub, I saw your scars." He slid one of his hands up under her sweatshirt and touched the skin of her stomach. She flinched. She couldn't help it. It was as involuntary as breathing.

"You have to do this. You have to own and accept what was done to you, or else you'll always carry fear about your body." He looked upon her with such intensity that she couldn't have defied him. And she didn't want to. Because, goddamn it, he was right.

She straightened her spine and locked eyes with him. He gave her courage just by his presence. Her hands fumbled with the tie on the pants she wore, but she got it loose and let them slide down her legs to the floor. Her knees wobbled as she stepped out of them, but he kept his hands still on her. One on her stomach. One on her waist. They anchored her—wouldn't let her fall.

Her hands shook so badly when she reached for the hem of the sweatshirt that she had trouble grabbing it. Not looking away from him, she pulled the material over her head, her gaze locking back on his once the shirt cleared her face.

Goose bumps pebbled across her skin. She stood before him wearing a cheap prison-issue bra and granny panties. And for the first time in a long time, she felt…a little bit free. As if shucking her clothing was akin to shucking the past.

"I'm going to look at you now." His tone was soft, his voice serious.

Her heart thumped against her chest wall and she reached out to him. Needing to touch him. He grabbed her hand in his, and affection and reassurance surged through her for the moment they touched, then he let her go.

His gaze slid down her face to her neck, then lower. She stopped breathing and fought the urge to close her eyes. She stared hard at him while he took in the damage. She expected revulsion. Disgust. But other than a slight tic in his jaw, he handled it remarkably well.

"Turn around." His voice was barely a whisper.

She did.

His hands landed on her hips, the weight of them, their roughness, reassuring. But then from each of the injuries on her back, she felt an upwelling of pain. As if a million splinters were working their way to the surface. It had to be in her head. Some psychological reaction to knowing that he was looking at the damage. She bit her lip to keep from gasping.

Something warm and wet and wonderful slid across her lower back, dissolving the discomfort with its touch. What was he doing? She looked over her shoulder and down at him.

He knelt behind her, his tongue gliding across her scarred flesh—licking her.

Licking. Her.

Licking her wounds. Healing her wounds. Healing her mind. Drawing all the bad out of her and consuming it himself.

It should shock her, disgust her, freak her out, but it felt so…right. His tongue was a balm to all her raw places—both in the flesh and the mind.

"What happened?" he whispered against her skin and then resumed licking her.

Not once in all her time in Fairson had she ever

spoken about what happened. If she had, she would've been labeled a snitch. And when she stopped talking, people stopped asking.

Words filled her mouth, needing to escape. "One night..." Her voice sounded rusty and thick. She cleared her throat. "The Sisters cornered me in the bathroom. They took turns. They kept..." The memories of the gang shanking flowed out of her. As she spoke, she felt lighter, as if each word carried a weight she hadn't known existed until she didn't have to carry it any longer.

He didn't jump up and down and scream and shout and act like a fool because she'd finally spoken. Instead, he kept licking the old wounds on her back until he'd covered all of them. Only then did he wrap his arms around her waist and hug her, pressing his face against the space between her shoulder blades. "Thank you for finally giving me your voice. It's the most beautiful thing I've ever heard." He kissed one side of her back and then the other. "All better now." And it was.

Then he used his hands to turn her so she faced him. He licked a scar that ran across her stomach. "How did you get this one?"

A low, simmering heat started in her belly. "One of the Sisters found a piece of wood with a nail through the end of it. She was trying to act like it was a sword and stab me." A bit of victory leaked into her tone. "I actually won that fight."

He kissed the scar. "Good for you." Pride infused his tone. And then he moved on to the next scar, licking and asking her to speak the horrors aloud.

Saying her truth made it more real, but at the same time less powerful. There was a catharsis in what he demanded from her. After her words always came his kiss. That simple kiss a benediction of healing as if he were sealing himself into each of her injuries.

Together, they cataloged her wounds.

Then he found the scar on her inner thigh. The old shame and panic jolted through her. She squeezed her legs together to hide the damage from him, but he'd already seen it.

"Don't hide from me now. Not when we've come all this way." His voice had a pleading quality to it. He wouldn't *force* her to show him the damage, but he *wanted* her to show him, and somehow that made it better. Put her in control. "Sit down on the edge of the bed."

She stared at him, still on his knees in front of her. And she realized every lick, every kiss, every stroke of his hand over her flesh was him worshipping her. Telling her with his actions that she was powerful, she was worthy and deserving of his love. And really, wasn't that the most important thing? Wasn't he the most important thing?

She knew what needed to be done—for him and for her. She shimmied out of her underwear and bra, then lay back on the bed and opened her thighs to him.

Chapter 13

ROBERT MALONE SAT BACK ON THE OLD COUCH, HAND IN HIS trousers, as the guy in front of him shucked his clothes.

What was the guy's name? Robert couldn't remember. Didn't matter anyway. In some way, all the men Robert brought here were Evan to him. Surrogates until he got the real Evan back.

In the darkened cabin, he could see that this Evan was a bony boy. Each vertebra of his spine poked out. The definition of his shoulder blades clear and sharp underneath his skin. But then all the Evans looked like this. They all lacked the health and vitality of *his* Evan.

This Evan dropped the last of his clothes and turned to him. His cock had shriveled to a nubbin in the chill of the shack. "What now." The Evan's flat tone lacked the caring and understanding *his* Evan's had possessed.

"Say it like you want it," Robert corrected.

The Evan gave him a petulant, entitled look.

A dull thudding started in Robert's left temple. Annoyance sizzled in his chest.

"What now." The Evan's voice was only slightly less apathetic.

The ache in Robert's head ratcheted up. He inhaled slowly, trying to calm the rising anger.

Through all the years and all the Evans, he'd only lost his cool once. And never since. But now he could feel his restraint unraveling. He closed his eyes, blocked out the Evan, and focused on remembering *his* Evan.

This little shack in the woods had been their secret getaway. Robert had preserved it. Never changed a thing about it in all the years Evan had been gone. This was where his memories of Evan and the reality of Evan collided. As though Evan's soul had imprinted on this little space and just needed a body to inhabit. In the arms of the other Evans, Robert could feel *his* Evan roughhousing and wrestling with him again—a prelude to their loving each other.

"You want the H?" Robert opened his eyes and nodded toward the white baggies sitting on the table.

The Evan looked at him with a *duh* expression on his face.

"Then. Work. For. It." Robert spoke slow and calm.

"What now?" This time when Evan spoke, his tone was slightly softer.

The shack wasn't large enough for a private bathroom. A sink and toilet stood side by side across the room. "There's pomade on the sink. Use it. Slick back your hair so it won't get in our way."

The Evan stared at him for a beat too long, glanced at the heroin with naked desire, then shrugged and went to the sink.

Anticipation hardened Robert's dick even more. Just smelling the pomade Evan used to wear had that effect on him. For many years after Evan's bitch wife killed him, the only way Robert could feel close to Evan was by using the pomade to jack off. That was until he started using the Evans.

The first Evan had been a mistake, of course. The way

all firsts usually are. Something about that young man had called to him. Maybe it was that mop of dirty-blond hair and the sharp, hard facial features. Whatever the reason, Robert had been drawn to him, but in his exuberance to taste what he and Evan had shared, he'd gone too far too fast and had to end the Evan before he even began with him. The cleanup had required accusing the man's girlfriend, a trip to court, and a lesson learned.

Now he only approached junkie Evans who agreed to payment for their time.

Robert leaned back and partially closed his eyes, leaving them open just enough to look through the fringe of his lashes. The Evan finished and turned around. If Robert focused only on the Evan's hair, if he ignored the Evan's face and his emaciated body, then he could almost pretend this was *his* Evan.

His balls tightened, and his hand got rougher. He was so close.

"You just want me to watch while you crank one off?" The Evan's belligerent tone killed the mood more effectively than if Robert had dipped his wick in a bucket of ice water.

Why was every Evan always so wrong? He'd never found a decent one. Some had been okay for a while. None lasted.

"I want you to speak when spoken to." Robert bent his tone to make it seem mild.

The Evan had the audacity to harrumph like an impatient woman.

"Come to me." Robert gestured toward the floor next to his legs.

The Evan moved closer.

"Down on your knees."

Reluctance infused every inch of the Evan's body as he knelt.

Good God. This Evan was getting compensated for his time and efforts—he could show a little gratitude. He didn't know Robert's whole plan for him. Robert yanked down his zipper. "Take care of me. Make it good, and you'll get a bonus."

The Evan bent over him and got to work.

This close, Robert could smell him—male musk. He drew in a deep, satisfying breath. His Evan used to smell like that after a long, hot day on the job or after they'd made love. He reached out and gently placed his hand on the back of the Evan's head. Pomade slid underneath his palm, the wonderful scent of it filling the air around them. Robert slit his eyes and looked through the fringe of his lashes again. He could smell *his* Evan and could almost believe the mouth wrapped around him was *his* Evan. Almost.

But he always knew the truth. Evan was dead. He was never coming back.

Evan's bitch wife was to blame. Evan only married the woman because it was expected of him. But then she'd killed him, and most of Robert had died too. The control it took not to murder her when she'd asked for his help in concealing what she'd done to Evan… That moment had been the biggest test of Robert's restraint.

He'd given her what she wanted. For a price.

He'd decided to spend the rest of his life punishing her. Punishing her body and her babies—the surest way to hurt her. He married her. Everyone thought it was so sweet that he'd taken her on after her husband *abandoned* her and their two kids. He'd done it to make her suffer. Make her children suffer. But nothing ever assuaged his loss.

Since the day Evan died, Robert hadn't been able to feel anything. He didn't care about his own son. Junior died a few weeks ago? A month? That's how much he didn't care. He'd always done enough to keep up appearances. That was all.

Now, for the first time since Evan's death, hope began to bloom. There was another who could take Evan's place.

It hadn't dawned on him until recent years how much Tommy looked like his father. The black hair of his bitch mother had disguised features that were purely Evan. Robert imagined Tommy with Evan's dirty-blond hair, imagined his mouth on him.

The orgasm began gathering in his balls, but he tried to hold back the pleasure.

It wasn't until Robert had fed the last Evan heroin, then set the scene, and requested Tommy from the BCI that he'd finally decided on a plan. It was gonna take some work because of the mistakes he'd made when Tommy was a child. He wished he could go back in time and take it all back. Treat the boy with love instead of the all-consuming revenge that had fueled him.

Tommy would resist as his father had done at first, but Robert was a patient man. One thing was on his side. Tommy never dated. Never. Was the boy saving himself for a man?

The orgasm crashed over him. He pushed the Evan's head down, and only when the last ripple of pleasure left did he let go of the guy.

The Evan sat back and looked at him, contempt and hatred shining in his eyes. Then he stood and walked to the sink and spat a mouthful of cum into the basin.

Robert needed to get used to that kind of reaction. Tommy would be furious with him at first, but eventually, he'd come around. Just like Evan had.

Chapter 14

AFTERNOON SUNSHINE REFLECTED OFF THE SNOW, FILLING the bedroom with an ethereal light, giving Helen a glow as if she were a celestial being instead of a flesh-and-blood human.

Heaven wasn't some place in the clouds where fat baby angels played harps and everyone walked around with a smile on their face. Nope. It was right here. In this moment. With her lying on his bed, legs spread wide open to him, baring her greatest hurt and, by that act, showing the immensity of her strength.

Gone were all her fears and uncertainty, replaced by a wanton beauty in wait for her man.

He knelt before her altar. The thatch of blond hair at her apex shimmered like spun gold.

He lifted her leg by the back of her knee, spreading her wider. The first glimpse of her juicy, pink lips caused his hips to buck forward in longing. There would be time for satisfying his dick later. Right now, she needed one last bit of healing.

The thick puckered flesh ran from the inside of her thigh all the way to her core. None of the other scars had seemed as vile as this one. It might not have been a life-threatening injury, but it was uglier for its intention. Humiliation.

His chest got tight. He had trouble pulling oxygen out of the air. Behind his eyes, he felt the sting of tears for all that she'd suffered. It was a miracle she'd come out the other side with any sanity left.

He bent his head and touched the damage with his tongue. The ridge and ripple of this scar felt different than the others. Appalling. He took his time, letting himself well up and flow into her. Trying with everything inside him to give her solace.

He followed the damaged skin until he found the center of her and slipped his tongue inside. Her flavor exploded across his taste buds—sweet, salty, and sultry. The best damn thing he'd ever tasted. He swallowed the essence of her; it warmed him and turned his already hard dick into a baseball bat. *Damn*.

Her hips bucked. He startled away from her. *Oh shit*. Did he hurt her? Never in a million years had he meant to cause her any pain. He should've been more aware of the injury, not losing himself in his desire for her. He opened his mouth to apologize, but she cut him off.

"Whatever you do"—she moaned a sound that his dick interpreted quicker than his brain—"don't stop."

No need to tell him twice. He shoved his nose into her golden curls and inhaled her carnal aroma. She smelled of sunshine on a summer day. His eyes rolled back in his head as the scent of her filled his lungs. He held her inside him. Aromatherapy at its finest.

And then he pressed his lips to her nub in a hard kiss, opened his mouth, and suckled.

With his fingers, he caressed her opening until her body thrashed, demanding more. He slipped two fingers into her. Her juices coated him, and she moaned a sound so sensuous that he dry humped air—couldn't control himself. He remembered every moment of being inside her and wanted so badly to be there again.

Bucking against his mouth and hand, she was resplendent in her abandon. Head tossed back, face flushed with pleasure. Watching her mounting pleasure was like gazing at a sunrise. A sunrise of his creation. Just before she peaked, he pulled away from her.

She growled a low, frustrated sound, and he couldn't help himself—he laughed. "Don't worry, we're not done."

"Better not be." Her tone was husky from desire. Dear God, he loved her voice. She could be reciting words straight from an owner's manual, and he'd cling to every vowel and consonant coming out of her mouth.

He got to his feet and gazed down at her while he unbuttoned his shirt. Couldn't go one more minute without his skin touching hers. He got lost in the beauty of her. Long, lean muscles decorated in badges of courage. Tight nipples an elusive shade between peach and pink. Wasn't that color called coral? Her breasts were the perfect size. Less than a handful, more than a mouthful. His mouth watered, imagining the flavor of them. For some reason, he suspected they'd taste sweet, like cotton candy. He licked his lips. He loved cotton candy.

She watched him with bald admiration, making him feel like a superhero. Her gaze stroked his chest as he let the shirt fall to the floor, then locked on his hands as he worked the button and the zipper of his pants. Slowly, he revealed his erection. Being the object of her adoration was sexier than hell.

A smile full of I-want-you fired on her lips. Seeing that look on her face reminded him of just how unbelievable life had become. He never wanted to take this for granted.

If ever there was evidence that she was meant to be his, it was right here. It was in seeing her lying there. Seeing the anticipation on her face and knowing it was because of him.

He lowered himself over her, bracing on one forearm.

Golden hair fanned out around her in a halo. "You are so beautiful," he whispered. "I thought so, the first second I saw you." He lowered his lips to hers.

Her fingers wound around his neck and into his hair. She pressed his face against hers as if she were starving for him as their tongues found each other. She tasted happy. The slide of her tongue against his, a vortex of sensation.

He pulled back to stare into her eyes, seeing himself reflected in her irises. With his free hand, he stroked her belly and the ridges of her scars. And then his palm found her breast, the density of her under his hand a fascination. It wasn't as though he'd never touched a breast before, but this felt like the first time. He lost himself in the satiny soft skin on the underside. He bent his head down and licked that perfect little spot, then captured her nipple between his teeth, biting gently as he stroked the tip with his tongue.

He'd been right—she tasted of cotton candy and every dirty fantasy he'd ever had.

Her hands were all over him. Pulling his hair, pushing his head harder against her, wanting more. And he intended to give her everything. She arched underneath him, and he settled himself between her legs, letting some of his weight fall on her. Everywhere their skin touched was fire and snow. Burning and cooling and beyond any sensation he'd ever experienced.

His dick strained, shifting forward those precious few inches to find its home. But he held off, wanted to wait just a bit longer.

Her hands smoothed down his back in a caress that was part tickle and part tail-fire of electricity. She grabbed his ass and squeezed, then lifted her hips underneath him. The center of her touched the tip of him. He slipped inside just a bit.

He brushed a strand of hair off her forehead and trailed his fingers over the place where she'd had stitches. He'd forgotten to ask her about that one. There'd be time enough for that later.

He met her eyes, locked on to her, into her in that way they had of seeing inside each other. "You're my miracle." He didn't exactly know what he was trying to say, only that he wanted her to understand how much she meant to him. How simply having her in his life changed everything.

Tears shimmered in her eyes. But these weren't sad or scared tears. They were the kind of tears a person had when they were deeply moved. "You brought me to life." She reached up, stroking the scar on his cheek. Her touch on his sensitive skin sent a shock wave of pleasure through him.

He pushed forward, the heat of her body bathing him in her grace. Her mouth parted, a small smile of pleasure tipping her lips. Her eyelids slid to half-mast. Her cheeks were flushed the same damned color as her nipples. Nothing could ever rival her beauty. The world paused, allowing him to take her in, memorize her, and tuck her away in his mind. This was his life now. She was his life. As necessary as his heartbeat.

"Please," she whispered.

It was the only word he needed.

Good intentions told him to go slow. His body didn't fucking listen. He slammed home, burying himself up to his balls. Distantly, he heard himself moan, but he was lost to everything except her. The ability to think vanished. All he could do was feel. And all he felt was her. Her soft body underneath him, surrounding him, cradling him, welcoming him, soothing things inside him that were sore, broken, and damaged.

She transformed him. Made him into something other than himself. A better version. Stronger. He could feel strength coursing through his muscles. Vitality surging through his veins. It was as if he'd taken a hit of some superdrug. Only it was all her. She did this to him.

"Do…you…feel…that?" He could barely speak as their bodies moved to a cadence of their making.

"Oh God. Yes. It's"—she moaned a low keening sound of pleasure—"amazing."

He hooked his arm under one knee, opened her wider, and slid deeper.

She gasped, her eyes going round, her body thrusting against his. "Please. Please. Please," she chanted.

He would deny her nothing. There was no thinking involved. Hell, he couldn't have formed a logical thought if he tried. She dominated his world. Nothing mattered except her.

They locked in the age-old dance of rocking and pumping and thrusting. Her hands roamed his body. On his chest, on his back, clenching his ass.

And suddenly he found himself in that strange place where his body teetered on the precipice of orgasm. He gritted his teeth, strained to hold off. Pain built and grew in his balls.

Her thrusts went messy and clumsy and more intense. "Thomas. Thomas. Thomas." She chanted his name like a prayer as she arched her back and groaned a sound so glorious, it went straight to his balls. He exploded, raw sensation ripping through him, tearing muscle from bone, heart from soul, mind from body, and then somehow mashing him all back together.

He didn't know how long it was before he finally emerged from the postorgasmic bliss. The first thing he became aware of was his face buried against her neck. He kissed her, nuzzling her skin, loving that little spot just beneath her ear. Her fingers gently trailed over his back, her touch light and ticklish and soothing at the same time. Then he realized he was lying completely on top of her. Her body a better cushion than the softest mattress. He lifted his head, blinking at the bright sunlight filling the room. He felt as if he'd just woken to a whole new life. "Am I crushing you?"

A brilliant smile fired on her face, the kind that contained enough wattage to power his heart for the rest of his life. "No. It feels good to have you on me. I feel safer than I have in years. Like you're my shield."

"You know I won't let anything hurt you." His tone was filled to the brim with I-swear-to-God truth.

No one got through life unmarked, but she'd been through enough. More than her fair share. And he was gonna make absolutely certain nothing caused her pain ever again.

She touched his face, her fingers cool as they stroked over the scar. He closed his eyes, absorbing the sweet sensation of her touch when his skin was normally so hot. "Tell me what happened," she whispered.

The old fear, the old resistance flared to life, but under her gentle touch, it dissipated. Oh, how quickly the tables had turned. He expected to feel some hesitation, some mental block to speaking his truth, but it seemed silly not to tell her. Especially when Helen had just bared her soul to him. What he'd gone through had been nothing compared to her suffering.

But the one thing he couldn't do was speak about it while still inside her. Didn't want the foulness of his past tainting her. He shifted, gently pulling himself out of her, the movement a delicate pleasure.

He slid his arm underneath her neck, and she used his shoulder as her pillow, nestling in to his side. He focused on the ceiling while he spoke, despising how his tone took on a dull quality and yet not being able to change it. He summarized a childhood of pain caused by his stepfather in a few sentences, but that didn't completely answer her question. "When I was five, he stomped on my face." She gasped. His gaze darted over her, trying to understand what was wrong, but then he realized she was responding to his words. "I've never told anyone. Not even my sister."

Helen shifted up on her elbow to look at him as if the damage on his face took on a new meaning to her.

And then he realized he needed to tell her all of it. It would be like telling a half-truth to stop now. Only he was frightened. Would she believe him? Would she think he'd lost his mind? The words came out in a rush. He told her about his black-and-white existence. He told her about the shadow of death. And through it all, she just stared at him, taking in the information. Her expression never wavered from compassionate and caring, and yet he couldn't help saying, "I know. It all sounds so…psychotic."

"Noooo…" Her voice soothed, and her eyes blazed. "It's not. It sounds terrifying. Especially for a five-year-old."

He reached up and placed his hand on Helen's face. Thumb and first finger on her cheek. Ring finger and pinkie on her forehead. Middle finger lifted away from her eye. "And when I touch a dead body like this and place my middle finger on their closed eye…the shadow of death shares that person's life with me."

He started to lift his hand off her face, but she grabbed on to him, holding him there. Showing him her acceptance. "What's my shadow of death look like?"

"You don't have one. You're different from every other human being I've ever met."

"I wonder why."

"I think it has something to do with this strange connection we have. I've felt it from the moment I saw you. You bring color to my life. *Color*. And I'm not just using that as a figure of speech. I mean I see all the colors when I'm near you. You have no idea what it's like living a black-and-white existence and now seeing the vibrancy of life. It's amazing. You're amazing."

Helen's expression didn't change. Didn't register horror or pity. Instead, she leaned over him as if to kiss his mouth but found his cheek instead. Her lips on him were soothing and… Wait… That wasn't her lips. Her tongue slid over the disfigurement on his face. Licking his wound the same way he'd licked hers. It was animal-istic, primal, and fucking hot as all shit. His dick went hard and pulsed as if saying *Put your tongue on me next*.

He closed his eyes, letting himself get lost in the slip and slide of her tongue on his skin. It was like drawing out an infection. The residual bad memories all came to the surface and evaporated under her tender ministrations.

"Now, I'll kiss it and make it all better." She rained loud, smacking kisses all over his face.

Laughter bubbled up inside him, and pure, undiluted joy flowed through him for the first time in…well, maybe ever. It felt great. "The moment I spotted you in the cemetery, I knew my life had changed." He stroked her golden hair. It still amazed him that her hair and her eyes were the exact same color.

"I was at the cemetery to visit Rory and my grandparents. Why were you there?"

"I was going to my mom's memorial service."

Her eyes widened, her mouth dropped open, and she sat up. "Thomas, why didn't you say anything? Oh my God. I'm so sorry." Her concern warmed his heart.

"Hey." He reached for her to pull her back down to him, but she grabbed his hand in both of hers, cradling it to her heart. "We weren't close. She pretty much let my stepdad do whatever he wanted to me, but that was nothing compared to what she did to my sister. That was inexcusable."

"What she did to you was inexcusable too." Helen's words were don't-argue-with-me firm.

In a way, he agreed. He'd never bought into the whole theory of forgiveness. Turn the other cheek and all that crap. He couldn't. Some sins were simply unforgiveable—especially those perpetrated against children.

Before he realized what was coming out of his mouth, he told her about the contents of his mom's posthumous letter. Mom's confession to murdering his father, his stepfather's role in covering it up, and the price he'd demanded. And then how the asshole had pulled a chickenshit move and run off. "There's a huge investigation into all this. Every case he ever testified in is going to file an appeal." Thomas sat up and threaded his other hand into her hair, holding on to her while he spoke his next words. "Yours included. My stepfather is Robert Malone."

Her head jerked as if an invisible hand had slapped her. Her eyes snapped to his. "All this time you've been talking about Robert Malone? He's your stepfather?" Before he could answer, she barreled on. "He lied. He told everyone he saw me get out of Rory's car. And then he checked on Rory, and he was dead." Her eyes blazed with such fierce intensity that if he hadn't already known she was innocent, he would've believed her. "It was a lie, Thomas. I swear to you I didn't hurt Rory."

"I know. You don't need to convince me. I knew you were innocent before I knew you were Helena Grayse. And you are still innocent now that I know."

"Just because you can't see a shadow of death around me?"

Her question surprised him. "No. Because I see you. I see all the pain, the vulnerability, the strength. I see your goodness." He wanted to say something that would make the past decade better, but no words existed that could erase the suffering. "This is such a fucked-up situation. None of what happened was fair. None of it was right." He pulled his gaze from hers. "I should've killed him when I was a kid. It wasn't like I didn't fantasize about it. Would've saved my sister and you so much hurt." Hindsight sucked.

"Don't say that. You were just a child."

He didn't know what to say to that, so he just opened his arms to her, and she settled against him, her cheek over his heart.

She spoke against his chest. "Do you really want to be with someone like me? A felon. Convicted of murder. People will always look at me differently." Her breath was warm against his skin.

He grabbed her by the shoulders and lifted her off his chest to stare into her eyes. He wanted her to see his truth when he spoke. "None of that—"

Bing bong bung. The doorbell went off.

"Goddamn it." Now was not the time for visitors. They were still resolving the past and figuring out the future.

Bing bong bung.

Bing bong bung.

Who the hell was out there leaning on the damn doorbell? It wouldn't be Dr. Stone. He was too polite to act like an asshole.

Bing bong bung.

"Let me get rid of whoever is out there. Then we need to finish this conversation." Thomas climbed out of bed and slid on his pants.

Bing bong bung.

"I'm coming!" He yelled loud enough to be heard a mile away.

Helen shrugged into the shirt he'd worn, but concern took up residence on her face. She was worried about the future. Their future. They had so much to figure out. There was the stuff between them—their connection, what it meant, how it worked. Then there was the whole wrongful-conviction suit. Because she had a case. A slam-dunk, home-run kind of case. Then there was Malone and the shit storm he'd created.

Bing bong bung.

Thomas left the room on a sprint, ready to shove the damn doorbell up someone's ass. Halfway down the stairs, he spotted Kent looking in through the leaded-glass panel next to the door.

He unlocked the door and ripped it open. "Dude. Seriously. What the hell?"

Kent held up his hands in a gesture of innocence and smiled. "At least I didn't bust it in this time. I call that an improvement."

"What do you want?" Thomas knew he sounded like an asshole, but he needed to get back to Helen and finish their conversation. "I'm kinda busy."

Kent took in Thomas's bare chest and waggled his eyebrows. "I bet you are. Sorry for interrupting. I've been calling for the past hour, and you weren't answering."

"I don't even know where my phone is." Must've left it in the truck last night.

"You've got a case."

"No thanks. Not today." The words popped out without thought. Working was the last thing on his mind. "The investigation is going on. I can't work."

"You know the case you had the other night? The addict lying dead in the middle of the road in the middle of nowhere?" Kent held out Thomas's credentials. Obviously Lanning had picked them up from where Thomas had dropped them at his mother's funeral. And now here they were, returned to him only a few days later instead of the months he'd expected.

Automatically, Thomas reached for them. "Yyyeeeaahhh." He stretched the word out into one long, suspicious sound.

"There's another one. Exactly like it. Lanning could call in the feds, but that would take a few days and a lot of bullshit, which seems kinda stupid when you're right here." Kent handed him a folded sheet of paper with an address on it. "Time is of the essence, especially since it seems we might have a budding serial killer on our hands."

Chapter 15

OUTSIDE THE TRUCK'S WINDOWS, THE DECEMBER NIGHT seemed ominous and oppressive. As if the sky was too low and the dark was too black. Each mile only made it worse. Didn't help matters that they were literally driving through the middle of Nowhere, Ohio. Despite being just one county over from Sundew, the fields were flat and the roads were straight, and it seemed as though they were lost in a vast nothingness.

A bad feeling gnawed on Thomas's gut. He glanced over at Helen asleep in the passenger seat. She seemed too far away over there, so he settled his hand on her leg. A sigh of contentment slipped from her lips, and the simple touch eased the tension brewing inside him. There really was something special about the two of them.

In the distance, faint blue and red lights strobed. *Ha*. The last time he'd seen the color of those lights, he'd been just a child.

He would've flat-out refused this job, but the prospect of the perpetrator becoming a serial killer was a game changer. Catch him early and the body count would remain low. Catch him late and the bodies would only pile up.

At least they were almost there. Communing with the shadow of death should only take a few minutes, and then they could be on their way home again.

Thomas pulled up to the scene. The flashing lights

came from an unmarked police car with a magnetized strobe attached to the roof. The only car on the scene. Everyone else must've packed up and headed home. It wasn't unheard of that only one deputy remained to guard the evidence, but since this might be the precursor to a serial, he'd expected some spectator officers. The kind who liked to be able to brag about being close to a big case.

He parked behind the car.

Helen didn't wake. If things went his way, she would sleep until he got back. She needed sleep. He left the truck running and quietly got out, shutting the door gently behind him.

From outside, he looked in at her. The dashboard lights etched her in a silver glow. She leaned against the passenger door, using her coat as a pillow. Just seeing her, watching her filled him up. Filled him with love and gratitude that she was his. But riding behind those feelings was the fear of losing her. Not once in his life had he ever possessed something he couldn't live without. Until now. Until her.

He imprinted her image in his mind to fortify himself for the pain to come, then headed toward the scene. Each step away from her was like slogging through wet cement. It felt wrong. But it also seemed wrong to wake her just so she could hold his hand while he worked.

An officer got out of the car, his shadow rising around him like the beginnings of a storm. The guy looked to be in his early fifties, hair graying and face lined with wrinkles from either job stress or bad living. With the way his shadow looked, Thomas was leaning toward bad living.

"I'm Thomas Brown from the BCI." He waited for

some reaction, but the guy said nothing and never met his gaze. "I'm supposed to connect with Ace Tetter."

The guy gave a curt dip of his chin. That was it. Guess he was the strong silent type.

"The scene's been cleared?"

Ace glared in his direction.

"Okay... Well, I'll get to it." Thomas walked by him toward the shapeless lump lying on the dark country road. No extra lights had been set up to provide illumination. None. Some counties had money for those little extras, and some didn't. Thomas nabbed his phone out of his pocket and used the flashlight app.

The stench hit. That triple threat—vomit, piss, and shit. He started breathing through his mouth. Hopefully the stink wouldn't cling to his clothes.

In the white light created by his phone, the remnants of the guy's shadow fluttered and flittered like wispy tendrils of fog. Careful to stay out of the shadow's range, Thomas walked around the body. It had been arranged in the same position as the one from the other night—in a slightly elongated version of the fetal position. The white globes of his ass like glow-in-the-dark balloons. A lot of details could be coincidental, but not that one.

This guy's clothing wasn't quite as filthy as the last guy's. Matted and greasy blond hair stuck to his head, and his eyes were half open, half rolled up in his head, giving him a decidedly demonic look.

No denying it now—they had the makings of a serial killer on their hands. Now Thomas just needed to do his job. Provide as much information as he could, and maybe they could stop the killer before the body count went any higher.

He inhaled and knelt next to the dead guy's face. Waves of warmth washed over him from the shadow. It always seemed weird that shadows looked so cold but were so very warm.

Gently, he brushed the guy's eyelids down.

Thomas's heart started vibrating, his insides trembled, and the air around him seemed oxygen-deprived. Instinct told him to run. And he wanted to. Wanted to sprint back to the truck and drive off into the night and pretend he'd never heard about this case. Pretend that this wasn't his job. That he was just some guy who worked in a factory or something. But he'd never run from the pain before, and he wasn't about to now.

His mind flashed back to only hours ago and touching Helen to demonstrate how the process worked. How painless that had been. How easy.

His hand shook as he reached out to place thumb and forefinger on the guy's cold cheek, ring and pinkie fingers on his forehead, and pressed his middle finger over the guy's closed eye. Heat blazed through his fingertips and up his arm, exploding in his own eye. Even though it was a familiar pain, a grunt slipped from between his lips.

Color burst to life behind his eyes, and this time, instead of desperately clinging to it, he let the colors slide by and watched as the shadow of death showed him this man's life. The man's experiences became Thomas's.

He time-warped through the guy's shitty childhood with his even-shittier parents—all those terrible experiences priming the guy for the escape heroin offered. Once addiction had him in a choke hold, he was like every other addict. There was nothing he wouldn't do for his drug.

The guy's story ended the same as the last body on the road. He had gone with a man who kept his identity in shadow. A man who forced him to overdose.

Everything went dark.

Thomas yanked his hand off the dead guy's face.

The terrible pain in his eye eased, but the shadow's heat didn't let go of him. It was inside him, burning him from the inside out. What was it about the last case and this one that made these men's shadows particularly awful?

He crawled away from the body, sweat soaking his skin. Everything inside him weak and wrong. Even blinking took too much effort. He planted his hands firmly on the pavement, waiting to feel the coolness seep into him, but he could feel nothing except the interminable heat and a terrible foreboding.

A large hand landed on his shoulder. He tensed. All muscles on high alert. He wanted to believe it was Helen behind him. But it wasn't. Her touch soothed. This touch felt malevolent and male. And Ace Tetter hadn't seemed like the touchy-feely, caring type.

"Tommy, what's wrong?" The words were daggers in the dark, each one finding a home in Thomas's gut. His blood congealed.

Tommy. Only one person ever called him Tommy.

He whipped around, expecting to see Malone, but his gaze landed on Helen. She stood, hands behind her back, duct tape over her mouth. Fucking duct tape. The expression on her face… Devastated. Destroyed. Demolished. He looked inside her. Saw the terror in her soul. Not for herself. No. She was scared for him. *For him.* She was his whole world, yet she stood before him with a pain he swore she'd never feel again on her face because she was worried about him.

A terrible realization slammed into him. He should've woken her up. Should've asked her to be with him while he worked. Never should've left her alone in the truck. Lathan's words echoed in his mind. *You want your woman safe? You want her unharmed and healthy? You don't fucking leave her side. You keep touching her at all times. Touching. That's the only way you are both protected. Nothing—I mean nothing—can hurt either of you when you're touching.*

This was all his fault. He should've listened. He knew they were special when together, and yet his own damn foolishness had caused this.

Like an afterthought, Thomas noticed Malone. Motherfucking Malone. His shadow dark and roiling like a pot of evil ready to boil over. Then he spotted the gun Malone aimed at him. Seeing the weapon didn't faze him. If anything, he expected it. The great equalizer. Malone was smart enough to realize Thomas could take him in a physical confrontation.

"H—" Thomas barely managed to stop himself from saying her name. Malone might not realize *who* she was—it had been ten years—and Thomas wanted to keep it that way until he figured out why Malone would go as far as he had to frame her. "Hey, are you okay?"

The unmarked car with Ace Tetter in it—if that was even the guy's real name—pulled away from the scene. *Fucking shit...* This had all been a setup. Thomas saw that now as all the pieces slid into place. Malone had called him out to that last scene. Malone was here at this scene. Malone had killed those men.

He'd killed to get Thomas to the previous scene and out here. But why? The man'd had unlimited access to Thomas as a child. Why wait until now to carry out some awful plan?

"What do you want?" Thomas's voice sounded stronger than he felt inside. His body was still locked in recovery mode, a sensation he'd only experienced with the last two cases. The ones Malone murdered. Was that why these men's shadows felt so awful to him? Because they'd also been Malone's victims?

"We don't need to talk about that now. I just want to make sure you're all right."

Thomas sent an if-looks-could-kill glare at Malone. He tried to get to his feet but couldn't get his arms and legs to move into the correct position. He was still too weak. Helen made a sound behind her duct tape and started toward him, but Malone nabbed her arm and kept her at his side. "Stay here." His voice sounded every kind of cordial and polite, as if Helen weren't standing with her hands tied behind her back and duct tape on her mouth.

"Don't you fucking touch her." Thomas lurched to his feet by sheer force of will. His legs quavered, and he wasn't sure he could manage a step forward yet, but at least he was upright.

With his free hand, Malone reached into his coat pocket and pulled out a plastic baggie—the kind mothers used when packing a sandwich for their kids' lunch. He tossed the baggie toward Thomas. It landed on the pavement between them. Next, he threw a pair of handcuffs. They clattered against the road.

"Please swallow what's in the bag, then put the cuffs

on." Malone's tone contained a friendly quality, so at odds with what he demanded from Thomas.

"No." The word popped out of him before he contemplated the consequences.

With an almost casual move, Malone flicked his wrist to the side and fired the gun.

Ppgglll.

The gunshot was loud and obscene in the quiet of the night. The sound of the shot didn't echo. Instead, it stretched out like a rubber band, getting thinner and thinner by the second until only silence stood between them.

Malone jammed his gun into Helen's side. "I'm sorry. Taking the pills is nonnegotiable."

Translation: Take the drugs or she'll get hurt.

Thomas's mind spun through the options. If he charged Malone and the guy shot Helen, wouldn't he be able to heal her? He'd healed her from the gunshot wound to her chest. He'd healed her waking sleep paralysis. But there was something fundamentally wrong about intentionally placing her in harm's way. Even if he did follow through on that scenario, Thomas would still have to deal with Malone before he could heal Helen. What if Malone shot him and he wasn't able to get to her, heal her?

Fuck. When the options were Helen hurt or Helen unhurt, he had to opt for unharmed.

Anger and defiance shone in Helen's eyes. She didn't want him to take the pills.

On wobbly legs, he walked forward and retrieved the baggie and the cuffs. His fingers were awkward and thick-feeling as he pried apart the bag's opening. "I take these pills, and she walks away from this?"

Helen shook her head violently. She didn't want him sacrificing himself. But what she didn't understand was that he wouldn't want to survive if anything happened to her.

Malone raised the hand not holding the gun in a swear-on-it gesture. "I promise."

Not for a second did Thomas believe the guy, but with a gun aimed at Helen, there weren't a lot of alternatives. He tossed the four round, white pills in his mouth. Immediately, they went chalky and tasted like ass. As if trying to win an Oscar, he pretended to swallow, while shoving the pills into the back of his cheek. He just needed a spare second to spit them out. But... he could feel them dissolving, filling his mouth with their awful flavor.

"They'll help you relax." Malone's volume hadn't changed, but there was something in his tone, something meant to soothe and cajole.

A heavy sensation started between Thomas's shoulder blades and traveled up the back of his neck. The fucking pills were already beginning to take effect. How long before he was completely out of it? Maybe only minutes.

"Take your coat off and lay it on the pavement for her." Malone gestured with his head to Helen. "We're going to have to leave her here, and we want her to be warm enough. Don't we?"

He kept using the word *we* as if they were a team— buddies or something. "She won't freeze, especially with your coat. We'll even leave your cell phone so she can call for help."

Thomas shrugged out of his coat and set it on the

pavement. Cold air licked his skin but offered no comfort. He met her eyes, tried to tell her that everything was going to be okay. That she would be okay. And he would be okay. He just needed to get Malone away from her. Despite the guy's words, Thomas knew the violence contained inside the man. "My phone is in my coat pocket. Call Kent. He'll know what to do."

"Actually, it would be better to call the Prospectus County Sheriff's Office. They are only twenty minutes away. They'll get here faster than anyone." Malone sounded ever so helpful. *The fucker*. As if this mess wasn't caused by him. "Here's the key to the cuffs she's wearing." Malone tossed the piece of metal on top of Thomas's coat. "See, Tommy? We're going to do everything we can to help her out after we leave. I just need you to put those cuffs on so we can go."

A loud whooshing started in his ears. The heaviness in his neck moved down into his body and up into his brain. He'd never felt like this before. It was odd, but not unpleasant.

What was he supposed to be doing? Thinking was getting hard. Holding on to a thought even harder, as if every thought had to be pulled out of a thick haze. Despite all his intentions, the pills were taking over.

Malone pointed to the cuffs. *Oh yeah*.

Thomas bent down and retrieved them, lost his balance, and stumbled a few steps before regaining his footing.

The metal cuffs were cold against his skin as he tightened them, the ratcheting sound coming at him as if through a wind tunnel.

"Tommy, I need you to get in the truck." Malone's

voice sounded oddly pleasant, almost like a father instructing his son.

Thomas's legs started moving, but he watched Helen. She was angry and scared, and he couldn't remember why. Then their reality came back to him. "Iloveyou. That'sallthatmatters." His words came out in a slow smear of sound.

Her eyes softened, and love reflected back at him. It cleared a bit of the fog encasing his mind and body. On the other side of this situation, they were going to be all right.

And then Malone was in front of her, and Thomas couldn't see what was happening.

His head seemed to weigh too much, and he let it fall forward on his shoulders. Time jumped forward a few minutes, and Malone was there, guiding him by the arm toward the truck. A distant part of himself didn't like what was happening, but he felt powerless to stop it. And he was so damn hot. Despite the cold winter air, sweat dripped off him.

"You don't love her. She's just tail."

Thomas heard the words but couldn't find any meaning to them. He was so tired. Every bit of him too exhausted to move. He just wanted to sleep. He let his eyes fall closed, but then remembered Helen. His eyelids snapped open, and he found himself in the passenger seat of his truck. How'd he get there? Where was Helen? Before he could open his mouth to ask the question, blackness wrapped its arms around him and hugged him to sleep.

Chapter 16

ILOVEYOU. THAT'SALLTHATMATTERS. TOMMY'S WORDS WERE slurred from the pills, but there was no mistaking what he said.

Who the hell was this woman? Tommy never dated. Never. And suddenly, he'd found someone he claimed to love? *No. No way. Not again.*

Reality and the past merged together for Robert, and he saw his Evan saying the same thing to Rosemary—his bitch wife. Back then, it had hurt to have to share Evan's love. Right now, with the knowledge of hindsight, it made him angry. Angry at not being enough for Evan. And even angrier that Evan had let a woman destroy them.

Never again. He strode up to the woman, aimed the gun right between her eyes. She didn't move. Just stood there, staring at him, her eyes flat and challenging. Not full of the fear they should've been. His finger itched to pull the trigger, but he wasn't one to murder frivolously.

Wielding the gun like a rock, he bashed her on the side of the head. The impact of the blow resonated up his arm. She fell back and to the side, collapsing in a messy heap on the pavement. He stood over her, daring her to move. She didn't.

He glanced back at Tommy, who leaned against the truck. The pills were doing their job, making him passive and pliant.

He knelt next to the woman, blocking Tommy's view. He lifted her head in his hands and for the first time really looked at her. She was beautiful in the classic sense of the word. High forehead. Arched brows. Pert nose. Plump lips. Something about her was vaguely familiar, but after so many years of being a public servant, everyone looked familiar.

It didn't matter who she was. He would not let another woman annihilate the good thing he was about to create. Anger from decades without Evan galloped through him. He slammed her head against the pavement. The solid *thunk* of flesh and bone against asphalt sickened and satisfied at the same time. He didn't intend to kill her. He just wanted to hurt her. Really hurt her.

He wanted to keep going, wanted to crush her skull and pulverize her brain, but time was not on his side. Every moment out here in the open was one of risk.

It hadn't been hard getting the BCI to send Thomas. Robert had known exactly what to say, how to say it, and who to pretend to be when he said it. Then it'd just been a matter of paying a less-than-ethical acquaintance to impersonate Sheriff Ace Tetter.

He turned toward the truck. Tommy waited for him. Hadn't tried to escape. Hadn't tried to help the woman. Part of that might've been the drugs, but still he'd waited. And that meant something.

For the first time since Evan's death, Robert felt something good. If he had to find a name for the emotion he'd call it...hmm...anticipation. Something amazing was about to happen. He could feel it.

"Come on, Tommy, time to go." He opened the truck door and motioned for Tommy to enter. Once he situated himself, Robert reached across and buckled him in like the precious cargo he was.

Tommy leaned back against the headrest, sighed heavily, and seemed to fall asleep. The drugs had hit him harder and quicker than anticipated. Robert unlocked Tommy's cuffs. On both wrists, red welts had formed.

"Aww… You put them on too tight." Robert rubbed the skin. The crisp hair on Tommy's wrists tingled against his fingertips. "That should be better." He lifted both wrists to his mouth and kissed each one lightly.

He stepped back and shut the truck door, then headed over to the driver's side. When he climbed in, the wonderful scent of Tommy—a mixture of soap and man that Robert found so damn alluring—hit him. A smile pushed up his cheeks. He was so close to getting his Evan back.

He shifted the truck in gear and drove around the bodies on the pavement toward their new beginning.

The night was his coconspirator on this mission. They passed no other cars, and the few houses they passed had no lights on. It was as if the world cooperated with his plan to remake Tommy into Evan.

Robert looked forward to the process. The pieces of himself that had been missing for so long started filling in.

After twenty minutes, he pulled into a wooded area near the Scioto River and followed a narrow set of tire tracks to his car. The truck's headlights splashed across the naked trees, creating a world full of mystery and secrets to be discovered.

He parked close to the riverbank, out of sight from the road. Leaving the keys in the ignition—if he was lucky, maybe someone would steal the thing—he got out and went to his car.

The gray sedan was so anonymous, even he couldn't remember if it was a Toyota or a Honda. Exactly what he wanted. He started the car and turned the heat up to full blast. Didn't want Tommy to be cold.

The next phase of his plan was about to begin. They'd drive to the little cabin in the woods where Tommy's transformation would take place. Anticipation put a skip in his step as he went to help Tommy out of the truck.

When he opened the truck door, all he could see was Evan. Evan's face. Evan's body. Evan's scent. The only difference was the hair. The hair always shattered the illusion, but he had a solution.

"Tommy." He cupped the side of his stepson's face, luxuriating in the sensation of stubble against his fingertips. "Wake up now." He spoke softly, soothingly.

Tommy groaned a sleepy sound. "Aw... Goddamn it. I'msofuckinghot." Sweat slicked his skin, and he sat there without opening his eyes.

Robert pressed his palm to Tommy's forehead. The man was burning up. Was he having an allergic reaction to the pills? Not one Robert had ever heard of. Or was he coming down with the flu? All he knew for certain was a body that hot needed to be cooled. He unbuttoned Tommy's shirt and slid it off his frame, all the while feeling the intense heat radiating from him.

"Don't worry. I'll take care of you." He rummaged in his pockets and found a tissue. Tenderly, he wiped the sweat on Tommy's face and looked at the scar, really looked at it, taking in all the nuances with an odd sort of remorse. He'd done that to Tommy. He'd never felt guilty about it until recently. But there'd be plenty of time to make up for it.

He grabbed the bottle of water sitting in the console and held it to Tommy's lips. "Drink for me."

Obediently, Tommy drank, then slumped back against the seat. Never once opening his eyes.

"Feel better now?"

"No."

Well, at least the man was honest. "We need to switch vehicles." Robert unbuckled him. "Come on." He tugged at Tommy to get his attention.

Tommy started to slide out of the truck, lost his footing, and went down hard on his side. He groaned but didn't try to get up.

"Careful. We don't want you to get hurt." Robert helped hoist him to his feet, then inserted himself under Tommy's arm and grabbed on to his waist. Tommy weaved and tipped, his balance nonexistent. The pills were doing a real number on him. Add a fever on top of that, and things were bound to get worse before they got better. When the drugs worked out of his system, the hangover was going to be a monster. But by then, the transformation would be complete and Robert would be there to care for him.

Chapter 17

THOMAS'S EYES WERE TOO HEAVY TO OPEN AS HIS MIND floated in a vast, open sky. His thoughts were clouds, shifting and changing, never solidifying. He drifted along, vaguely aware of a nagging sensation that there was something important he needed to remember, but he couldn't seem to find the memory.

A sharp chemical tang in the air offered only slightly more clarity. He recognized that he sat slouched in a chair, head hanging off the back of it, and his skin was on fire. His insides melting.

Cold water suddenly doused his head. He startled but relaxed into the soothing coolness. Then the water was gone and hands massaged his scalp, but they were hot, burning against him. He tried to move away, but his body didn't fully cooperate.

"No, no, no. Just hold still while I finish rinsing your hair," a familiar male voice cajoled.

Thomas couldn't make sense of the words, but relaxed again as the cold water returned, dousing the heat. But then it stopped.

"Evan...I need you to help me get you back to the bed." That voice again. How did he know that voice? And who was Evan?

Distantly, he felt his arm being lifted, felt someone insert himself underneath. "Okay. Try to stand up."

He tried, or at least thought he did as he weebled and

wobbled to his feet, each step taking an act of concentration while the person helping him served as a living crutch.

"Okay. You can sit down now."

His body collapsed more than sat. Cool sheets against his hot cheek. Even though he lay on a bed, his body felt weightless, carefree. Exactly how it felt to be around Helen. As if everything that had been wrong had been forgotten. She was beauty and peace and color all rolled into one.

Helen.

She was the only solid thought he could find. The image of her on his bed—his mouth between her legs, while her body writhed in pleasure—flitted through his mind.

An urgent and desperate longing for her burned through him.

"Helen?" Her name slipped from his lips in a slurry plea. Blindly, he reached out to her, feeling along the mattress, searching for her body alongside his. "Where are you?"

Ssmmkk. Pain exploded in his cheek. His head wrenched to the side. White stars flared behind his eyes. He recognized the sensation well—he'd just been slapped.

"You will not speak that name." Fury threaded the man's tone. "You will not think about her. You will forget she ever existed."

The man's words were abhorrent, wrong. "That would be like asking me to forget about my heart. I love—"

Ssmmkk. A ball of agony flared over his cheek again. A wimpy whine slipped out of him.

"Every time you mention her name, you will be punished."

His brain might not be fully functioning, and he might not be able to get his eyelids to rise, but he understood cause and effect. *Say Helen's name. Get hit.*

An ice-cold cloth was pressed against the sting on his cheek, cooling his face and the never-ending heat burning deep inside him. He leaned into the comfort like an abused dog finding solace when his master decided to stroke his fur. What was wrong with him? This wasn't him. When he'd been a boy, he'd been quiet and compliant in order to survive. But the moment he'd gotten old enough to fight back against Malone, he'd never backed down.

Malone. Recognition crashed over him. His insides jerked. That familiar voice was Malone. He was with Malone. And that heat was Malone's shadow of death.

Memories jammed into his brain. *Helen.* Oh God, where was Helen? Was she all right? Was she alive? He sensed her presence in the world, an invisible lifeline connecting him to her. He turned his head to the left— she was in that direction. He could feel her as if her heart were inside his, the two of them beating together.

His eyelids weighed twenty pounds, but he forced them up to half-mast.

A black-and-white world greeted him. He shouldn't have been surprised, and yet he was. Helen had given him color, and it had felt so right, so natural, that his normal vision seemed wrong.

The room swung back and forth on a giant pendulum. *Rrriigghhtt…Then lleeeffttt…* The dizziness made it hard to define his surroundings. Slowly, he was able to make out the room around him. A kitchen area, a dining table, a couch. And a sink, toilet, and shower out in the open for all to see. He blinked. Was he seeing that right? *Yep*.

His gaze shifted to the man sitting next to him. The black shadow around Malone throbbed, yet the man sat there staring at him with a smile on his face. A child's terror gripped Thomas—the kind that happens when the monster under the bed turns out to be real.

Adrenaline bucked through him, offering him the gift of clarity.

He gasped and jerked away, but he ran into something solid and unyielding. A wall.

"Shhh… It's okay," Malone soothed and reached toward him.

Thomas scrambled away from Malone on all fours, falling off the bed onto his hands and knees. The combined impact resonated through his body, but he forced himself to standing and caught sight of a man across the room. A man he recognized. A man he knew.

His father. His fucking dead father.

There weren't very many pictures of his father. As a child, Thomas had pilfered one of the few photos and spent hours staring at the man, begging the image to rescue him from Malone. For years, that picture represented hope. Until Thomas grew up enough to realize no one was going to save him.

Thomas recognized the man's dirty-blond hair, the sharp features, the downward tilt to his eyes. It was almost like staring into a mirror. Only… *Fuck*. It really was a mirror he was looking into. He could see the scar on his cheek. He was looking at his own damned self.

He raised a hand to his hair. *His* dirty-blond hair. "What'd you do to my ha—"

A sudden sting in his ass whirled him around. Malone held a syringe. "I didn't want to do this to you, but if it's the only way to keep you compliant…"

A heavy black wave poured over Thomas, drowning out the rest of Malone's words.

Thomas didn't wake all at once. Each of his senses yawned and stretched, warming up before finally engaging.

He felt the solid presence of Helen spooning his back. She reached around his waist, pulling him in tighter to her. He nestled into the feeling, but he was so hot. Her hand wandered over his hip, his abdomen, then lower, gripping him through his underwear.

He tried to enjoy the sensation, but her hold on him was too hard, too aggressive, almost painful. And he was so damn hot.

"Hey. Slow down." He opened his eyes as he rolled over to face her. "We have all the time in—"

Malone lay with him, his shadow rising and roiling, his disgusting hand on Thomas's dick.

Thomas bucked away from the man's touch, sat up, and shot a fist at Malone's nose. Cartilage crunched underneath his knuckles. Malone squeaked, a high-pitched, childish sound. Thomas slammed a fist into the man's gut, then delivered an uppercut to his jaw, snapping his head back.

Malone collapsed back on the bed, and Thomas scrambled out. He stole a moment to loom over the asshole, willing him to move, to twitch, to even breathe—because if he did, Thomas wasn't sure he'd stop at just a few blows. He might beat the man until all that remained was a pile of bloody meat. This man had not only stolen his childhood but tried to take his dignity as an adult.

His gaze snagged on the image in the mirror across the room. His fucking blond hair. Didn't have the time to think about that now. Only one thing was important. Finding Helen. Just thinking her name, he sensed what direction she was in. To his left.

He nabbed a set of keys off the counter, then threw open the only door in the place, and ran out into the snowy night.

His feet were bare, his body clothed only in a pair of tighty-whities. He didn't even want to think about what had happened to his pants and shirt. Getting out of here and back to Helen mattered above all else.

Snow burned his feet. His muscles locked in a battle to retain their heat, but he forced them to move. Forced himself to run along the shoveled path to a car.

"Evan. Stop. Don't run." Malone yelled from behind him. His tone was the same one that used to ram a rod of fear directly up Thomas's spine. But he'd turned a corner. Gone was that scared little boy. In his place was an enraged man who would've enjoyed hurting Malone as much as Malone had hurt him. But getting back to Helen mattered more than revenge. There'd be time for vengeance later.

Something pinched his shoulder. He flinched away from it, but then his body stopped working. He went weightless, snow rushing up to him. He hit hard. Hands. Chest. Knees. Pain rocketed through his body.

He couldn't move, his body convulsing as if plugged into a lightning bolt. He couldn't yell. He couldn't think. All he could do was feel. And it felt as if he were being ripped apart on a cellular level.

The all-consuming pain vanished, but his muscles remained locked into tight spasms that refused to relent.

"I told you not to run. You're not leaving me this time. We'll be together until our end."

Thomas lay facedown in the snow, gulping air, his body twanging. He should've turned the guy into hamburger meat before leaving the cabin. *Shoulda. Woulda. Coulda.*

He turned his head—all the movement he could manage—in time to see Malone's sock-covered foot rushing toward his face, ending things between them the exact way they'd started.

Before impact, he closed his eyes and somehow, impossibly, he heard Helen's voice in his head. "I love you. Stay alive. I'll find you."

Chapter 18

WHITE EVERYWHERE, EXPANDING TO INFINITY.

She was inside another dream, about to fight for someone else's life when the only life that mattered to her was Thomas's. Why the hell was she dreaming right now anyway? She needed to wake up. She needed to help Thomas.

"Hurry up. Let's get this over with."

She felt the shimmer start low on her abdomen, spreading through her entire body. Her mouth opened, and the same words she'd heard the last two times came out. "You are the warrior. It is your destiny to teach others how to survive."

The environment morphed and changed. Color emerged. Browns. Dark Blues. Tan. Splashes of cream. Just like a jigsaw puzzle being put together one piece at a time, a room formed around her.

She lay on a cold, hard surface—a table maybe? Her shoulder blades and tailbone points of pressure beneath her. Malone moved into her field of vision. Oh God, was she sharing a dream with Thomas? Teaching him how to survive? This was one fight she was definitely going to win.

She tried to roll away from Malone but couldn't move. Not even an inch. She lifted her head, looking down the length of her body. Thick black straps covered her hips and chest, locking her naked torso to the table. More of those straps sheathed her ankles and her wrists. Even though she already knew she couldn't move, she had to test them all. She flexed all her muscles, pulled and pushed with everything inside her, and...nothing.

"This is a fight you cannot win by force. You must give him what he wants." The words came out of her mouth but weren't in her voice.

Oh, hell no. Everything inside her rebelled. She was the goddamned warrior and this thing in her dreams was asking her to give in, give up when Thomas's life was on the line? *No. Never.*

Malone moved to stand beside her head. Both of his eyes were ringed in purple, and his nose looked swollen and painful.

"Evan..."

Evan? Who the hell is Evan? Where's Thomas? She opened her mouth to speak the words, but no sound came out.

He reached out and stroked her hair. Such an oddly gentle gesture. And the way he looked at her, or Evan, overflowed with a sad kind of love.

Where is Thomas? she screamed, but her mouth didn't move, and no sound came out.

"Every time you hurt me, I will hurt you worse. This time, I'm not going to martyr myself for you. This time, Evan, you will suffer for me." Malone's tone offered no room for question or disagreement. "You broke my nose. And my toe."

She saw his fist rushing at her face too late. Didn't have time to turn her head. Force and pressure. Lights and stars. Hot blood gushed over her skin, drained down into her throat. She turned her head, coughing and choking on the goop, but not feeling the pain of the blow.

Tears burned in her sinuses, then filled her eyes and spilled to race to her hairline. These weren't sad tears. They were angry tears. Tears filled with fight. She wanted to hurt this man who hurt Thomas as a child and was trying to hurt some guy named Evan now.

Where is Thomas? Again, she tried to ask him, but nothing came out. Her only option was to wait until the end of the dream when Evan would finally appear to her. Then she'd ask him if he'd seen Thomas.

"Here now," Malone's voice soothed. "None of that." Tenderly, he wiped at the tears drizzling from her eyes with his fingers. Her body wanted to recoil from him, but something locked her into place, forcing her to endure his touch.

Her mouth opened, and words flowed out of her. Words that didn't come from her. "I've made some terrible mistakes." Her hand lifted in the restraint as if it were seeking his. He grasped her hand with his, twining their fingers together in a lover's knot. She squeezed and looked him in the eye. "The past is over and gone. No matter how much I wish I could change it, I can't. I'm sorry I screwed up, but those are only words. Give me a chance to show you that I won't leave and won't hurt you ever again."

What the hell was coming out of her mouth?

He bent and kissed her knuckles, rubbing his smoothly shaven cheek against her hand. Her insides recoiled at his touch, but her outsides didn't move.

"God, I've missed you. You have no idea what it's been like all these years without you."

"I've missed you too. I was stupid. I wasted so much time."

He swept his arm around the space. "I changed

nothing. Kept it all the same." He sounded like an excited little boy showing his momma an A he'd gotten on his report card.

Under the control of something else, her head turned and her eyes roamed the setting, as if taking it all in. Her mouth opened. "I've always loved it here. It's so quiet. So peaceful. So...ours." Where the hell were these words coming from?

He let go of her hand and stroked her face. "Evan...I love you. And I'm sorry for what I'm about to do. I hadn't expected you to wake so soon. I had wanted you to remain asleep for this part, but maybe this is as it should be. So you will be aware of the consequences of your behavior." His tone carried a sadness and regret that scared the shit out of her. He let go of her hand and walked down to the foot of the table. Only then did she see the tools. Pliers. Screwdrivers. A hammer. A saw.

"For both of us, I'm going to make sure you never again run from me."

"Wake up," a female voice intruded. "Come on. Time to open your eyes."

Helena felt a hand on her shoulder, felt her body jostle.

―――

Her eyes popped open to a hospital room and a perky, petite nurse disappearing behind the curtain partition.

No. She'd been woken up before she finished the dream. *Oh God... Evan...* Whoever he was, he was going through hell at Malone's hand, and she hadn't been able to finish helping him. And didn't find out one thing about Thomas.

She tried to sit up but couldn't move. A spurt of

panic launched through her system, but she doused it before it latched on too tight. This was just that sleep paralysis thing bleeding over into wake time.

Just give it time, and she'd be able to move again. Then she'd figure out how to find Thomas and how to find Malone so she could save Evan. She closed her eyes and concentrated on trying to move her fingers and toes.

Minutes ticked by as sensation and the ability to move returned at the same time as a pain in the back of her head grew. When full feeling returned, she reached up to touch the spot, but her hand moved only an inch before it caught on something. A shiny, silver handcuff encircled her wrist, latching her to the bed rail.

Her heart caved in on itself. It was futile and stupid, but she couldn't help herself. She tugged against the cuff, hoping beyond hope that it would magically release and she would be free—not for herself, but free to find Thomas. She would endure a lifetime in Fairson as long as he was alive and well out in the world.

She closed her eyes. *Thomas. Thomas. Thomas.* She could *feel* him. She turned her head to the right, seeing through her eyelids, the walls, and the miles that separated them to a ramshackle cabin in the woods. She wanted to see Thomas to confirm for herself that he was all right, but her vision ended at the cabin. "I love you. Stay alive. I'll find you." Like a rubber band, her vision snapped back, and everything she'd seen disappeared.

Her eyes popped open.

Using her free hand, she reached up and found a thick gauze bandage wrapped around her head. What had happened to the back of her head? She remembered

Malone punching her in the side of her head with his gun, not the back of the head.

She reviewed every moment of interaction out on the road with Malone. He'd seemed polite. Almost as if he was trying to ease Thomas's mind by leaving her a jacket and a cell phone and keys to the cuffs. But that seemed so at odds with the man who'd hurt Thomas so badly as a child.

Why would he want to take Thomas now? What could he possibly gain from that?

A nurse bustled in, saw she was awake, turned on her heel, and was out the door before Helena could even open her mouth. *Great*. That was probably the nicest reaction she was going to get. Being Helena Grayse carried no perks. Tenderly, she scooted to a sitting position, her head not happy with the change in equilibrium.

The curtain surrounding her little space was flung back. A man in khaki pants and a black polo shirt stood there. His gray hair was overly thick and rode just above his brow line, making him a dead ringer for a Neanderthal.

He stared at her with one of those hard, assessing looks that only a law-enforcement officer could pull off. As if he had some special power to see all her sins. *Ha!* Only Thomas could do that.

Behind him, a gaggle of nurses gathered, all of them staring. None of them bothering to hide their curiosity. Obviously, they all knew she was Helena Grayse. Felon. Murderer. None of them would be an ally to her.

"I'm Detective Brody with the Prospectus County Sheri—"

She shifted her attention back to him. "Do you know where Thomas is? Robert Malone took him. Are you looking for him?" Each word she uttered felt as if her brain wanted to blow out the back of her head.

Her words didn't startle the detective. Instead, he went very still. "You're telling me that Robert Malone is involved in this?"

"Yes. He took Thomas." *Oh God.* Her head was killing her. She reached up and gently settled her hand over the thick gauze on the back of her head—another layer of security to prevent her brains from leaking out. "You have to find him. Malone's going to hurt him. He—"

The detective held his hand up in stop motion, then slowly, almost as if he was trying to annoy her with his turtle speed, he reached into his pants pocket and pulled out a small notepad, then a nubby stump of a pencil. Casually, he flipped the pad open and one by one leafed through the pages, scanning each before finding the perfect one to use.

She knew the tactic. He sensed she was desperate, and if he could send her over the edge, she might lose control and confess. She wanted to scream. She didn't scream.

"Let's start at the beginning. Give me your name and date of birth."

It took everything inside her, but she calmly played twenty questions with him. Then she told him every single detail from the moment Kent showed up at Thomas's door to now.

Detective Brody stared at her as if she'd just read him a boring bedtime story. Not once during the entire time she'd spoken had he bothered to use his paper and pencil.

Rule number one: Nobody believed a felon.

"Then who was the DB out on the road?"

She smothered an eye roll. With the way her head hurt, she wasn't even certain she could've pulled off the maneuver without going cross-eyed. The detective had the ability to hear and comprehend; he was simply trying to trip her up. "I don't know. Thomas was called in to investigate."

"So you're telling me Robert Malone, who everyone suspects left town days ago, has been hanging around waiting for an opportunity to kidnap his stepson who he abused as a child? And when Thomas Brown wouldn't go with him, he somehow forced him to take some drugs, and that's why he OD'd and is in the morgue right now."

For a split second, Detective Brody's words were worms in her brain. Could Thomas be in the morgue? Could he have died? *No*. The word echoed through her soul. He was in that cabin in the woods.

The detective was trying to steer the narrative in the direction he wanted it to go because the truth wasn't easy and sure as hell wasn't convenient.

"No. I'm saying that the body in the morgue is the one Thomas was called out to investigate. I'm saying that Malone forced Thomas to take drugs to make him compliant by threatening my life. I'm saying that Malone took Thomas."

"How about you tell me a different story? One that corresponds with the *evidence*." The detective crossed his arms. "Because you say you were punched in the side of the head, but you also have a deep wound in the *back* of your head that you can't explain. You say you were cuffed, but you weren't when you were found. You say there was a phone and a coat at the scene, but we didn't find any. You say to call this mysterious Kent, but you don't even know his last name, and his number is in the magical disappearing cell phone." He raised an eyebrow at her—the equivalent of saying *liar, liar, pants on fire*.

"He works with Thomas at the BCI. Call them."

"Here are the facts. You've admitted to being with Thomas Brown. Staying with him. Having a relationship with him. And driving out there with him. Evidence points to there being a fight. You have a bruise on your face and a head wound. We haven't had any reports of a dead body lying out in the middle of the road. And we certainly haven't called in the BCI. Here's what I think happened. Thomas Brown popped a few too many pills, and you all got into a fight. He knocked you out but then OD'd." His eyes searched every bit of her face, looking for confirmation. "We all know what happened to Rory Ellis. What I don't get is why you'd think we'd be stupid enough to believe this cock-and-balls story."

Cock-and-balls story? Wasn't it supposed to be cock-and-bull story? But who was she to correct his speech? "Do a little research, and you'll find out that body *isn't* Thomas Brown." She tried to rein in the sass in her tone. Failed.

"Okay…so let's say that body *isn't* Thomas Brown, and someone really did take him. There's just one problem with that. Nobody has filed a missing person report for Thomas Brown."

This guy was either playing dumb to get on her

nerves, or he was dumber than a box of boogers. She was leaning toward the booger box.

She spoke through gritted teeth but managed to keep her volume in the normal range. "Of course no one has reported him missing. No one knows he's missing except me." She tugged at her wrist cuffed to the bed rail. "Am I under arrest? You can't detain me unless you're going to arrest me." At least she was pretty sure that was the rule.

"I can hold you for twelve hours."

She glanced at the clock above the nurse's station. It was 3:07 a.m. Twelve hours would be an eternity.

Chapter 19

ONE OF THE FLUORESCENT LIGHTS IN THE INTERROGATION room buzzed and flickered. After ten hours in this miniature-sized room, answering the same questions over and over and over, Helena had a low-grade migraine and high-grade irritation. "Are you going to charge me or let me go?" She made sure her tone didn't carry any attitude. Didn't want to give Detective Brody any reason to conjure up some charges.

If what he'd said was true, he technically had two more hours before he had to make a decision. She wasn't going to do anything to jeopardize her potential freedom.

"A lot can happen in two hours. I guess you'll just have to wait and see." An almost teasing quality entered his tone, but his face remained deadpan and flat.

He had no evidence. He had no proof. Which should have eased her mind, but she had no faith in the justice system that had convicted her without evidence or proof.

The only glimmer of goodness was that sometime during the past hours of questioning, he'd shifted the narrative away from the idea that it was Thomas's body out on the road and onto a line of questioning that demanded she tell him the body's identity. Maybe Brody was finally realizing Thomas was missing.

To her credit, she hadn't uttered the l-word. Lawyer. Any mention of the word would be an unofficial admission of guilt. Or at least that's the way law enforcement looked at it. She was keeping the lawyer card in her back pocket in case he kept her over the twelve-hour limit.

Abruptly, Brody stood, opened the door of the interrogation room, and looked out into the hallway. "Hey, Mikey. You wanna escort her to one of the holding cells?"

"We got a full house this afternoon," an officer answered.

Brody gave her an asshole's smile. "Perfect." He stepped back to let a young officer enter the room. Mikey... His name perfectly matched his appearance. He might be in his early twenties, but he had one of those boyish faces dominated by freckles and a prominent cowlick in the front of his short-trimmed hair.

"Come on." Mikey's tone carried none of the attitude that Brody's did. He motioned for Helena to precede him.

Outside the interrogation room, those familiar institutional scents—stale air and unwashed flesh— automatically called up a decade's worth of prison memories. None of them good.

Two more hours until Brody decided to charge her or release her. Only two more hours.

"Can I make a phone call?" She wasn't sure if she was entitled to a call, but it didn't hurt to ask.

Officer Mikey motioned for her to precede him down the hallway to a pay phone hanging on the wall. He lifted the receiver, punched a code into the phone, then held it out to her. "Just dial your number."

She stared at the thing before taking it. It had been her idea to ask for a phone call, but she hadn't expected the request to be granted. Who was she going to call? There were only two numbers she knew by heart. Her grand-parents and... An idea, fully formed and far-fetched, whacked her upside the head. Before she could over think it, she typed in the number.

On the other end of the line, the phone rang. Once. Twice. "Hello." His voice, his tone, his inflection glued her lips together, and her tongue felt too big for her mouth. She tried to say something but couldn't figure out how to form words.

"Hello?" Aggression punched through that friendly word.

Thomas's voice spoke in her mind. *This fear you have... You're letting them win.* And she was sick to damned death of being afraid. "CO Holbrook." Her voice croaked. She cleared her throat and spoke with force. "I need to speak with Mrs. Ellis."

"Who is this?"

"Lena." Saying her prison name out loud made her skin prick. Terrible memories bombarded her mind. She shoved all that away. There was something greater at stake than her old past fear. Thomas's life was on the line. "Helena Grayse. And if you and Mrs. Ellis want my help to escape the charges that are going to be piled on you both, you'll let me talk to her."

Holbrook said nothing else. But he didn't hang up. She heard the sound of a hand being cupped over the receiver and a muted conversation. No words were distinguishable, but the angry inflection was loud and proud. She couldn't help the smile that twitched the corners of her mouth. Bet neither of them had expected a phone call from her.

Someone breathed into the receiver, then Mrs. Ellis

spoke. "What do you want?" If words could kill, those would've been convicted of murder.

Helena didn't have the time for explanations and niceties. "You want to know what happened to Rory? Not the bullshit you've chosen to believe all these years, but the truth?" She didn't wait for Mrs. Ellis's answer. "I can take you to his killer. He'll tell you. All I need you to do is meet me at the Prospectus County police station in two hours. If I don't come out after two hours..." This was where she might lose the woman. "Then I'm gonna need you to bail me out of jail."

"I can't believe your audacity. That you'd ask anything of me when you've already taken everything from me." The woman was riding the ridge of rage.

"I'm offering the truth. Not some lie that's easy to believe. The truth. Take it or leave it." She slammed the receiver into the cradle.

The bottom dropped out of her stomach. What had she been thinking? That Mrs. Ellis would care about the truth after she'd invested a decade in a lie? Not likely. Not to mention that she was lying to Mrs. Ellis about taking her to the real killer. Helena knew she could find Thomas, knew it on an instinctual level, and also knew that she would lie, cheat, and steal to get to him. She had figured that once they found him, then they both could explain Malone's true nature.

"Your people coming?" Mikey asked, pulling her away from her thoughts.

"No..." She stared at the phone, unable to take her eyes off it.

"You need to make another call?" Helpfulness, kindness filled his words.

Should she call the BCI and ask for Kent? She'd never actually met Kent. Would he believe her if she told him what happened? She was Helena Grayse. Felon. Murderer. Law enforcement would automatically be biased against every word coming out of her mouth. Calling him might lead to wasted time answering questions that didn't matter when all she needed was to get out of here so she could find Thomas. There was a *slim* possibility she might be released soon. No way did she want to jeopardize that opportunity. No, she wouldn't call BCI. At least not until she knew if Brody was going to charge her or release her. If he charged her, she'd call them as a last resort.

She realized Mikey was still waiting for her to answer. "No... There's no one to call."

Mikey motioned for her to precede him. "Head down to the end of the row." He spoke from behind her.

Desperate, degenerate women filled the two other cells she passed. Women who'd gotten lost on the wrong side of life and hadn't found their way back yet.

And then she was there at the last cell, waiting to be locked in.

Blood rushed out of her head. The world tilted a bit. Panic threatened to open its gaping maw and swallow her whole. *Not again. I can't go through this again.* Another, stronger voice spoke in her head. *This is a temporary holding cell. Not jail. Not prison. Temporary.*

Mikey unlocked the door and slid it open.

On the outside, she projected calm acceptance as she walked inside. There was a pecking order to these places. Show weakness, and every woman would capitalize on it.

Five other women were in the cell. Some were coming down from a high, some dressed for their work in the sex trade, and one slept sprawled across the only bench like she'd bought and paid for the thing. Recognition shot a warning flare through Helena's system. The woman lying on the bench was a former Sister. A freaking Sister. Could things get any worse? *Hell yeah*. Things had already gone bad just by being on Brody's radar, and they'd gotten worse when she was placed in this cell with a Sister. They'd go in the shitter if the Sister woke up. But it'd been a few years since the Sister had been released. Maybe she wouldn't remember Helena.

"I know you." One of the women sitting on the floor slurred. Her eyes were glassy, and her head seemed unsteady on her neck. "You mmmuurrddeeerrreeed someone."

Every set of eyeballs turned in her direction, even the Sister's. Helena witnessed the moment the Sister recognized her. It had nothing to do with her body, nothing to do with her facial expression; it was all in the alert energy the Sister focused on her. Her thoughts so obvious, Helena didn't need to be psychic to understand their meaning. The Sister was trying to figure out how to kill her in front of all these witnesses.

Helena clenched both hands into fists. Never back down from a fight. Always meet it head-on. Maybe she really was the warrior from her dreams. Now if she could just conjure some of that shimmer stuff...

She locked eyes with the Sister in a silent challenge, but the woman never moved from her position on the bench. Finally, the Sister slung her arm over her face, feigning sleep. But Helena knew she was contemplating murder.

"Sister. Don't waste your time." Helena's words were heavy with warning and laced with promise.

The Sister wrenched herself upright.

Helena knew intimidation when she saw it and head butted it. "You're wondering how to get word to CO Holbrook that you succeeded where everyone else failed. I got news for you. CO Holbrook is under investigation. Your payday just dried up. You hurt me, and all you'll get is more time—and I'll be the one walking out of here toward freedom."

The other women scuttled into the opposite walls of the cell, well out of the path between the Sister and her. No one wanted to be in the line of fire when this shitter exploded.

"You talkin' now, bitch?" The Sister stood.

Helena wasn't a short girl. She was five eight and used to looking down at most women. But she'd forgotten just how tall this Sister was. Six feet at least and hefty, not fat. No, this Sister was a semi, and she was a compact car.

Fear threatened to gallop out of control, but Helena grabbed the reins with both fists. "You can't kill me. You can try. You might even think you can succeed, but I won't die. I won't. Never have. I can take a shankin' and keep on crankin'."

Something shifted in the Sister's eyes. Hesitation? Uncertainty? Helena was gonna jump all over that. "You were part of the gang shanking. How many times did you stab me? Ten? Twenty? Fifty? And look..." Helena opened her arms wide. "Here I am. You didn't kill me then. And you can't kill me now."

The Sister's top lip peeled back over her teeth,

revealing two front teeth capped in gold. "Eighty-seven. I fucking stabbed you eighty-seven times. And that ain't counting how many the others did."

Helena smiled, but the expression was more of an I-told-you-so smile.

"Helena Grayse," an officer called from outside the cell.

Her name hung in the air like a hot air balloon to salvation. The officer unlocked the cell.

Without taking her eyes off the Sister, she exited the space. Only when she was free and the door firmly locked behind her did she dare to turn her back on the Sister.

The officer impatiently motioned for her to walk in front of him. She followed his curt directions through the facility, finally stopping at a thick metal door. He unlocked it and motioned her into an empty waiting area. The only other person in the space was another officer behind a glass-enclosed window. The door clicked shut behind her, leaving her alone in the room.

What the heck was going on? Was she going to be charged? Sent to jail to await arraignment? She walked up to the window and waited while the officer pointedly avoided looking at her. It took everything inside her to not knock on the glass. But any demands she made would be met with resistance. It was a universal rule. If an inmate wanted something, the guard would do the opposite.

She watched the second hand of the clock behind the man and started counting. One. Two. Three. After she counted off 135 seconds, he glanced at her.

"I'm Helena Grayse," she rushed to say before he looked away.

He grabbed a piece of paper out of a printer and shoved it at her through the slit in the glass.

RETURN OF PROPERTY.

She read the top line of the form again. RETURN OF PROPERTY.

She was being let go? Just like that?

"You need to sign it." The officer spoke in a flat, toneless voice.

She grabbed the pen tethered to the desk and scribbled her name on the blank line, then slid it back to him. Two minutes later, she walked out the door of the police station a free woman. Not a word, not a thanks, not even a screw-you from Detective Brody.

It was late in the day, and the sky was a low shroud of gray. The kind of sky that made you feel lonely and depressed. Cold air snapped against her skin, but after breathing institutional air, it smelled pure and pleasant.

Now she had to find Thomas. *Thomas*. On the steps of the station, she closed her eyes and called his image to mind. She pictured him as he'd been that first night. In her little tent. The firelight from outside casting him in a bronze light. The kindness in his eyes. Him staring into her, seeing her damaged soul and not being repulsed.

Her body turned automatically, and she felt a tugging inside her chest as if her heart were a divining rod pointing the way to him.

Someone grabbed her arm. Adrenaline flashed through her, readying her body for a fight. Her eyes snapped open.

"Don't make a scene," CO Holbrook growled in her ear.

Helena forced herself not to fight or struggle. She

had called him and Mrs. Ellis; she just hadn't thought they'd show up.

He guided her down the sidewalk to an SUV idling at the curb and opened the back passenger door. "Get in."

Mrs. Ellis sat there in the back, looking innocently bundled up for winter—except for the gun she aimed at Helena.

Flashes of memories played on a loop in Helena's mind. Being in that bathroom with her. Her rage. Her pulling the trigger.

Self-preservation told Helena to run. Self-sacrifice told her to stay. This wasn't about her. It was about Thomas. She'd lead Mrs. Ellis to Thomas, under the pretense of leading her to Malone. Everything else, she'd figure out on the way.

She climbed in and shut the door. CO Holbrook got in the driver's side.

Mrs. Ellis looked exactly the same as she had right before she'd shot Helena—ravaged by grief. "Tell me this *truth*"—spit flew from her mouth—"you think I don't know."

Holbrook drove them out of the parking lot.

Helena's body felt off-kilter, almost as if it were tilting to one side. But it was more than her body. It was an urge. She felt drawn, pulled, tugged in a different direction.

"Go that way." Helena pointed to the direction where instinct told her to go. "That's the way."

Holbrook looked in the rearview mirror, awaiting Mrs. Ellis's approval. The woman dipped her chin.

Holbrook followed her instructions. "So where are we going?"

"I don't know." Helena focused on the sensation inside her body, on making sure they were traveling in the right direction. Yes, they were. If someone pressed her to define how she knew it, she'd have no logical answer. It was a feeling more than anything. Almost an expectancy. As though she could sense the distance between her and Thomas diminishing.

"You playing games with us?" Holbrook used the tone that put fear in most of the inmates.

She tried to explain without being completely truthful. "I don't know the address, but I know how to get there."

Mrs. Ellis jabbed the gun at Helena like a bayonet. "Tell me the truth."

"I. Didn't. Kill. Rory." No plainer way to say it.

"The hell you didn't." Mrs. Ellis pressed the barrel between Helena's eyes, the metal cold and unforgiving. Helena didn't flinch away, didn't fight. Part of her realized she should be frightened that the woman would pull the trigger—the best predictor of future behavior was past behavior—but she could find no fear. Only a determination to keep herself alive long enough to find Thomas.

She met Mrs. Ellis's eyes as best she could around the barrel. "Haven't you ever considered that Robert Malone might've been lying? How about now when he's on the run for covering up a murder, child abuse, and corruption? After all that, you've never stopped to consider that I might be innocent?"

"No. Because I *know* it was you." Mrs. Ellis's face twisted up in a snarl of aggression.

"Why? What had I ever done that would make you

think that about me?" Stupid tears pricked in Helena's eyes.

"Because you were always odd. Everyone knew it. You were too polite. Too quiet. You walked through the world differently than other girls your age. You never cared about makeup and hair and clothes."

"And that makes me a murderer?" Helena felt a sob rise in her throat but caught it before it came out. All those feelings of being condemned unfairly came back to her. As an adult, she realized how petty and cruel all the judgment had been. As an eighteen-year-old girl, every bit of it had hurt.

A bit of doubt crept into Mrs. Ellis's eyes, but that's as far as it went. The foundation of her hatred was built on grief and anger. Take away the anger, and her hatred would crumble. But she wouldn't let go easily.

"I'll take you to Malone. He knows the truth." Slowly, Helena reached up and wrapped her hand around the barrel of the gun and pushed it away from her forehead. "Point this gun at him and ask him about Rory."

Chapter 20

WORRY SWALLOWED HOPE, HOURS SWALLOWED MINUTES, and night swallowed day. Helena stared out the car window at the isolated countryside. Inside the SUV, the heat blew a constant stream of warmth, but she couldn't get warm. Not that Holbrook or Mrs. Ellis cared. No one spoke. No one needed to. The tension between them wrote an encyclopedia on contempt.

Holbrook caught her eye in the rearview mirror. "You lying about knowing where Malone is?" He pinned her with a look that was the equivalent of truth serum.

With no hesitation, she shook her head. Her entire plan hinged on convincing them that they were taking her to Malone when they were really taking her to Thomas.

Inside her chest, that strange sensation started again. Her heart shifted on its axis, leaning in the direction it wanted her to travel. "There." She pointed at a narrow lane almost hidden by a thick screen of barren trees.

Holbrook slammed the brakes, the SUV fishtailing on the pavement. "You could've told me sooner." He sounded like the asshole she knew and hated. But one thing she'd discovered over the course of their road trip—the man inexplicably loved Mrs. Ellis. Loved her enough to try to arrange Helena's murder to give Mrs. Ellis peace and closure. The woman had suffered so much and somehow gained a man who cared for her beyond sense and sanity. In a weird way, it kinda endeared him to Helena. Anyone who could love that hard couldn't be all bad.

"Turn off the headlights. You don't want him escaping out the back while we pull in the front." Her tone left him no room for argument. Holbrook complied and slowed to inch up the narrow drive. She sounded so sure of herself, sure that Malone was going to be in there. The only thing she knew for certain was that Thomas was in there. She could feel the strength of his presence pulling her to him like a tractor beam into his force field.

An anonymous silver sedan came into view. Before Holbrook parked the car, Helena cranked at her door handle. Locked. Irrational panic tickled the back of her mind, wanting her to freak out that she was confined in another sort of prison. But now was not the time to let fear take hold. Now was the time to be strong.

"You're sure Malone's in there?" Holbrook didn't hide his skepticism.

"Yes." She made sure to pack her tone with absolute certainty. "He's in there." A necessary lie. A lie to save Thomas's life. Because the only thing that mattered was Thomas. Once she found him, everything else would work itself out. "Please, let me out." She pulled on the door handle again.

Holbrook turned in his seat to look at Mrs. Ellis, waiting for her command. The woman dipped her chin. Holbrook turned off the SUV, got out, and opened Helena's door.

She rocketed out of the car like a runner hearing the starter's pistol, her footsteps gobbling the ground between her and Thomas.

From inside the house, a savage yell of anger and anguish reverberated into the dark. She didn't want to believe that terrible sound came from Thomas, but it did. Relief that he was alive warred with rage over whatever had caused him pain.

Ppgglll.

The crack of gunfire from Mrs. Ellis or Holbrook startled her into a hitched step but did nothing to slow her speed. Only a kill shot would prevent her from getting to Thomas.

Helena rammed full body into the door at the same time as she turned the knob and ran inside. In a flash, she recognized the place from her dream of Evan. But instead of another guy lying strapped to the table, Thomas lay there.

She locked eyes with Thomas, and everything around them ceased, as if God had hit the world's pause button. They stared at each other for an endless moment out of time, communicating in their special way.

I'm here now.

I love you.

Everything will be all right.

I love you.

She cataloged the scene before her. The most unexpected thing, the thing that shocked her beyond his bruised and battered face, was his hair. It had been colored a bizarre shade of blond. Why would Malone color his hair and call him Evan?

And then the reality crashed over her. Malone stood near Thomas's feet, holding—her stomach did a backflip off the high dive of revulsion—a saw. Malone's face was grim and pale, as if disgusted by his own actions.

But a miracle had occurred. Whatever terrible price Malone intended to require of Thomas's flesh hadn't happened yet. She'd arrived in time.

"Nobody move." Holbrook's voice broke the bubble of shock she'd locked herself inside.

Helena ignored Holbrook and rushed to Thomas. He tracked her every movement, unblinking as if afraid she'd disappear.

"I'm here. You're going to be okay." She stroked his damaged cheek, a jolt of lightning passing between them. He gasped, tensed, then relaxed into her touch, his gaze going soft and languid but never leaving hers.

In the periphery of her attention, she heard Mrs. Ellis, Holbrook, and Malone, but nothing they had to say carried any importance.

Her hands shook as she worked on the restraints around Thomas's wrists, releasing one and then the other, then began loosening the one around his chest.

"Are you real?" he asked, his hands skimming over her face, her hair, her body as if he couldn't take all of her in at once.

"I'm real." She half sobbed, half laughed and bent to kiss his mouth. His lips were too cool. Was he going into shock?

"Don't kiss my Evan."

"He's not *your* Evan. He's *my* Thomas." The words flew from her mouth, the weight of them slapping Malone's face. He bellowed and rushed at her, bashing into her like a bull bursting through a gate. She went weightless, then impacted with the wall. Breath whooshed out of her, her limbs jangled. But she was ready. A decade of fighting for her life had trained her for this.

She became a wild thing. Her body twisting and writhing, punching and pulling. Soft tissue—she aimed at his throat, his gut, his balls. If he got in any blows, she didn't feel them, her rage a shield against all pain.

Shouts and crashing noises sounded in the room. Thomas. Was Holbrook or Mrs. Ellis hurting him?

"Stop." Thomas's voice bellowed through the room, freezing Malone midaction. "Let her go. Come to me."

Suddenly, she became aware of Malone's grip around her neck loosening, then leaving her altogether. Everything went silent. Too silent. It was silly, but she realized her eyes were closed. She opened them to see Thomas standing over them, his hand on Malone's shoulder, guiding him away from her like a pied piper. When Malone was out of range, Thomas let go of him, then came back to her.

Mrs. Ellis and Holbrook rushed in between them and Malone.

Thomas fell to his knees in front of her. She crawled to him. And then they were inside each other's arms, clinging to each other. Both of them were breathing heavily, chests rising and falling in perfect cadence. The strength of him around her soothed all the worry. Something warm and sweet flowed from her into him—he absorbed a part of her. He buried his face in her neck and clung to her. They didn't need words. All they needed was each other.

"Did you kill Rory?" Mrs. Ellis screamed, pulling

Helena out of the dazed wonder of being in Thomas's presence. The woman shook her gun at Malone as if that would encourage him to answer.

Malone's face had gone ashen. His lips moved as if trying to answer, but he had eyes only for Thomas. "Evan..." He raised a hand toward Thomas, imploring him, but ignoring Mrs. Ellis.

"Rory. Rory Ellis. Did you kill him?" Mrs. Ellis yelled at Malone.

Thomas lifted his head, stared straight at Malone. "You want me?" A dead quality entered Thomas's tone. "Then tell the truth."

"I thought he might be my Evan." Malone spoke to Thomas in a small voice. "But he wasn't. He wouldn't stop yelling. He threatened to report me. I couldn't let that happen. Not after everything I'd gone through. I killed him."

Helena gasped. Mrs. Ellis gasped. And just like that, the truth was out there. Floating around in reality for all five of them to hear.

Holbrook's face drained of color, and he couldn't stop looking back and forth between Helena and Mrs. Ellis—the realization of all the pain he'd orchestrated written on his features. Helena didn't have time for his guilt or self-condemnation. She needed to save Malone's life.

"Mrs. Ellis." She spoke slow and firm.

The woman didn't look away from Malone.

"Mrs. Ellis, you need to listen to me." She raised her volume a bit. "You didn't believe me when I told you the truth. You tried to have me killed in prison. You made me suffer. None of that took away the pain of

Rory's loss. Killing Robert Malone won't take it away either." She looked at Holbrook, who still stared at her and nodded with her head toward Mrs. Ellis in a get-the-gun-from-her gesture. "But you can make amends. You can let him live so he can exonerate me. So that he can spend the rest of his life in prison for what he did to Rory and to me." She took a deep breath. "I want my life back. I want my innocence back. And you're going to do this one thing for me."

―✺―

Golden rays of hopeful sunshine lit Thomas's hospital room, but all the light in the world couldn't vanquish the shadow on Helena's soul.

Thomas lay in the bed, head turned away as though he couldn't bear to look at her. Yet she couldn't look away from him.

She was worried about him. Not about his health. Despite the terrible bruising, no bones were broken in his face. They were waiting for the doctor to give him one more exam, and then he would be discharged.

No, what she worried about was *him*. The man inside the body. There was a reluctance, a resistance, a *rejection* from him that she'd never experienced before. And it scared her more than all the Sisters in the world.

She sat in a chair pulled as close to the bed as it could get. For the hundredth time, she reached out to him, settling her hand atop his. An instant jolt of warmth and comfort arced between them.

"Don't," Thomas whispered. His tone wasn't angry or outraged, but resigned and sad. So sad, her heart wept giant, bloody tears for the private pain he endured. He shoved his hand under the covers so she couldn't touch him anymore.

She closed her eyes and let her head fall forward on her neck. There was a storm raging inside him, and she didn't know what to do other than simply stay by his side. It was selfish of her to let his rejection hurt her. He was holding himself together in the only way he knew how. She recognized that much. She'd lived a decade in that space.

A knock sounded on the door. She turned in her seat to see a dark-haired beauty and a big, scary dude with his arm possessively wrapped around her. The woman had the same black hair that Thomas had before Malone had colored it, and those same midnight-blue eyes. This had to be his sister. Evanee.

Helena got to her feet. How would they react to her? Thomas said his sister was excited to meet her, but that might've been just words. She braced for the couple's fear and suspicion.

Evanee rushed out of her husband's arms. "What the hell did that asshole do to your hair?" she gasped as she bent down and embraced her brother. Thomas didn't react, just lay there, enduring the contact.

Helena glanced at Evanee's husband. The man nodded to her with what she thought was meant to be a friendly gesture, but it kinda missed the mark because of his intimidating appearance. He was tall and broad, and that tattoo on his cheek made him downright frightening. He moved in next to his wife, wrapping his arm around her waist and tucking her in to his side. She snuggled against him.

This was Thomas's family. She was the intruder

in this reunion. Leaving him alone went against the grain, but Helena didn't want to force herself on these people who might want a private word. "I...I'll...I'll step out for a while so you all can talk." She backed toward the doorway.

"No," Evanee's husband said, his voice a bit louder than it should have been, freezing Helena in place.

"No, you won't." Evanee motioned to the chair Helena had been sitting in next to Thomas's bed. "You'll stay right here with him where you belong." Her words might've been bossy, but her tone was friendly. "You're family now."

A pleasant warmth stole over Helena's face. *Family.* She hadn't had a family since she'd gone to prison.

Helena looked at Thomas to see if he felt the same as his sister, but he wouldn't meet her gaze. He was avoiding eye contact with all of them.

The wild smile on Evanee's face faded, her brow wrinkled, and her mouth turned down on one side. She could see there was something wrong with her brother too. She placed her hand on his shoulder. He flinched at the touch. "I know. I...know..." Savage understanding dominated her tone. "It will get better, I promise."

Evanee aimed an uninterpretable look at Helena. It wasn't quite blame but was riding close to that ridge. She reached up and touched the tattoo on her husband's face. "I'm going to take Helena out in the hallway for a chat. I'll stay where you can see me."

Her husband's eyes absorbed every word, as though he saw them rather than heard them. "Okay." There was hesitation in his voice. Not the kind that came from an abusive, controlling asshole, but the kind that came from anxiety and fear. What had these two been through that they were afraid to be apart?

Evanee headed for the doorway and grabbed Helena's hand and tugged her out into the hallway but was careful to look in and see her husband standing, arms crossed, watching them. Helena stood where she could see Thomas lying in bed.

She fortified herself for the onslaught of anger Evanee was going to fire at her. "I'll stay out here until you leave if you want, but I'm not leaving him. And just so you know the truth, I'm innocent. I never killed Rory Ellis. Malone confessed…sort of. I would never hurt Thomas. I only want to be near him and help him." She ran out of words and steam at the same time.

Evanee threw herself at Helena. Suddenly, she was locked in a bear hug. *What? Why?* She stood there, not sure how to react. Maybe she should embrace the woman back.

Evanee pulled away and stared into Helena's eyes. "Thank you. Thank you. Thank you. For finding him. We didn't know any of this was going on, or we would've been there to help you."

Of all the things Helena thought might've been said, this hadn't even been on the radar. How was she supposed to respond? *You're welcome* sounded stupid.

Evanee placed her hand on Helena's arm. "How much do you know about how this thing between us works?"

"I… Um… Us? I just met you. I'm not sure what you mean."

"By us, I meant Xander and Isleen, me and Lathan, and you and him." She must've seen a total blankness on Helena's face. "The connection." Her tone almost carried a *duh* quality. "Dr. Stone was supposed to tell you about it." Before Helena could find a response, Evanee was talking again. "You know you can heal him, right? Body and mind." Urgency born of concern dominated her tone.

Helena's head bobbled sideways. "What..." She couldn't figure out what to say beyond that one word.

"You have bad dreams, right?" Evanee spoke so fast, Helena had a hard time interpreting the words.

"How do you know about that?"

The corner of Evanee's mouth lifted. "Isleen and I have terrible dreams. Your nightmares started the night you met him, right?"

Helena nodded slowly. How did Evanee know all these things?

Evanee stared into the hospital room at her husband, naked love shining on her face, making her radiant. "The moment you met him, you knew something was different, right?"

Helena's mind flashed to the cemetery, to the instantaneous connection she'd felt. "Yeah. How—"

"And you found him at that cabin. Like needle-in-the-haystack found him." The weight of Evanee's implication landed on her.

What she had done *was* impossible. There was no rational explanation for how she'd known Thomas's exact location. "Yeah."

"I could spend hours telling you how all this stuff between the couples works, but I found it easier to understand when Dr. Stone told me the story of Fearless and Bear—"

"The old totem alongside the road? I know the story.

My grandpa used to tell it to me. What does the story of Fearless and Bear have to do with anything?"

A gleeful surprise lit Evanee's eyes. "Then here's the crib notes version: You're Fearless, and he's Bear. You can heal him. All of him. And look at him. He's suffering in a prison of his mind's creation. I know the feeling. I've been there…locked in a place where I didn't think I deserved to be healed or helped."

"Me too." Helena's voice sounded small but carried a decade's burden.

"Oh, sweetie." Evanee drew her into a tight hug. "I know you have. We all have. It's why we have these abilities. 'Sacred are the wounded, for they shall balance the earth.'" She drew back and stared into Helena's eyes. "You go in there, and you touch him. Touch is healing. Just like with Fearless and Bear, if you're touching, nothing can harm you."

A sudden thought occurred to Helena. "Is that why your husband doesn't like to let you out of his arms and out of his sight?"

"That's exactly the reason. We're only truly safe when touching." She motioned for her husband to join her. She didn't speak until she was safety ensconced next to him. "Now go in there and heal my brother. He needs you. We'll stop by the house tomorrow and explain everything."

Helena watched them walk down the hallway, arms around each other, the love they carried for each other a tangible thing. Visitors and nurses and doctors all turned and watched them pass, a look of longing on all their faces. To be loved—to be really loved—was a rare thing.

She went back into the room. Thomas lay in the same position he had been in, looking anywhere but at her.

She sat on the edge of the bed and stared at his bruised face. Beneath all the damage, she saw the beautiful man she loved. *Loved. Yes.* She loved this man more than she'd ever thought possible. She'd known the love of her grandparents; she'd known the love of a boy. But she'd never known that love could feel this scary and soothing at the same time.

"Please…please look at me."

His jaw clenched, a muscle twitched in his cheek, but he wouldn't look at her. She had no choice. She was going to use his words against him. "You have nothing to be ashamed of. Nothing. The scars on your body are evidence of Malone's shame, not yours. They don't define you unless you let them. They don't own you unless you let them. They can't change you unless you let them. This self-condemnation you've got, this fear you have… You're letting him win. You're letting him have control over you, and he isn't even here."

Slowly, his gaze shifted. Their eyes locked, and she tumbled into him, into his mind, into his soul. Saw the doubt inside him. Not doubt in her, but doubt about himself. Doubt that he deserved her. That he was worthy of her. He blamed himself for all her pain, his own pain, and even his sister's pain. She witnessed his thoughts. Witnessed how he believed he should've killed Malone as a child, and then none of this would've happened. And worse, how he'd left her alone in the truck, and if he'd never done that—if he'd listened to his soul—none of this would've happened.

Tears of guilt and shame and regret welled in his eyes.

One lonely tear slipped down his cheek. She pressed a kiss to it, tasting the salt on her tongue before putting her mouth to his. She spoke against his lips, breathing her words into him. "I regret nothing. All of it led me to you."

She crawled into bed with him, slipping her arm under his head and holding him to her.

A pleasant warmth radiated from her center outward to all the places they touched. He kept very still but then latched onto her, squeezing her tighter and tighter and tighter until it was impossible to tell where she ended and he began.

His breath came in ragged bursts, and she felt wetness against her skin from his tears as he began talking of the horrors done to him. She wept with him, but these were good tears. Healing tears. He'd taught her that. And now he was learning the lesson.

Chapter 21

THE COUNTY JAIL'S WAITING ROOM WAS EMPTY, THE SPACE bizarrely quiet. Almost as though the entire building held its breath. Or maybe just Thomas was holding his breath. He forced himself to suck in some air and then exhale.

Helen sat beside him, her body as tense as his, but for different reasons. She stood and walked to the waiting-room doorway, peered out into the hallway, then came back, stopping in front of him.

There was no hiding how he felt about being here — not from her anyway. He wasn't frightened or scared of what he was about to do. More like wary, vigilant, and on guard. The peace he'd found with Helen over the past few weeks was a balm to all the old and new pain.

A worry line pinched between Helen's brows. "You don't have to do this."

Thomas stood, staring her in the eye so she could see the determination inside him. He slid his hand partly into the hair at her temple and used his thumb to massage the worry wrinkle away. Touching her soothed him, just as it eased her. "I *want* to do this. For me. For you. For my sister. For the families of the men Malone murdered." That last word hung in the air. Malone had killed three people — Rory Ellis and the two men he'd used as bait to get Thomas out to those crime scenes.

The whole Malone mess could go to trial, but that

would mean months and months of dragging out all the past pain. A trial would keep the wounds fresh and bleeding, when they all just wanted to heal and move on. Even the prosecutor wanted it over ASAP, just to end the media circus surrounding the case. The best way to package it up and put it away fast? Get Malone to confess and plead guilty.

"Malone will listen to..." He'd been about to say *me* but caught himself. "He'll listen to Evan."

When he'd first gotten home from the hospital, he'd intended to shave his head to get rid of all that hair that made him look so damn much like his father. The hair that shoved Malone over the line from seeing him as Tommy, his stepson, to seeing him as Evan, his lover. Just as he'd been about to buzz it all off, a thought had occurred him. Why not use this hair against Malone?

From the doorway, Kent cleared his throat. "Malone is ready now."

Thomas and Helen turned to face the guy. A uniformed officer stood waiting next to Kent. Both men's shadows were thick and white, displaying the innate goodness each possessed.

Thomas stared into Helen's golden eyes and tried to reassure her. "I'll be fine. And you'll be right here when I'm done. So no matter what, I'll still be fine." He was trying to make a joke about them being able to heal each other, but it fell flat.

She didn't say anything further but grabbed his hand in hers and pressed it over her heart. Underneath his palm, the strong, steady beat entered him and fortified him for what was about to come.

When he was ready, he gave her a peck on the lips,

then walked toward the doorway. "Don't leave her, Kent. Not for a minute. Not for a second. You understand me?" His voice contained a little too much force to sound like a question.

Kent's expression was serious. "I'm not going anywhere."

Thomas wasn't sure how much Kent knew about the connection between him and Helen, but the guy seemed to understand the importance of keeping Helen safe. Maybe it was because Kent had seen her that day in the bathroom with a hole in her chest, gushing blood, and had recognized the miracle that had occurred.

Thomas turned his attention to the uniformed officer.

"You know the rules, right?" the officer asked.

"Yeah." No way in hell was he about to violate any of them.

The officer led him down a hallway, then stopped outside a door to unlock, then open it.

Thomas braced his shoulders, held his head high, and walked into the room.

Malone's shadow of death seemed less threatening today, less dark. Hell, almost subdued. The man sat at a small table. In all Thomas's life, he'd never known Malone to be anything but freshly showered and shaven. Now, scruff fuzzed Malone's cheeks and chin. And he smelled...like he'd gone a few days without the benefit of a shower.

It was weird, but this guy didn't seem like Malone. He seemed pathetic and small and harmless. Especially the way his leg shackles locked him to a large ring in the floor and his hands were lashed to the belt around his waist.

Apathy dulled Malone's features, but everything changed when he saw Thomas. A smile lit his face. A real smile. The kind that Malone never aimed at Thomas or his mom or his sister, the kind reserved only for Evan.

If Thomas didn't know better, he might've been swayed by the affection on Malone's face. It was obvious that Malone had loved Thomas's father and the loss of his love had deeply cracked his psyche. In an odd way, Thomas almost understood. If something happened to Helen, his rage and wrath would be nearly uncontrollable. But he could never hurt a child.

A calm settled over Thomas. He pulled out a chair and sat across from Malone.

"Evan..." Malone breathed the name like a prayer.

The one funny thing about this whole situation was that despite Malone believing Thomas with colored hair was Evan, the guy was still mentally competent to stand trial. Competency rested on the ability of the defendant to recognize the difference between right and wrong. And Malone clearly recognized the difference—he just thought all his actions were justified because they were a means to an end.

"Oh, Evan. I've missed you. I wasn't sure if they'd let me see you."

Thomas had spent the past few days rehearsing what he'd say to Malone, but here in front of the man, all Thomas's prepared words vanished. Or maybe they boiled down to one essential thing. "I need you"—he paused for effect—"to do me a favor."

Excitement and anticipation lit Malone's eyes. "Anything for you. For my love."

Bile rose in Thomas's throat, but he forced himself to

look Malone in the eye. "I want you to confess. Confess all of it. Tell everyone how much you loved me and what you did in the name of love."

Malone reached out to Thomas but only got a few inches with his hands cuffed to his waist. "I will. I will for you." Naked love shone in Malone's eyes. And suddenly, Thomas felt like a shithead for using that love against Malone.

Malone didn't deserve any kindness, but Thomas settled his hands over Malone's cuffed ones for a few moments.

That was the difference between the two of them. Thomas could forgive. But Malone couldn't forget.

Thomas stood and walked to the door, where he paused and looked back. "Thank you. Thank you for this one gift."

—⁓—

The courtroom was packed with spectators and media, but for Thomas, only two people existed. Malone and Helen. Evanee and Lathan had refused to attend. Thomas understood. They'd already found their peace. They didn't need this. But he and Helen did—their futures rode on this.

They sat in the back row, directly behind Malone to make it nearly impossible for the man to spot them. Not that it would've mattered. Thomas had buzzed all the blond hair off after his meeting with Malone. His black hair had already grown out an inch. Now, Malone would likely just see him as Tommy. The boy he'd abused.

Helen tucked herself in to his side, while his arm rested across her shoulders. Her nearness soothed and strengthened. Without her, he wasn't sure he'd be able to tolerate hearing his childhood of abuse spoken about so publicly.

In the front of the room, Malone stood and cleared his throat.

Thomas held his breath.

And then Malone started talking. He confessed his part in covering up the murder of Thomas's father. He admitted the depth and breadth of his love for Evan Brown and his plan to punish Thomas's mother by hurting her children. He admitted all the foul things he'd done to them.

Thomas's face stung while he listened to his personal pain being put to words. Helen grabbed hold of his free hand and squeezed, the simple act comforting all the wild emotions flaring to life inside him.

And then Malone spoke about Rory Ellis's murder. Helen's body went on alert. He pulled her in tighter to him and pressed his lips to the top of her head. Across the room, Elaine Ellis sobbed quietly while Holbrook tried to comfort her.

Elaine Ellis turned in her seat, her gaze searching the space and lighting on Helen. Thomas was ready to launch out of his seat and give the woman a beatdown right here in front of everyone, but then the woman covered her heart with her hand and mouthed to Helen, *I'm sorry. Forgive me.*

Helen dipped her chin once in acknowledgment, then turned away and buried her face against Thomas's chest. She didn't sob, but he felt the wetness of her tears through his shirt. And these weren't all tears of sadness or pain. They were ones of relief. Malone had just publicly exonerated her.

The man had destroyed so many lives because of love and hate. People always thought hate was the opposite of love, but it wasn't. Hate was the angry, ugly side of love.

When Thomas and Helen walked out of this courtroom, they would not hate Malone. No, the man would mean nothing to either of them. He'd be nothing more than a footnote in the great adventure that was going to be their lives.

Epilogue

Christmas Eve

"WAIT, WAIT, WAIT—WE HAVE TO LOOK AT IT WITH THE lights off." Helen rushed over to the overhead light. "Close your eyes."

Thomas obeyed. Through his eyelids, bright color shone, then went dim. "Can I open them now?"

Helen slid in next to him and wrapped her arm around his waist and leaned her head against his shoulder. "Okay. Open them."

In the darkened room, the twinkling golden lights from their Christmas tree glowed warm and magical. They'd spent the past hour decorating the tree with ornaments from her childhood—many of them ones that she'd made as a girl. Thomas loved those the best. Maybe it made him sound sappy, but he couldn't wait until they had a little girl of their own to make ornaments for the Christmas tree.

He'd surprised Helen with the Christmas decorations. Back when he'd moved into the house, it had felt wrong to throw away all the things that seemed to matter to the people who'd lived there. Instead, he'd packed everything up and stored it in the basement. Now he realized an unconscious part of him had been preserving Helen's legacy.

A contented sigh slipped from her. "It's lovely, isn't it?"

He pulled her in tight and kissed the top of her head, inhaling the flowery scent of her shampoo. "It is," he breathed, his voice containing an awe that he'd never expected to feel. And yet standing here in their living room, he marveled at all the beauty in his world. It all stemmed from her. Not only did she bring grace to his life, but she also brought meaning, and most importantly, she brought love. And love changed everything.

Bing bong bung. The doorbell chimed a descending tone that sounded like the prelude to the apocalypse.

Helen giggled and looked up at him. "It's like doomsday every time someone comes to the door. It means so much to me that you didn't change anything in the house, but we *need* a new doorbell."

"I couldn't agree more." He gave her a quick peck on the lips, grabbed her hand, and headed toward the foyer. Along the way, he flicked on the lights.

Through the foyer windows, he saw Pastor Audie and his niece on the front porch. Both were bundled up against the cold. Pastor Audie wore that same red knit winter cap with the jaunty yarn ball on the top and matching scarf wrapped around his neck. It really was like looking at Gandalf wearing modern winter gear.

Thomas's mind flashed back to the day that seemed a lifetime ago when he'd last seen Audie—the day of his mother's memorial service. Looking back at himself, Thomas didn't recognize the man he'd been. He'd been so angry, suffering in his own mind from the disease of the past. He was a different man now. He had Helen in his life.

"It's Pastor Audie and Charity." Helen raced to the front door, unlocking it while she looked at Thomas.

"He used to stop by every Christmas Eve on his way to candlelight services. My grandparents were good friends with him. I should've expected him." She threw the door open. "Pastor Audie." She rushed into the old man's arms. "You came. I've missed you."

The old man's face brightened with happiness that eliminated half a century of wrinkles.

"Oh, Helena. I've missed you too." He hugged her back, tears brimming in his eyes. "Your grandparents would be overjoyed to know you're home and you're happy." Pastor Audie held on to her shoulders and looked her over. "They missed you desperately and never gave up on you. Even when you gave up on yourself."

Tears filled Helen's eyes, but she nodded and swallowed. Thomas was next to her in an instant, wrapping his arm around her, wishing he could absorb all the pain of her past but recognizing these moments were healing for her.

"Come on in." He motioned the pair into the foyer.

Audie gestured toward his niece. "Have you met Charity? She's my niece and my chauffeur at night."

Helen aimed her attention at Charity. "We met…" Her voice trailed off, then she moved forward and hugged the other woman. "I'm so sorry. Last time I saw you, I wasn't myself."

Charity laughed and hugged her back. "Girl, it's all good. Everything always works out exactly how it's supposed to." When Helen stepped back, Charity shoved a wrapped package at Helen and one at Thomas. "I made these for you. My only request is that you open them right now so I can make sure they fit."

Thomas and Helen tore into the gifts at the same

time. He found a dark-blue hat and scarf that looked exactly like Audie's.

Helen held a sweet pink scarf and hat. She stared at them a long time as if lost in thought, then shoved the hat down on her head and wrapped the scarf around her neck. "It's like the one you have… Exactly what I wanted." She hugged Charity again as if they were long-lost friends. "Thank you so much."

Thomas put his hat on too and wrapped the scarf around his neck. It was warm and fit perfectly. "It's awesome. Thanks so much. Come on in." He gestured toward the living room. "I'll get you a mug of Helen's spiced cider."

Audie's eyes widened, then a warm smile spread across his lips. "Your grandmother's special spiced cider?"

"Yes! Grandma's recipe. When Thomas moved in, he saved all the picture albums, all the Christmas decorations, and all Grandma's recipe books." Helen gazed at him with a look of wonder laced with love. "Can you believe he did that?"

Audie met his eyes. "He sure is special." Then he groaned. "We can't stay. We're on our way to candle-light services, but it would be worth being late for a cup of your grandma's spiced cider." He turned to Charity. "Seriously. This stuff will rock your world."

They all laughed at the old man's choice of words.

"How about I put it in a travel mug for you so you aren't late?" Thomas offered.

"Wonderful." The old man clasped his hands together like an excited child.

Thomas understood. The spiced cider was on the same level as nectar of the gods. He gave Helen a squeeze, then headed into the kitchen still wearing his hat and scarf. Normal things like this were a part of his life now, and it felt so damn good.

He filled two travel mugs and returned to the foyer, handing one to Audie and one to Charity. Audie flipped up the lid and took a sip. He closed his eyes and was silent for a moment. "Don't mind me. I'm just saying a prayer of thanks that I got to taste this again. I have so many good memories attached to this cider."

Charity took a sip. "Oh my... This is amazing." She tried it again. "Would you be willing to share the recipe?"

"Of course. Grandma always said good recipes were meant to be shared. Give me your cell number, and I'll text it to you. It's really simple, just takes a while for all the spices to infuse."

After Charity and Helen exchanged information, Audie took another sip and eyed Helen. "I'm so happy everything has finally worked out for you."

It was such an innocuous statement, but underneath was so much more. Malone had confessed to *all* his crimes. The newspapers had done a good job of covering the case so everyone already knew she was innocent. It was only a matter of time before she was officially exonerated.

"Me too." Helen twined her fingers with Thomas's and squeezed gently. "Things worked out better than I ever dared to dream."

Audie groaned. "Okay, you two, we've got to go. It won't look good if I'm too late."

Helen stepped forward and hugged the old man, then hugged Charity.

"Thanks for stopping by." Thomas reached out to

shake the old man's hand. "You're both welcome to stop by any time." He found himself hugging the guy instead.

"I'm glad you've found happiness." Audie patted him on the shoulder in a fatherly gesture of affection that warmed Thomas from the inside out.

Wearing their new caps and scarves, they followed Audie and Charity out into the cold night air. They waved as the pair honked and drove off toward town.

Outside, the world was still and quiet, the only sound the distant hum of Charity's car, and soon, even that evaporated. The moon was nearly full, and the sky glittered with stars. "Even when I couldn't see color, I always thought moonlight on snow was pretty, but now it's magnificent."

Helen snuggled in to his side. "The night sky reminds me of your eyes."

They both stared upward. A flash of color streaked across the heavens and then disappeared so quickly that Thomas wasn't sure what he'd seen.

"A shooting star." Helen turned in his arms and stared into his eyes. "Make a wish."

He looked into her and saw the amazing life they were about to lead. "All my dreams have already come true."

Keep reading for an excerpt from the first book in
Abbie Roads's Fatal Truth series

SAVING
MERCY

Chapter 1

It's a sad testament to the state of humanity that we elevate serial killers to the level of mega-celebrity.
—Ellsworth Garyington, MD, *Journal of Human and Philosophical Studies*

THE AIR REEKED OF DIRTY PENNIES AND DEATH. THE BODIES had been removed days ago, but Cain Killion could still *feel* the desperate energy of the dying and almost—*almost*—hear the echoes of their screams imprinted on the bones of the house. He abhorred the sight of blood, and yet here he was, standing in another murder house in front of another wall smeared, splattered, and sprayed with gore.

His heart banged against the cage of his ribs, trying to bust out and make a break for it. A bead of sweat slid in agonizing slowness down the center of his spine.

"You don't look so good." MacNeil Anderson stepped into Cain's line of sight, diverting his attention from the blood. The furrows around Mac's eyes cut deeper than normal, and three days' worth of old-man stubble fuzzed his cheeks, giving him a haggard and homeless appearance. Not exactly the look the FBI was going for when they promoted Mac to *senior* special agent.

Cain almost smiled at his own thoughts, but laughter no longer existed in this place. Only horror could thrive here now.

"Do I ever look good when I'm about to...?" Yeah. There wasn't a name for what he did. To the bureaucrats with their thumbs jammed up their asses, Mac called it profiling—had to call it something. But it wasn't profiling. Not at all. What Cain had to do with the blood was something worse than profiling. So much worse.

"This is different." Mac reached up and put his dry palm on Cain's forehead. "You sick? Have a fever?"

Cain might be thirty years old and had lived on his own since he was eighteen, but Mac had never outgrown the role of his adopted dad.

"You can always walk away." Mac made this offer at every kill scene.

And every time, Cain's legs twitched with the urge to run. Only determination, masochism, and the promise of sick satisfaction kept him locked in place. "I'm staying. I always stay."

"I'd stop calling you out for these cases, but I know you'd just find someone else who would." Mac's words were slow and glossed with sadness.

"No one else has the history I have. No one else can do what I do. No one else can give you the information I can." Yeah. His *profiles* were more accurate, more detailed than anything a traditional profiler could come up with. In the majority of cases, his work guided law enforcement directly to their perpetrator. "It'd be stupid not to call me." Not to mention he *needed* to be around that dynamic duo—blood and death. They stripped away his mask of normalcy, leaving him naked to the one truth about himself he could never forget.

He was Killer Killion's Kid—*Triple K*, the media called him. The spawn of a killer with the genetic predisposition to be a murdering machine. One of the only ways Cain had found to curb the ugly urges was to force himself to attend these murder scenes. Force himself to witness the destruction.

His deepest, darkest, dirtiest secret—the thing he would never utter out loud because it terrified him: sometimes he enjoyed himself.

"Son, you don't have anything to prove. Not to me." Mac used a caring tone, but that word—*son*—threatened to transport Cain back to his childhood. Back to his biological father using that word like a curse.

Not going there.

Cain stepped around Mac and moved to look out the window. The Victorian home sat on a miniature peninsula of land that jutted out into a large pond. Such an odd place for a house. A beautiful place—breathtaking and yet eerie in its loneliness and total isolation. Just the kind of place Cain loved.

Had location been a consideration for the killer? Had he finished with his bloody work, then stood in this very spot staring out the window at the water?

Cain sucked in a breath, held it for as long as his lungs would allow, then blew it out slowly. "I know I don't have anything to prove to you. I do this for me." He tried to make his tone firm, but it came out a little shaky. Mac the-FBI-guy would hear it, but Mac his-adopted-dad wouldn't press. Time for a change of subject. "You notice anything odd about this place?"

"It's not the typical." Mac's words were spoken on a sigh. "Not that there is a typical. This just isn't like any other location I've been called to investigate."

"Yeah. Victorian house. In the woods. On a pond. I get why our guy would like the isolation of this place. But there's something more. It has to do with…" He had trouble finding the words to describe the gut-level truth inside him. "…all of it. The house. The woods. The pond. The family. It's like this guy wanted the complete package."

Mac nodded, his expression serious as a gravedigger. "You get that from the blood?"

"Just a feeling I have." It was the kind of place he'd choose if he were going to plan a murder. Kind of like how salt and sweet tasted so good together, this was violence and peace in one location.

Enough stalling. Cain turned away from the window and faced the room.

Three walls were covered in Victorian-era wallpaper—rich gold background, red blossoms on a vine, and fancy peacocks. *Ostentatious* was the word that came to mind. One wall—the longest, largest wall—had been painted the same color as the paper's background. Yeah. Four walls of peacocks and posies might've caused bleeding eyeballs.

Finally, Cain forced himself to look at the blood on the wall. Rosettes of red seeped into the wallpaper, the fat watercolor splotches almost blending in with the flowers.

Mac cleared his throat as if gearing up for a formal speech. "The techs released the scene this morning. They worked 'round the clock to get everything cataloged and bagged so we could get you on this ASAP. The blood is, of course, clean. I wouldn't have called you in otherwise." He pointed to the three distinct blood pools. "The family—Dad, Mom, girl—was found here. Killed here too. Forensics places their time of death at—"

"Mac." Cain spoke the name loud enough to smother whatever the guy had been about to say. "Quiet." He needed the absence of sound to *see* what happened. And he needed to do it now before he pussied out.

Mac clamped his lips closed, nodded, and moved across the room—out of the way.

Just fucking get it over with.

Cain knelt at the altar of blood. The sweet scent of rotting biological material was an abomination to his nose, and yet foul anticipation crawled underneath his skin. His mind slid sideways like it always did around the red stuff. Back to his childhood. Back to a time when he was very much his father's son. Back to when blood covered his skin—the slick, silky warmness of it so wrong and yet so horribly soothing at the same time.

He slapped his hands down into the congealed sludge. The coldness sent pleasant shock waves up his arms. He didn't want to feel pleasure, didn't want to enjoy this, but that *other* part of him had terrible intentions. Helpless to stop himself, he smeared his hands around in the red like a kid playing with finger paints. Only when his fingers and palms were coated with the family's blood did he raise them to his face.

A minuscule part of him rebelled against what he was about to do, but the rebellion was quashed before it began. He spread the blood over his forehead, his cheeks, coating his skin in the thick, sweet goo. He

painted his neck, his bare arms, then lifted his T-shirt
and wiped his hands on his chest.

His head fell back on his shoulders. His breath came
in shallow, hyperventilating gulps. From a distance, he
heard himself moan—only it wasn't a moan; it was more
like the yowling of a feral cat fighting for its life. Or
getting ready to mate.

Blood did that to him, was a pleasure and a pain. A
gift and a curse.

He had a complicated relationship with blood. He
hated it. He loved it. Blood was a conduit, a link, a connection between him and those who slayed souls. Blood
opened a doorway, allowing him to step into the minds
and bodies of those who found bliss in ending life. He
became the killer. He saw what the killer saw. Did what
the killer did. Felt what the killer felt.

An incandescent light flashed behind his eyelids.
Cain was gone. He was now the killer.

He stood on a ladder, rolling simple white primer
on the wall.

A song had been locked inside his head for months,
and only now was it time to give voice to the words.

> Lift your feet when you
> Dance around the old well,
> Be careful or you'll tumble pell-mell.
> Look into the dark, dark, waters
> For the blood of your fathers.
>
> Show some courage, young man,
> Find your calling, young man.

He loved the song. He hated the song. But that was life, wasn't it? It was all one big paradox.

A breathy sound intruded. He turned on the ladder to see the ones on the floor.

They were laid out in a neat row in the middle of the room. Each of them on their stomachs, hands bound behind their backs and tied to the shackles on their feet, mouths obliterated by duct tape. The male's wrists were hamburger, dripping blood from fighting against the metal cuffs. But none of them struggled now.

Their faces were wet from tears, or maybe sweat—didn't really matter—and splotchy red and pale. The child grunted.

"Do you want to sing along?" He used a soft tone, the same as he would if he were cajoling a whipped dog. "I will let you, but you must sing it properly. No mistakes."

More tears slicked the girl's face and dripped on the drop cloth underneath her. A bubble of snot blew from her nostril and hovered there waiting to pop. She shrank from him. The female seal-humped herself up and over the girl as if to hide the child beneath her body.

Oh well. He wouldn't allow them to destroy the pure freedom of this moment. He turned back to his task, losing himself in his song once more.

> *Save pomegranate seeds*
> *as payment for the ferryman,*
> *Offer red, red wine*
> *as payment to the bar man.*
> *Carve some red, red meat*
> *as food for the hungry man.*

Show some courage, young man,
Find your calling, young man.

And then the wall was done, the completion of it sneaking up on him like a surprise party. He stepped off the ladder, moved it to the side to have an unobstructed view, and then unzipped his painter's coveralls and let them slide down his body.

The cool air whispered over his naked flesh like an endearment, the sensation wonderful after the confines of the material. His head fell back on his shoulders, and he stood there absorbing and savoring. Everything from this moment to his finish would be carefully recorded in his memory. No matter what happened, no one could erase his memories. They were his alone—safe and untouchable—to be lovingly replayed until his death.

The female sobbed, deep throaty sounds similar to gagging. He faced the ones on the floor and used a gentle voice. "I do understand this is distressing for you, but I"—he dropped his tone a couple of octaves to show his seriousness—"Need. Complete. Silence." He took his time, meeting and holding each one of their gazes before he continued. "I need to rest now."

Only when they all quieted did he sit on the couch he had moved to face the wall. The material he'd spread over the cushions—couldn't risk leaving DNA when he left—scratched against his ass and testicles, but that couldn't be helped. He lay back and stretched out, waiting for his body to relax.

The blank canvas before him was a beautiful thing. All the potential in the world was right here. A picture waiting to be born.

He emptied his mind of all thoughts and feelings and stared at the wall. He stared, unblinking, until his vision yellowed and then darkened into something that looked akin to an X-ray. He stared until tears watered his cheeks and his eyes burned like hot coals in their sockets. Only then did he catch a flash of what needed to be created—all he needed was a glimpse.

Wings. He saw wings.

He was about to create a masterpiece in blood.

A sense of timelessness came over him as he killed and painted. Painted and killed. He lost himself in his work. Not thinking about anything, just letting his hands wield the brushes, mindless of the image he produced. When the blood in his paint container was nearly gone and an image had been born upon the wall, he came back to himself.

He stepped away from the wall, taking more and more of it in with each footstep until he stood on the other side of the room, taking in the full magnitude.

The color contrast of blood on white was as breathtaking and beautiful as a flock of cardinals against the brilliance of snow. Tears burned his eyes. His face stung, and a wild freedom he'd hadn't experienced in years surged through him. He recognized the feeling. In this moment he was God. The author of destruction. And creation.

The image he'd painted was so... No words existed to convey the gloriousness. Words were small and meaningless compared to this wall.

On the wall—a man knelt, head bowed, hair falling forward, shielding his face from view. Even in that supplicant's position, supremacy and authority radiated from him. He looked like the strongest of warriors after a great battle—exhausted, but not weak. No, never weak. There wasn't an ounce of vulnerability in his sinew, muscle, and bone. Nor was there any delicacy to the lacework of scars marring the skin of his arms. And on his chest, directly over his heart, were two crisscrossed slashes that dripped blood down his torso.

Surrounding him was a magnificent pair of wings. Not the kind you'd see on a sparrow or even on a chubby cupid, but the kind of wings that conveyed power and strength and utter indestructibility.

He loved the picture as he loved himself.

An incandescent flash and Cain returned to reality, to the stench of decomposing blood smeared over his face.

His brain recategorized everything that he'd just seen and done into the it-wasn't-really-me file. But that didn't take the *feelings* away. The awe spreading through his chest at what he'd seen. The guilt sinking into his gut because he'd had no remorse.

A dull thumping started behind his eyes. Usually when he did his blood work, he was there for only a few seconds before skipping on to the next images and the next. Those flashes gave him a migraine every time, but seeing entire scenes like this... The migraine was gonna be a badass bitch today. He had maybe ten minutes before the pain ratcheted up to the level of ax-buried-in-his-brain.

Mac handed him a black towel—black disguised the blood better than any other color.

"You back?" Mac knelt next to him, his face full of concern, but Cain could see the concealed disgust in the way Mac's mouth turned down at the corners, like he was fighting an outright grimace.

That look—especially when it was aimed at him—always took him back to the moment Mac had found him. Cain had been covered in snot and blood and shame. He had to give it to Mac. The guy had tried to hide his horror, tried to pretend Cain was just a kid, when he'd never been a kid. He'd been more monster than anything else.

Cain scrubbed the material over his face, his arms, wiped his hands. The blood on his body—so thick and dry it smeared *into* his skin—would only come off after a good scouring down in a scalding shower.

He turned his attention to the image on the wall. But...there was no image. Instead, the wall had been painted gold, perfectly coordinated with the rest of the room. Mac must've called him back from his vision before the killer covered up his work with the paint.

Holy.

Fucking.

Christ.

Cain's legs wobbled when he stood. His hand shook like an alcoholic in need of his jolly juice, but he pointed at the wall. "He painted a picture." His brain bashed against the backs of his eyeballs. He wanted to press his hands to his eyes to keep them from exploding out of their sockets, but his hands were smeared with the family's blood. The pain was only beginning.

"I-I don't know what you mean." Mac's tone was full of question.

"He painted the wall white—made a blank canvas. Then he used the family's blood to create a portrait of some guy..." Cain closed his eyes, seeing on the back of his lids the scars lined up and down the man's arms, the slashes over his heart, just like the ones on his—

"Fuck!" His lids popped open. His gaze automatically sought the wall, hoping to see the actual image again, but gold paint pulsed in his vision from the thumping inside his head. He held his arms out in front of him. Underneath the thin coating of blood on his skin, a network of white slashes ran from his wrists to his shoulders.

The wounds had healed decades ago, but the scars still remained. He pulled his shirt up high and looked down at his chest stained with drying blood. A thick, white crisscrossed scar rested over his heart—cut into his flesh by his father. Every scar on his body, placed there by the man.

"What is it?" Mac's tone was full of question, mixed with a bit of suspicion. "You've got to talk to me. I don't know what's going on."

Cain's heart galloped up and down his rib cage, but he forced himself to speak slowly and quietly—in deference to the ax beating against his skull. He told Mac everything he'd seen and everything he remembered about the artwork in blood. "It's there. You can't see it, but it's there. *I'm* there. Underneath that gold paint."

It took a lot to catch Mac off guard, but score one for Cain—he'd just done it.

Mac's mouth was slightly open, lips twitching like they were trying to form words, until one finally spilled out. "Infrared." The word came out soft and hesitant. "We might be able to see the image using infrared photography." Things went quiet for a moment while Mac stared at the perfectly painted gold wall. "Why paint you? Why not paint Killion? I mean, people are obsessed with you both, but why choose you over him? And this guy made it clear it was you he painted. Without those scars, we would've thought it was Killion."

Yes. Cain was cursed with looking too much like his father—like one of the world's most horrendous killers. It usually took a double take and some head-scratching before people realized he wasn't Killer Killion.

Mac shook his head. "But then our guy covered up what he'd painted. Probably thinking we'd never know the image was there."

"He even fucking signed it." Cain didn't realize until the words exited his mouth that he *had* seen a signature.

"He put his name on it?"

"Not his name. A symbol." Cain wiped his hands harder on the towel, then dropped it on the floor. He yanked his cell from his back pocket and tapped on the ArtPad app. The white light from the phone lasered into his skull. It was all he could do to keep his eyes open and not groan out loud. He drew a Christian cross, then put a hook on the bottom of it that looked like an upside-down question mark. "You've seen this before. I've seen this before."

He showed the image to Mac and watched the guy's face turn pink, then tomato with recognition.

"Yeah." Cain voice was straight as a line. "It's from my father's last kill. But he didn't do this. Not unless Petesville Super Max allows weekend furloughs."

Mac snorted. "Only way he's getting out of there is in a body bag."

Couldn't happen soon enough. His father was a stain on humanity. "So we know he didn't do this."

"But…" Mac's words disappeared for eight thumps of Cain's brain. "The girl—Mercy Ledger—made that mark on the wall as she was bleeding out from your father cutting…from her throat being cut. It didn't mean anything. It doesn't mean anything."

"*Didn't* mean anything until today. That symbol was at that scene twenty years ago, and it's here now."

Mac shook his head slowly, like an old dog with neck problems. "No one ever questioned her about it. The prints on the wall were hers. Jesus, we need to find Mercy Ledger."

Mac didn't say it, but Cain knew how the man's brain worked. Mac thought Mercy must've done this. "She didn't do this. She's been locked down in the Center of Balance and Wellness for the past few years." The words popped out of Cain's mouth before he censored them. And he really should've censored them.

He lifted his arm, pressed his eyes against a clean patch of material near his shoulder, and spoke without looking at Mac. "I…" Yeah. Just what was he going to say? It wasn't like he could confess that he'd been checking up on Mercy Ledger for the past twenty years. That would make him sound like a damned stalker. And stalking was considered the gateway drug to killing. "Liz told me." Bold-faced, flat-out, flaming-bright lie. And Mac would know it. The guy was trained to spot a lie at thirty paces. And yet Cain would rather endure the cost of the lie than spend the truth. Call him chickenshit—he would own it. He kept his eyes closed against his shoulder.

"Isn't that a violation of confidentiality or something?" Mac worded it as a question, but it sounded like a statement. "Liz could lose her nursing license."

But Liz hadn't *actually* told him. He'd guessed. He'd

known Liz long before he'd met Mac. In those dark days of childhood, his father had forced Cain to work with him at the Center. Liz had been a night nurse and the only person ever to show kindness to him. Even after his father had been caught, she'd remained a part of Cain's life—babysitting him when Mac was away for work. She was one of the few people Cain considered a friend and the closest thing he'd ever had to a mother. And now he'd tossed her in front of the bus because he was a pussy.

The quiet closed in around him. His head felt like it was about to burst off his shoulders. His stomach started rolling.

"The Center?" Mac finally broke the quiet. "That's a horrible irony."

And it was. That Mercy Ledger had lived the past few years of her life among the same hallways his father had roamed as a janitor was beyond irony. It was downright wrong.

Chapter 2

In a recent online auction, the knife Adam Killion used in the Ledger family murders sold for a record-breaking $2.3 million. The Son of Sam law prohibits convicted felons from profiting from their crimes, but someone just made a fortune.

—J. C. Brown,
criminalnewsinvestigations.com

MERCY LEDGER SAT IN THE THERAPY CIRCLE WITH ELEVEN other crazies from Ward B. The pungent funk of unwashed bodies and rotting chicken—thanks to Bo Coray and his chicken fetish—hung heavy in the air. The suicidal, homicidal, or just plain psychotic didn't care about trivial things like hygiene.

Dr. Payne wore his usual attire—three-hundred-dollar shirt, perfectly tailored pants, and shoes so shiny that when he stepped in front of her, she could see her reflection in them. He looked too *GQ* to be a psychiatrist in this underfunded, overpopulated dump of a mental hospital.

He handed her a sheet of paper. In what had once been bold letters, but now were more in the realm of fuzzy gray from over-photocopying, it read:

GRATITUDE JOURNAL
Practice an attitude of gratitude!
List three things you are grateful for today!

Gratitude? Seriously? After two years on Ward B, there wasn't a whole lot to be thankful for.

Dr. Payne held out the box of crayons to her. They didn't trust the residents of Ward B with pens or pencils. Guess no one had ever gotten shanked with a Crayola. "What color are you going to choose?" His words themselves were benign, but each syllable was threaded with judgment.

Her pulse pounded in her veins, her face got hot, and her hand holding the paper began to shake.

The vibe that came off Dr. Payne was something she recognized. Ever since that long, terrible night with Killion, she'd been able to sense people's bad intentions as if she had an early warning system. It had to do with their energy—it connected with her differently than with most people. But then most people hadn't survived what she'd survived.

Her mind's early warning system flashed her snatches of tomorrow's session with Dr. Payne. If she selected the yellow or orange crayon, he would say she was trying too hard to be cheerful. If she picked red, he would accuse her of having angry or violent thoughts. If she grabbed blue or gray, he'd declare her depressed. If she chose black, he'd claim she wanted to disassociate. Whatever the color, he would make sure she was wrong, forcing her to spend all of tomorrow's session defending tonight's color selection. And if she wasn't successful in her defense, he'd use that as an excuse to have more private sessions with her.

"Mercy. Take a crayon." Dr. Payne's voice sounded like a calm ocean, but underneath the surface, hungry sharks swam.

Shit. She grabbed the purple crayon.

"I can stay after group to help you process your reluctance." His tone was full of fake helpfulness.

"No. I'm sorry. I was just daydreaming." Great. Now she was going to have to come up with a reason why she'd stared at the damned crayon box so long without choosing one. It wasn't like she could tell him the truth—that she knew what he wanted and had been trying to outthink him. The level of control he had over her life scared her nearly as much as Killion had all those years ago.

He moved on to Bo, handing him the paper and giving him a crayon, but she still felt the burden of his gaze on her: watching her, assessing her, looking for an excuse—any excuse—to have more one-on-one sessions with her.

She settled her hand over the six-inch ridge of puckered skin scarring her neck. The old injury was always cold, and the heat of her palm soothed something inside her, reassuring her soul that she had already survived the worst of life—and she would survive Ward B and Dr. Payne too.

But she'd better get her hand off her neck before he decided she needed to talk about Killion again. Dr. Payne enjoyed her tragedy too much.

She moved her hand away from her throat, and the scar went cold. She held the purple crayon by the fingers of both hands.

"For tonight's education group…" Dr. Payne used his Moses-parting-the-seas voice and took the empty seat next to her. He *always* sat next to her. "…we're going to talk about happiness and some of the research being conducted in the field of positive psychology. A group of Harvard psychologists have found that happy people have a particular set of habits."

None of the patients on Ward B gave two shits about happiness. They were all too damned crazy to care about such an elusive term. Now, if this evening's group had been about how to score smokes, line up conjugal visits, or get extra pudding cups, most of the patients would have been taking notes.

"I'm already happy!" Bo let out a high-pitched little-girl giggle that sounded nine kinds of wrong coming from a three-hundred-pound guy. "I'm Bojangles! See!" He framed his face with his pudgy hands and smiled an open-mouthed, deranged clown smile.

He called himself Bojangles, partly because of his chicken fixation and mostly because the name sounded like a clown's name, and that's exactly what Bo thought he was—a clown. That crazy smile and his carrot-colored Afro only solidified the delusion.

"I'm so happy!" Bo swayed violently in his seat, bumping into her and knocking her into Dr. Payne, whose arm went around her, locking her against his hard body. He held her too hard and too wrong. The room fell away. Bo's shouting vanished. The only thing that existed was his horrible strength, trapping her against him, and the urge—the almost uncontrollable urge—to scream.

"Are you all right? If he hurt you…" Dr. Payne's breath fanned across her cheek, smelling of sweet tea and summer. He should be the one who smelled like rotting chicken. Her body went into rigor mortis. She couldn't move or breathe or think.

Bo jumped to his feet and moved into the center of the circle. Dr. Payne let her go. What had felt like an eternity of being pinned against him had probably lasted only two seconds, since no one seemed to notice.

"Let's be happy together!" Bo hollered at the top of his volume range and began twirling like a morbidly obese ballerina. "Bojangles. Bojangles. Bojangles." He sang his name at an ear-throbbing volume.

Dr. Payne didn't move, didn't blink, just watched Bo with an expression of absolute indifference on his face. That was part of how Mercy had known he was a sociopath. He never reacted normally—and he didn't have the excuse of being pumped full of anti-psychotics and sedatives like the rest of the group. He never seemed threatened, no matter the situation. Probably because he was always the biggest threat in the room.

Bo pirouetted to a stop in front of her. "Dance with me, baby doll!" He snatched her up against his flabby body and hurled them around. His rotten-chicken stench assaulted her nose, but no matter how bad he stank, she wasn't scared of him. Bo would never intentionally hurt her or anyone else. He was like a mastiff pup. He didn't understand how big he was, or how strong, or how his size could intimidate.

"Bo, I don't feel like dancing right now." She pushed against his pudgy man boobs.

His bottom lip jutted out, shiny with saliva, but he stopped and let her go, just like she knew he would.

His chest bellowed, his lungs wheezed and whistled.

Hauling around three hundred pounds would do that to a person.

"Now why don't you sit down, catch your breath, and let Dr. Payne finish tonight's—"

Bo began toppling over sideways, taking his time to fall, the way a giant tree goes down in a thick forest. She reached out to grab him, but his momentum and weight were too much. He landed—knee, hip, then shoulder— the sound of flesh slapping concrete punctuated by the thud of heavy bones. Where Bo had been only a second before, Dr. Payne now stood, staring at her. Not at the man on the floor.

And that's where her ability to sense bad intentions fell short. Spontaneity. When someone acted without planning, her internal warning mechanism failed every time. She could never fully rely on it.

"What'd you do to him? He was done. He was going to sit down." The moment the words flew out her mouth, she wished she could suck every syllable back inside and swallow them down whole.

An unnatural silence engulfed the room. No one in the group moved, no one spoke, no one checked on Bo. They all stared at her. At her. As if she'd done something wrong. And she had done something wrong. She'd challenged Dr. Payne—talked back to him instead of being subservient. And worst of all, she'd shown caring for Bo.

There was a terrible pattern to her life, one she tried to deny, one she tried to tell herself wasn't real. But the undeniable truth, the thing that loomed over her ever since that night with Killion, was that if she cared for someone, they were bound to get hurt.

But didn't anyone else care about Bo? Or that Dr. Payne had somehow caused Bo to fall? She wanted to scream at the group, at Dr. Payne, but clamped her lips firmly closed.

Click. The sound was a mini explosion in Mercy's head. Her gaze shot to the panic button clipped to Dr. Payne's belt and his finger just lifting off the pad.

Her stomach kicked. *No, no, no.* He wouldn't have hit the button because of her words. He wouldn't put her on Ward A just for questioning him. Or would he? On Ward A, he'd have supreme control over her. No interaction with anyone except for him. Just what he wanted and what she'd managed to avoid for the past two years.

Dr. Payne's eyes were black and unfeeling, his lips pinched in a promise of terrible things to come. He reached into his pants pocket and withdrew a syringe, uncapped it, and took a step toward her.

An odd buzzing sound started in her ears, and her vision narrowed until the only thing she saw was that syringe held between his perfectly manicured fingers. She couldn't let him inject her. Couldn't let him knock her so completely out that she would be unconscious and then in a sedated, vegetable state for days afterward.

Dr. Payne jammed the needle in Bo's ass cheek. Mercy sucked in a lungful of air—she hadn't realized she'd been holding her breath.

Two security guards and two male nurses rushed into the room. She moved away from Bo and stumbled back to her chair, collapsing so hard on the metal seat her tailbone rang.

"Transport him to Ward A." Dr. Payne returned to his place beside her. "I'll be down to assess him in a few minutes."

She wanted to cringe away from him, but forced her body to stillness and watched as each member of the security team took an arm or leg and dragged Bo out of the room. He weighed too much to carry.

"We'll be cutting group short tonight. Everyone fill out your papers, return them to me, and then go to your rooms."

Dr. Payne passed her a fresh sheet of paper and the pink crayon, her paper and crayon having somehow disappeared in all the commotion. Using her leg for a solid surface, she scribbled the same thing on all three lines.

I'm grateful to be alive.
I'm grateful to be alive.
I'm grateful to be alive.

Without glancing at Dr. Payne, she handed in her paper and crayon and strained to walk from the room, instead of run. Because she wanted to run. She wanted to be far away from Dr. Payne and Ward B and this miserable existence where everything she did was under a microscope.

In her room, she didn't bother with the overhead fluorescents. She went straight to her barred window and stared out into the night. There were no distant lights dotting the horizon, no stars twinkling in the sky. Nothing to indicate an entire world existed beyond her pane of glass. Just a void—a massive, black nothingness stretching on to infinity. The emptiness, the illusion of being alone, soothed her.

Her door clicked and swung open. She clamped her teeth together and breathed a quiet huff of frustration. Privacy didn't exist on Ward B. To the staff, privacy equaled delinquency. The wavy image of a person reflected on her window. Liz—the charge nurse—always checked on her after she'd done everyone else. She understood Mercy's need to experience the only peaceful moments of the day.

"All good here. I'll get in bed in a few minutes." Mercy forced lightness into her tone. If she let any irritation or tension leak into her voice, she risked Dr. Payne finding out.

"Mercy—" A man's voice.

She startled, a jerking of muscle so violent it felt as if she'd been electrocuted. She whirled from the window to face him.

"—I need to make sure Bo didn't hurt you."

Her mind rebelled against the message her eyeballs were sending. Dr. Payne stood in her doorway. He never entered a patient's room. And male staff were not permitted in the rooms of female patients. But here he was and here she was, and this wasn't going to end well.

Her heart went off like a cannon.

"I'm responsible for you. You're under my care. I won't let anyone interfere." Dr. Payne wore a grin, his deep dimples giving him a look all the women—staff and patients alike—adored.

"I'm fine. No harm done." There was only a slight tremor in her voice. Maybe he wouldn't notice. She cleared her throat and aimed for a stronger tone. "Liz knows my routine. She'll be in to do a check in a few minutes." Yeah. Remind him that someone might catch him if tried anything. "She's fine with me being awake as long as I don't bother anyone else."

Dr. Payne took a step into the room. "Liz is dealing with Bo."

Slowly, silently, the door began to fall shut behind him. The light from the hallway pinched off inch by inch until only darkness stood between them. The barely audible click of the latch sent a cold rush of adrenaline through her limbs.

Her internal warning system went off, and she knew—knew in the way of instincts and reflexes and urges, knew with a clarity beyond understanding—what he had planned for tonight. For her. The images flickered through her mind almost like memories, but they were of things to come. Him forcing her facedown over her bed. Him taking what she wouldn't give. Him making it hurt. Him making her bleed. Him marking her as his.

Fear licked down her spine and bit into her guts, but she refused to cower before him. She wouldn't be an easy victim. Not her. Never her. Never again. And if he didn't know that, it just went to prove how much he sucked at his job.

She would handle this. She'd been through worse. She'd *survived* worse. This time, all she needed to do was get to the hallway where the lights were on and the cameras were rolling and there was always someone at the nurses' station. Ten feet. That's all that stood between her and safety.

She walked toward him. Better to be on the offensive instead of being forced to react. She put an extra sway to her hips and prayed he'd be too distracted to realize she was going for the door—not him.

He watched her, that dimpled predatory smile never leaving his lips. Her heart somehow exited her chest, floating up into her head and pounding in her ears. She stopped a mere foot away from him.

Calm. Keep calm. Breathe in slow. Exhale slow. She could freak all she wanted later. But not now. Not when it really mattered.

Slowly, she shifted to his side, a mere two feet from the door. No sudden movements. Not yet. Not until she knew she could grab the handle and get out into the hallway before he stopped her.

"What do you think you're doing?" His words were liquid nitrogen to her blood. She froze.

He turned to face her, moving farther into her space. He wasn't much taller than she was, his dead eyes and taunting mouth right on the level of hers— only inches away.

Do something. Do anything. Don't let him touch you. Her mind screamed the words to be heard over her heart thundering in her ears.

With every ounce of force she possessed, she rammed her knee into his knobby knockers.

He didn't make a sound. He didn't move. Didn't react.

Had she missed?

He struck out with his fist so fast she didn't have a chance to flinch, block, or move. The impact sent a shock wave of agony through her face, the sensation so intense she couldn't feel the epicenter. She stumbled backward, lost her footing, and landed on her ass. The impact vibrated through every bone in her body like a plucked violin string.

Dr. Payne bent double, cupping his pulverized parts.

He shuffle-walked the one step to her, drew back his foot, and slammed it into her ribs. Air whoofed out of her. She collapsed back, rolling and writhing to escape the fire in her side.

How long she lay there, she didn't know. But suddenly, Dr. Payne's face was in her line of sight, and his intentions were in her head. Her mind flashed through images of the stark walls of Ward A, of herself drugged beyond awareness, of Dr. Payne amusing himself with her mind and body.

She tried to move toward the door, but her body wasn't able to comply. She was lost in an inferno of pain.

Dr. Payne ruffled his hands through his hair, making it messy. He pulled at his perfectly tucked-in shirt, making it sloppy, then knelt down next to her.

She scooted away from him, but he grabbed her hand, forced her fingers open, gripping her middle finger in his fist. Was this some new form of torture? He yanked her finger to his face, jammed the nail against his cheek, then scraped it down over his skin, leaving a red trough of blood. He slammed her hand against the floor, but she had reached a familiar place. A numb place. A place where physical pain no longer hurt her. He could slit her throat like Killion had, and she wouldn't feel it.

He stood and hit the panic button, then pulled another syringe from his pocket.

"You were the reason Bo acted out tonight. You stormed off from group without completing your assignment. I came here to check on you. You attacked me. You called me Killion. You've had a break from reality."

The whimpers and whines of a wounded animal filled the room. The sound came from her, and no matter how hard she tried to shush herself, something deep inside had broken and wouldn't be soothed.

He raised the syringe over his head and slammed it down with all the force of a large hunting knife, stabbing her in the thigh. She watched as the clear fluid emptied into her body.

"I think it's time we stepped up your treatment. ECT should help. I'll plug you in a couple times. See how you behave toward me then."

A wave crashed over her, but it wasn't a wave, it was her body. No, it wasn't her body moving, it was the drug hitting her system, pounding its way to her mind. The world went gray. She fought to stay on the surface, to not let the sedative pull her under, but the world went dark and she drowned under the drug's effect.

Acknowledgments

My first and last thank-you always belongs to Dan. Without your unconditional love and support, I wouldn't have had the courage to keep riding this crazy roller coaster called Being a Writer. Your steady presence and encouragement are the roots from which I continue to grow. Thank you for loving me.

All the thank-yous in between belong to Brinda Berry. I owe you so much. You're a mentor. A friend. A critique partner. You're the first person who reads my stories, and you always keep me from looking stupid! That in itself is priceless! Thank you for just being fabulous you!

And my final thank-you belongs to my darling readers. Each and every one of you who read my books matter to me. That you devoted time from your life to read my story warms my heart and makes me smile. Thank you times a million.

About the Author

Abbie Roads is a mental health counselor known for her blunt, honest style of therapy. By night, she writes dark, emotional novels, always giving her characters the happy ending she wishes for all her clients. Her novels have been finalists in RWA contests, including the Golden Heart.

Also by Abbie Roads

FATAL DREAMS
Race the Darkness
Hunt the Dawn

FATAL TRUTH
Saving Mercy